Stories of Old Greece and Rome

CW01072642

Emilie K. Baker

Alpha Editions

This edition published in 2024

ISBN : 9789362924698

Design and Setting By
Alpha Editions
www.alphaedis.com
Email - info@alphaedis.com

Contents

CHAPTER I
IN THE BEGINNING

IN the days of long, long ago when men built altars, and burned sacrifices, and worshiped their gods in temples of pure white marble, Jupiter, the greatest of the gods, sat upon his throne on high Olympus and looked down upon the doings of men. The topmost peak of Mount Olympus was covered with clouds,—so high it was above all the hills of Greece,—and its slopes were thickly wooded. Just how high the mountain really was could only be guessed, for no man had dared to climb even as high as the first cloud line; though the story goes that once upon a time a wandering shepherd, looking for a strayed lamb, had ventured far up the mountain side and had soon lost his way. He groped about blindly, as the mists began to thicken all around him, and the sound of his own footsteps terrified him in the dreadful silence that seemed to be suddenly creeping over him. Then a mighty tempest broke over his head, and the mountain shook to its very base. From the hand of wrathful Jupiter fierce thunderbolts were hurled, while the lightning flashed and gleamed through the darkness of the forest, searching out the guilty mortal who had dared to climb too high.

No human eye had ever seen the glories of Olympus, no human foot had ever stepped within its sacred halls, where the ceiling was of gold and the pavement of pearl and the thrones of the gods shone with a thousand glittering jewels. Here

"the gods have made,
So saith tradition, their eternal seat;
The tempest shakes it not, nor is it drenched
By showers, and there the snow does never fall.
And in the golden light that lies on all
Day after day the blessed gods rejoice."

—*Odyssey*, Book VI, line 53.

Of the life that was lived among the dwellers on Olympus, not even the poets could claim to know; but sometimes a tired soldier dozing by his camp fire dreamed dreams of this wonderful country where the immortal gods walked by night and day; and sometimes a lonely fisherman, looking across the blue waters of the Mediterranean to the crimsoning sunset, saw visions of youth and beauty and life that lasted for ever and ever and ever.

It was long before the memory of man that the gods first came to live on Mount Olympus, and it was still longer ago that all the great powers of the universe fought with each other for the right to rule the world. In this mighty war, which rent the very heavens with the crash of battle, Jupiter at last conquered all his jealous enemies, and made himself ruler of the gods and of the world.1 On that day he established his dwelling place on Mount Olympus, and set the earth below him for a footstool. From his throne in the high heavens he looked down upon the kingdoms that he had portioned out to each of his brothers; and he saw Neptune, the god of the sea, driving through the waves his chariot drawn by huge, misshapen sea-beasts that beat up the thick white foam until it glistened on the sea-king's beard and on his crown of shells and seaweed. The other kingdom was so far away that even the all-seeing eyes of Jupiter were strained to catch any glimpse of the shapes that moved noiselessly there, for this was the realm of Pluto, god of the underworld, that dread country of darkness and unending gloom, where no ray of sunlight ever came, and where the sad spirits of the dead wept for the lost world of love and light and laughter.

Sometimes the great billows of clouds that rolled at the foot of the red-gold throne shut out for a moment all sight of the earth at his feet; but however thickly the mists gathered, Jupiter could always see old Atlas standing on the shore of Africa with the heavens resting on his bent shoulders. This giant had stood so long that forests of huge trees had sprung up around his feet, and they had grown so tall during the ages and ages that had passed, that their topmost branches reached to the giant's waist and almost hid him from the sight of men. No one offered to relieve him of his burden, not even his two brothers, Prometheus and Epimetheus, to whom had been given the less difficult task of creating man and placing him in the rich gardens of the earth. There was every kind of plant and animal life in the gardens, and all things were very beautiful in this morning of the world—so beautiful that the gods, who must forever dwell in Olympus, felt sad that no eyes like their own could look upon the green meadows and flower-covered hillsides. So they bade Prometheus and Epimetheus fashion a being which should be like and yet unlike themselves. There was nothing but clay out of which to make this new creature called man, but the brothers spent much time over their task, and, when it was finished, Jupiter saw that the work was good, for they had given to man all the qualities that the gods themselves possessed—youth, beauty, health, strength,—everything but immortality.

Then Prometheus grew ambitious to add even more to the list of man's blessings; and one day, as he sat brooding by the seashore, he remembered that there was as yet no fire on the earth; for the only flame that burned in all the world was glowing in the sacred halls of Jupiter. For a long time he sat on the seashore, and before night fell he had formed the daring plan of stealing some of the divine fire that burned for always and always on Mount Olympus, and carrying it to the earth that men might revel in its warmth and light.

It was a bold thing to dream of doing, but Prometheus forgot the fear of Jupiter's wrath, so determined was he to carry out his plan; and one night, when the gods were in council, seated around the great red-gold throne, he crept softly into the hall, unseen and unheard. The sacred fire was burning brightly on a hearth of polished silver. Some of it Prometheus secreted in a hollow reed and hurried with it back to the earth. Then he waited, with terror at his heart, for he knew that sooner or later the vengeance of Jupiter would search him out, even though he fled to the uttermost parts of the earth.

When the council of the gods was over, Jupiter looked down through the clouds and saw a strange light on the earth. For a while he did not realize that it was man, building himself a fire; but when he learned the truth, his wrath became so terrible that even the gods trembled and turned away in fear. In a moment Prometheus was seized and carried off to the Caucasus Mountains, where he was securely chained to a rock, and a hungry vulture was sent to tear out his liver and devour it. At night the vulture, having gorged itself, slept on the rocks above its victim's head; and at night the liver of the wretched Prometheus grew again, only to be torn out and eaten by the vulture as soon as the sun rose. This terrible punishment kept on for years and years; for though Jupiter heard the cries of Prometheus, and many tales were told of his sufferings, the ruler of the gods never forgave the theft of the sacred fire, nor would he set Prometheus free. But the story tells us that at last there came an end to this cruel vengeance, for Hercules, son of Jupiter, went wandering one day among the mountains, found the tortured Prometheus, and broke his chains, after killing the vulture that had been enjoying this hateful feast.

Though the gods were rejoiced at his freedom, the name of Prometheus was never spoken on Mount Olympus for fear of Jupiter's all-hearing ears; but on the earth men uttered his name in their prayers and taught their children to honor the Fire-giver as one of the greatest among heroes.2

Jupiter

CHAPTER II
THE STORY OF PANDORA

IN the early days of man's life on the earth, when everything was beautiful and new, there was no sickness anywhere, nor any pain, nor sorrow. Men lived to be very old and very wise, and everywhere was happiness such as has never been since in all the world. Now Jupiter had not forgotten about the stealing of the sacred fire, and it angered him that man should light his own fires and kindle the cheerful blaze which should by right be glowing only in the halls of Olympus. The suffering of Prometheus had not softened his wrath. He would not be satisfied until punishment was visited upon those who had received the stolen fire. Accordingly he called a council of the gods and spoke to them of his desire. Though none of the deities wished to see misfortune brought upon the race of man, they did not dare to dispute the will of Jupiter. So they agreed to carry out the plan that he unfolded, and before many days had passed they had fashioned, out of the same clay from which man was made, a creature that they called woman. To her each of the gods gave a gift such as softness, or grace, or wonderful fairness; but Jupiter added one other quality, curiosity, and he gave the woman the name of Pandora, which means "the gift of all the gods."3 Then he bade Mercury, who is the messenger of the gods, take this new soft thing down to the earth and give her to Epimetheus for his wife. Now Epimetheus had mourned apart from his fellows ever since he learned of his brother's dreadful fate; and he sat day and night in the cool silence of the forest, brooding over his sorrow. But one day he saw some one coming toward him, led by the hand of Mercury, and all at once he forgot to be sad; for the sunlight was shining on the woman's golden hair, and her white arm was stretched out to him in greeting.

For some time Epimetheus and Pandora lived happily in the gardens of the earth, and every day Epimetheus thanked the gods for their last and best gift to man. He never tired of watching Pandora chasing butterflies through the tall meadow grass, or making cups out of broad leaves, that she and Epimetheus might drink from the clear, cool spring. One day as they were resting under the trees and eating their simple meal of dates and wild honey, they saw a traveler coming toward them. He was walking very slowly and seemed heavily burdened with what appeared to be a large box. While he was yet some distance off, Pandora ran to meet him and asked him to come into the shade and rest. The stranger was old, and the chest that he carried bent his shoulders almost to the ground. He looked hungry and thirsty and tired, so Epimetheus urged him to stop and rest, and offered him some freshly gathered dates. But the traveler—who was none other than Mercury in disguise—replied that he could not tarry with them, for he had a long distance yet to go. He asked them, however, to take care of his great oak chest, for with that burden off his shoulders he could hurry on and reach his journey's end before nightfall. He promised to come back for the chest a few days later. Epimetheus and Pandora were delighted to be of service to a stranger, and promised to guard the chest with great care. The traveler thanked them and turned away; but just as they were saying good-by, he mysteriously disappeared, and whichever way they looked there was no trace of him to be seen.

Epimetheus was not at all eager to know what was in the mysterious chest; but as soon as they sat down again under the trees, Pandora began to ask a thousand questions as to who the traveler might be and what the chest contained. Epimetheus begged her not to think any more about it, as nothing could be learned of the old man or his burden; but Pandora refused to be silent, and talked still more of the probable treasure that they were guarding for the stranger. At last Epimetheus got up angrily and walked away, wearied with her insistence. Pandora then went over to the chest, and kneeling down beside it, she examined the exquisitely carved figures that were on all its four sides. Then she studied the fine golden cord that bound the chest. It looked soft enough, and yet it was very strong; for it was made of strands of twisted gold and was tied at the end with a curious knot. There was no lock to be seen, and apparently nothing hindered eager fingers from opening the lid when once the knot was unfastened and the golden cord unwound. Pandora's fingers itched to try her skill on the knot, and she felt sure that if she worked at it long enough, she could finally loosen it. The figures carved on the lid were groups of dancing children, and in the very center was one figure whose face was so strange that Pandora sat for a long time staring at it. Now and then she turned away, and when she looked at the face again, it had a different expression from the one she had seen on it before. She knew that this carved thing was not alive, and yet each time she gazed into the strange eyes of the wooden face they were quite unlike the eyes that had smiled or frowned or mocked at her before.

She went to see whether Epimetheus had come back, and finding that he was still away, she returned to the chest again, but would not let herself be tempted into so much as touching the golden cord. As she stood wondering what to do, she thought that she heard some little voices coming from inside the chest, and they seemed to say:—

"Open, Pandora, please, please open and let us out."

Pandora looked quickly around to see whether Epimetheus were in sight, then she came a bit nearer to the chest and put one hand on the golden cord. Again she heard the small voices, this time very distinctly, and they said:—

"Open, Pandora, please, please open and let us out."

Pandora's heart was now beating fast. What *could* be in the chest? What poor imprisoned creatures were calling to her, begging her to set them free? She put both hands on the golden cord, then she looked guiltily around; but no one was in sight, no one was watching her except some inquisitive squirrels who were peering down at her from the branches just above her head.

Swiftly and deftly she untied the knot, which yielded easily to her eager fingers; but even then she hesitated, fearing the anger of Epimetheus.

The little voices cried again:—

"Open, Pandora, please, please open and let us out;" but still she hesitated, not daring to raise the lid. Just then she heard her husband calling to her, and she knew that there would be no chance now to explore the contents of the mysterious chest. She must wait for that pleasure until another time; meanwhile she would take just one peep inside to be sure that the voices were not mocking her. So she raised the lid very gently, but no sooner had she made the smallest opening than out poured a host of tiny creatures like brown-winged moths; and they swarmed all around her, biting and pinching and blistering her soft skin until she cried out in fear and pain.

She tried to fight them off, and rushed away to find Epimetheus; but the tormenting little sprites followed her, buzzing about her ears and stinging her again and again. In vain she strove to brush them away, for they clung to her dress, her hair, and her poor swollen skin. When she reached Epimetheus she was crying bitterly, and it did not need any questioning to find out the trouble, for the malicious little creatures were so numerous that hundreds of them encircled Epimetheus, and bit and stung him, just as they had done to Pandora. In the unhappy hour that followed, while husband and wife bound soothing herbs on their bruised skin, Pandora told Epimetheus how her fatal curiosity had led her to open the chest and set free the host of evil things.

It was not, however, until later that they realized the extent of Pandora's folly, for the little brown-winged creatures were all the spirits of evil that had never before entered the world. Their names were Sickness and Pain and Sorrow; Envy and Pride and Jealousy; Hunger, Poverty, and Death. All these ills had envious Jupiter put into the oak chest, and bound it with only a golden cord. He knew that sooner or later Pandora would open the chest, and then man's life of untroubled happiness would be forever at an end. Never again could the gardens of the earth be places where man might hope to find peace. Evil things had taken up their dwelling there, and they would stay for always and always and always, as long as the world should last.

When Epimetheus and Pandora saw the hateful winged creatures settling down on the leaves and flowers so as to be near at hand to torment them, they wept bitter tears and wished that the gods had never created them. In the midst of her sobbing Pandora had not, however, forgotten about the chest, and she was still wondering what else might be inside it, for she was sure that those mothlike things could never have wholly filled it. Suddenly she heard a wee soft whisper coming from within the chest, and it said: "Open, Pandora, please, please open and let me out."

Pandora stared in surprise, for she had thought that all the evil sprites had rushed out in that moment when she raised the lid. Was there, then, another host of tormenting things still there; and if so, should she let them out to add to her misery and pain?

Again the little soft voice cried: "Open, Pandora, please, please open and let me out."

Pandora now called to Epimetheus, and together they listened to the pleading voice which was so very soft and sweet that they were sure it could not belong to any evil thing. Still Epimetheus was unwilling to risk bringing any more trouble into the world; but in spite of her remorse, Pandora was curious to see what it was that was begging so plaintively for freedom. So with Epimetheus's consent she opened the lid once more, and out fluttered a tiny little creature with beautiful gauzy wings. She flew straight to Pandora, then to Epimetheus, and at her touch all their hurts were healed and all their pain forgotten.

The name of this gentle messenger was Hope; and she had been hidden in the chest secretly by one of the pitying gods, who grieved that Jupiter was sending so many ills to fret mankind. The host of evil beings, once set free, could never again be shut up in their narrow prison; but wherever they flew—even to the remotest corner of the earth—Hope followed them and brought healing in her wings; and when the world grew wicked, as it did in the days that came after, so that men neglected the altars of the gods, Hope was still remembered with votive offerings and her shrines kept garlanded with flowers.

CHAPTER III
THE DELUGE

THE children of Epimetheus and Pandora wandered in the gardens of the earth just as their parents had done; and the generations that followed them lived peacefully and were happy, in spite of the brown-winged sprites that went about doing mischief. Men helped each other to cultivate the fruitful soil, and offered sacrifices to the gods in return for a bountiful harvest.

This golden age of the world's history might have lasted forever if men had continued to reverence the gods; but after a time they ceased to offer prayers for health and safety, and boasted proudly of their own strength. They looked no more to high Olympus for help, but each man trusted to his own right arm. Then strife and discord arose, and fierce wars were fought among all the peoples of the earth. Brother killed brother, and fathers strove with their own sons. Every man's hand was against his fellow, and he knew no law but that of his own will. Seldom now were the fires kindled on the neglected altars, and the smell of burnt offerings dear to the gods no longer mingled with the smoke that rose up to the white clouds around Olympus. The sacred vessels moldered in forsaken temples; around the shrines of the gods the snakes crawled lazily; and the bat and owl dwelt undisturbed among the pillars of the temples.

For a time the gods sat patient, believing that this state of things could not last; but seeing that mankind was growing worse instead of better, year by year, they determined to put an end to godlessness and to destroy the whole race of man. Then Jupiter called a council of the gods to decide on the most effective way of wiping out every vestige of human life so completely that not one soul would be left to tell to his children the story of those evil days, when men neglected to worship the immortal gods and allowed their temples to decay.

The most terrible punishment to visit upon man would be to set the whole world on fire, to make of it one great sacrificial altar on which human victims, and not the garlanded ox, would burn night and day, and from which the smoke would rise up into the heavens so thickly that it would shut out the sight of a blackened and smouldering earth. The one objection to carrying out this plan was the fear lest the flames would leap so high that they would reach even to lofty Olympus, and so endanger the sacred throne of Jupiter. Though the fire might not utterly destroy it, the gods could not bear to think of its burnished red-gold base being touched by any flame from earth's unholy fires.

The only other effective method of destruction was water, and this the gods decided to employ. So on a certain day when men were everywhere feasting, and singing songs, and boasting of their victories in battle, Jupiter rent the heavens with a mighty thunderbolt, whose crashing drowned all sounds of merriment, and made men turn pale with fear. The skies opened, and the rain poured down in torrents; the rivers became swollen and flooded their banks; the waves of the sea, rising higher and higher, swept in great fury over the land, washing everything before them like so much chaff. Æolus, god of the storm, opened the cave where he kept the winds securely bound, and let them loose to work havoc on the earth. Soon all the lowland was covered with water; not a dry spot remained anywhere but on the hills, and thither the terrified people rushed in the vain hope that the flood would subside before the mountains were submerged. But the waves rose higher and higher; and the winds, rejoicing in their freedom, beat up the water until it almost touched the clouds. The frail boats to which men had at first desperately clung were shattered to pieces in the fury of the storm, and on the crest of the waves the bodies of the dead were tossed like playthings. Higher and higher rose the water, until at length the mountain tops were covered, and all dry land had disappeared. So were the gods avenged.

There was one spot, however, that was not yet hidden under the waters, and this was the top of Mount Parnassus, the highest hill of Greece. To this place of refuge had fled Deucalion and his wife Pyrrha, two virtuous souls who alone, of all the people on the earth, had lived uprightly and worshiped the gods. When Jupiter saw them standing on the top of Mount Parnassus and weeping over the universal destruction, he remembered their piety and decreed that their lives should be spared. So he gave commands that the rains and the floods and the winds should cease, and the dry land appear. Then Æolus brought the winds back from their mad wanderings and bound them again in the cave. Neptune blew upon his conch-shell, and the angry waves returned again to the sea. Little by little the tree-tops showed above the water, and the green earth smiled again under the warm rays of the sun.4

But it was upon a desolate and unpeopled world that the eyes of Deucalion and Pyrrha rested, and in their utter loneliness they almost wished that they had perished with their friends. They went slowly down the mountain-side, not knowing where to go, being led blindly by the will of the gods to the temple at Delphi5—the only building that was not destroyed. To this sacred spot men had been wont to come in the old, god-fearing days to consult the wishes of the gods and to learn their own destinies. Here was the divine oracle that not even the most daring mortal would refuse to obey.

When Deucalion and Pyrrha found themselves at the temple of Delphi, they made haste to consult the oracle, for they wished to repeople the land before another morning's sun could look down upon a lifeless earth. To their surprise the oracle returned them this answer:—

"Depart from here with veiled heads and throw your mother's bones behind you."

This command seemed impossible to obey; for they could never hope to find any grave, when all landmarks had been washed away; and, even could they do so, it was an unheard-of sacrilege to disturb the bones of the dead. Deucalion sought, therefore, to explain the strange words of the oracle in some other way; and at length he guessed the meaning of the god's answer. It was no human remains that he was commanded to desecrate; the bones referred to were those of Mother Earth. So husband and wife left the temple with veiled heads; and as they went they gathered up the stones at their feet and threw these behind them. All the stones that fell from the hands of Deucalion turned into men, and those that Pyrrha dropped became women.

Thus it was that through the kindness and wisdom of the immortals the earth was repeopled with a new race of men that feared evil, and reverenced piety, and walked humbly before the gods. Never again was Jupiter forced to send a deluge on the earth, for men no longer let the altar-fires burn low, nor did they neglect to offer sacrifices because of forgotten prayers.

CHAPTER IV
MINERVA

I

ALTHOUGH the brown-winged spirits of evil were kept busy flying up and down the earth, their mischief-making never reached those immortal ones who dwelt above the cloud-wrapped summit of Olympus. It was, therefore, a most unheard-of happening when the Father of the gods complained one day of a terrible pain in his head. Some of the gods were skilled in the art of healing; but no one could relieve Jupiter's suffering, nor tell what might be the cause of his pain. The trouble grew worse and worse until it was too severe for even a god to endure; so Jupiter bade his son Vulcan take an ax and split open his head. Not daring to thwart the divine will, Vulcan tremblingly obeyed; and at the first blow a marvelous thing occurred, for out of Jupiter's head sprang a maiden clad in armor and bearing a spear in her hand. This was Minerva, goddess of wisdom, so called because she came full-grown from the mighty brain of Jupiter. So wise did the Ruler of the gods find this child of his to be, that he kept her constantly near him, and sought her counsel in dealing with the affairs of men, while Juno, his stately wife, stood jealously by, envying the warrior-maiden her place at Jupiter's side.6

Being born equipped for battle, Minerva delighted in war, and had no feminine shrinking from the noise of clashing steel or the cries of struggling men. No Trojan hero gloried in the war more exultingly than she, as she carried aloft the terrible shield of Jupiter—"the Ægis"—and bore in her hand the mighty spear, "heavy and huge and strong." When armies met in battle, the goddess was never far away from the fighting hosts; and ofttimes a dying soldier, turning his eyes for a last look at his comrades, saw the glint of her spear or the flash of her shield as she led the favored ones on to victory.

But the azure-eyed Minerva was not always on the battle-field, for in spite of her warlike appearance she had many very feminine tastes, and among them was a love of weaving. Often would white-armed Juno taunt Minerva with her unwomanly fondness for warfare; but when the goddess took up her weaving, even jealous Juno could not withhold her praise, for the hand that could wield a spear like a man had also the delicate touch of a woman.

Now there lived on the earth a maiden named Arachne, who was very proud of her skill in weaving, and boasted that in the whole length and breadth of the land there was no one to equal her in this art. Whenever people spoke with her, she could talk of nothing else but her work; and if a stranger stopped to rest at her door, she would be sure to show him her weaving and to ask him whether in all his wanderings he had seen anything to surpass it. Soon she grew so conceited that she dared to compare herself with the goddess Minerva, and boasted that her own work was as beautiful as anything that hung in the halls of Olympus. Her friends grew frightened at her rash speech, and begged her not to let her foolish pride go too far, lest some whisper of her boasting should reach Minerva's ears. But Arachne only grew bolder, and said openly that she would not be afraid to challenge the goddess to a contest. These words were overheard by Apollo's raven, who flew quickly back to Olympus to tell what he had seen and heard.

Minerva had known for some time of Arachne's boasting, but she had not deigned to notice it. Now, however, when she learned that a mortal maiden had dared to claim superiority to a goddess, she grew very angry and determined to punish such presumption. So she cast off her glittering armor and laid aside her long spear, and went down to earth in the disguise of an old woman. She found Arachne seated on the doorstep, weaving; and as she stopped to admire the girl's work, even Minerva was forced to admit that the weaving was beautifully done. Soon Arachne began to boast proudly of her skill and told the pretended old woman that she hoped some day to challenge the goddess Minerva to a contest. The listener seemed shocked at these daring words, and begged the maiden to be more humble and not to presume too far; but Arachne only tossed her head and laughed, saying that she wished the goddess would hear her and accept the challenge.

At these bold words Minerva's anger broke out, and throwing off her disguise she commanded the astonished girl to fetch two looms and set them up in the doorway. Then she bade Arachne make good her boast. For hours they worked in silence, each weaving with practiced fingers an exquisite design in the tapestry; and neither one turning her head to watch her rival's progress. When the last thread was tied and the work finished, Arachne looked anxiously at the goddess's loom, and one glance was sufficient to assure her of her own failure. Never in all her life had she seen work so faultlessly done, and the beauty of it was like that of visions in a dream.

Humiliated at her defeat, and too proud to endure the taunts that she felt awaited her from those who had heard her boast, the unhappy maiden tried to hang herself. But Minerva would not let the world so easily forget how a mortal had dared to challenge a goddess; so when she saw Arachne's body hanging by a rope, she quickly changed her into a spider, and bade her spin and spin as long as she lived. Thus when strangers came from all the country round to see the maiden whose skill in weaving had been noised far and wide, there she hung—an ugly black spider in the midst of her dusty web—a warning to all mortals who presume.

II

Many, many years had passed since Epimetheus and Pandora wandered in the gardens of the earth; and many, many generations of men had come and gone since the day when Deucalion and Pyrrha looked down from Mount Parnassus upon an unpeopled land. Cities had been built, with marble palaces and costly temples. Towns had sprung up on river-banks and by the sea. Everywhere man was making for himself a home, and journeying into strange and distant lands. The gods, seated in the council-hall of Jupiter, watched the changes taking place upon the earth; and as each new city was built and the flames of its altar-fires rose up toward the white clouds around Olympus, they smiled upon the work of man's hand and made it prosper. Nowhere was the worship of the gods forgotten, but in each undertaking the protection of some deity was sought and a sacrifice offered that success might be assured. Scattered throughout the land, in town or by the wayside, were shrines where the farmer laid his offering of doves in return for a rich harvest, or a soldier hung some trophy of victory upon his safe return from the war or a sailor, starting on some uncertain voyage, burned spices and incense that the gods might grant favoring winds to all those who go down to the sea in ships.

But in every city there was one temple more beautiful than the rest, and this was dedicated to that particular deity who had named the city and was its especial protector; and as city after city was built throughout the fair land of Greece, each of the gods wished to have the naming of it that he might thereby receive added worship and honor. There was much jealousy among them on this score, and they watched eagerly each thriving inland town or seaport, knowing that in a few years it would become a great city, building costly temples and erecting statues to the god whom it delighted to honor.

So once, when a certain town on the coast of Greece began to grow into a large and prosperous city, there was much dispute in the council hall of Jupiter as to who should have the privilege of naming it. Perhaps the gods were looking far into the future and saw what this city was destined to become; but however that may be, the gods and goddesses argued so fiercely over the matter that Jupiter was obliged to interfere, lest some murmur of this unusual discord should reach the earth. Then one by one the various contestants withdrew until only Neptune and Minerva were left to dispute over their respective rights to the naming of the city. There being no ground for either's claim, Jupiter at length decided to give the much-coveted honor to whichever of these two should present the most useful gift to the people of the city.

Neptune then struck the ground with his trident, and where the earth opened there sprang out a horse with snow-white mane and arching neck and a splendid body on which a king might be proud to ride. The gods and goddesses who had assembled to witness the contest were delighted with Neptune's gift, and waited impatiently to see what better thing Minerva would be able to offer. Surprise, amusement, and contempt were written on the faces of the spectators when the goddess stepped forward, holding in her hand an olive branch. But Jupiter, wisest of them all, did not smile, for he was listening while Minerva told of the great value her gift would have for the people of the new city. She described all the uses to which its leaves, its fruit, and even its bark could be put, adding that the olive branch was to be a sign of peace among all nations, and was therefore of more true service to man than a war-horse, which would bring upon him only bloodshed and disaster. To these wise words the gods were forced to agree, so to Minerva was granted the privilege of naming the city; and as she was called Athena, by the Greeks, she named the place Athens, which it is called to this very day. Before many years passed a splendid marble temple was built on the hill just above the city, and this was dedicated to Athena, whose colossal statue, carved by the famous sculptor Phidias, adorned the interior. They called this temple the Parthenon,7 and from the ruins that still remain we know that the hand of man has never built anything to equal it in beauty.

CHAPTER V
APOLLO AND KING ADMETUS

THERE would have been but little trouble between Jupiter and his stately wife if no one but Minerva ever gave the watchful Juno8 cause for jealousy; but other goddesses, and even mortal maidens, found favor in the eyes of Jupiter, and for their sake he often left her side. From his throne in the high heavens the ruler of the world saw not only the goddesses, with their glory of immortal youth, but also the daughters of men endowed with that same beauty and grace which the gods themselves had bestowed upon the first woman. Though Juno "of the snow-white arms" alone enjoyed the title of queen of heaven, she knew that she had many rivals for the love of Jupiter; and it was this jealousy of all loveliness in woman that made her ever watchful and revengeful. Perhaps it was the cause, too, of the very changeable temper that her husband accused her of possessing.

Apollo Belvedere

Whoever won the affections of Jupiter was sure to be persecuted by "cruel Juno's unrelenting hate," as the poet Virgil says; but this did not hinder the ruler of the gods from leaving very often the marble halls of Olympus to wander, in some disguise, about the earth. It was after such an absence that the watchful Juno learned of Jupiter's love for fair-haired Latona, goddess of dark nights. As this new rival was not a mortal maiden who could be punished with death, the wrathful queen was forced to be content with banishing the goddess forever from Olympus, and compelling her to live upon the earth. Not satisfied with this, she decreed that any one who took pity on the unhappy goddess, or gave her any help, would incur the lasting displeasure of Juno.

For days and nights Latona wandered, not daring to ask for food or shelter, since all men knew of Juno's decree. She slept at night in some spot where the trees offered protection from wind and rain, and her only food was the scanty store that she could gather by the way—berries, nuts, wild honey, and sometimes bits of bread dropped by children in their play. One day, being very thirsty, she stopped beside a clear pool to drink; but some reapers who were passing by saw her, and hoping to gain favor with Juno they stepped into the pool and stirred up the water into such muddiness that poor Latona could not drink. Angered by such uncalled-for cruelty, the goddess prayed to Jupiter that these wicked men might never leave the spot where they were standing. Jupiter from his throne in the high heavens heard her prayer, and in answer he turned the reapers into ugly green frogs and bade them stay forever in the muddy pool. And ever afterward when men came upon slimy ponds, where rank weeds grew and the water oozed from muddy banks, there they found the blinking frogs—even as Jupiter had willed.

After wandering some miles further Latona came at last to the seashore and here she begged Neptune, "the god who shakes the shores," to come to her aid, for she knew that Juno's power did not extend to the ruler of the sea. Seeing her distress, and pitying the poor persecuted goddess, Neptune sent her a dolphin, who took her on his back and swam with her to the floating island of Delos, which the kindly sea-god had caused to appear out of the depth of the ocean. Here Latona landed, and was for a time content; but the rocking of the island soon grew unbearable, and she begged the aid of Neptune a second time. He obligingly chained the island to the bottom of the Ægean Sea, and Latona had no further cause for complaint. On this island were born her two children: Apollo, god of the sun, and Diana, goddess of the moon.

When the children were grown, Jupiter took them to Olympus, though not without much protest from the ever-jealous Juno. The young Apollo's beauty and his skill in music gained him great favor among the gods, and found him worshipers in every town and city throughout the land of Greece. So conscious of his power did Apollo become, that he sometimes dared to assert his authority, unmindful of the will of Jupiter; and on one occasion he so angered his divine parent that he was banished to the earth, and made to serve Admetus, king of Thessaly.

In spite of his disgrace, Apollo managed to cheer his lonely hours of labor with his music; and as his work was no more difficult than to care for the king's sheep, he had abundant leisure to play upon his lyre while his flocks grazed on the sunny hillsides. As soon as he touched the strings, all the wild things in the forest crept out to hear. The fox came slinking from his hole among the rocks, and the timid deer drew close to the player and stayed beside him, listening. The strains of the wonderful music were carried across the meadows, and the mowers stopped their work, wondering where the player might be. One day they brought word to the king that some god must be among them, for no mortal could produce such music as they had heard. So Admetus sent for the shepherd, and when the youth stood before him, he marveled at his great beauty, and still more at the golden lyre that Apollo held in his hand. Then when the young musician, in obedience to the king's command, began to play, all those who heard him were filled with wonder, and felt sure that a god had come to dwell among them. But Admetus asked no questions, only made the youth his head shepherd and treated him with all kindness.

Though a god, and no true shepherd, Apollo served the king faithfully, and when, at last, his time of service was over and Jupiter called him back to Olympus, Apollo, wishing to show some favor in return for the king's kindness, begged for Admetus the gift of immortality. This request the wise Jupiter granted, but only on the condition that when the time came for the king to die, some one could be found to take his place. Apollo agreed to these terms, and Admetus, knowing the conditions on which the gift was made, accepted his immortality gladly. For a time all went well; but the inevitable hour came when the Fates decreed that Admetus's life was ended, and that he must go the way of all mortals unless some one would die in his stead. The king was much beloved by his people; but no one's devotion to his sovereign was great enough to inspire him to make the needed sacrifice.

Then Alcestis, the beautiful wife of Admetus, learned of the price that must be paid for her husband's immortality and gladly offered her life in exchange for the king's. So, in all her young grace and beauty, she went down into the dark region of Hades, where no sunlight ever came and where her joyous laughter was forever hushed in the silence that reigns among the dead. Thus Admetus gained immortality; but his happiness was too dearly bought, for as the days went by he mourned more and more for his beautiful young wife, and in his dreams he saw her walking like a shadow among the grim shapes that move noiselessly in the silent halls of death. Bitterly he repented of his selfishness in accepting the sacrifice of her life, and his immortality grew hateful to him since each day only added to his sorrow. So he prayed to Apollo to recall his gift, and to give him back his wife Alcestis. It was not in the power of that god to change a decree of Jupiter's; but the Ruler of all things looked down from heaven, and, seeing the great grief and remorse of Admetus, he withdrew the gift that had cost the king so dear, and sent Hercules to the kingdom of Pluto with commands to let Alcestis go. Very gladly the god carried this message to the gloomy realm of Hades, where amid the myriad shadow-shapes he sought and found Alcestis; and out of the dreadful darkness in which she walked alone, Hercules led her back to earth again.9

CHAPTER VI
APOLLO THE MUSICIAN

I

WHEN Apollo left King Admetus and returned to the halls of Olympus, he had not rested there long before he found that there was further service for him to render on the earth. Among the many noted deeds that he performed, the most famous was his slaying of a monstrous serpent called the Python, which was born of the slime that remained on the surface of the earth after the Deluge.10 Apollo killed the creature with his golden arrows, and then went to the help of Neptune, who, though a powerful deity in his own realm, was often obliged to ask help of the other gods when he wished to accomplish anything on land. Hearing that Neptune wished to build a great wall around the city of Troy, and remembering the aid that the sea-god had given his mother Latona in her great need, Apollo went down to the sea and offered his services to Neptune. Of course no son of Jupiter could be expected to do the work of a slave, but this was not necessary, even in the building of a wall; for Apollo sat down on a grassy bank near by, and, with his lyre in his hand, began to play such exquisite music that the very stones were bewitched, and rising from the ground of their own accord took their places in the wall. Still under the spell of Apollo's music, others followed in quick succession, and the wall rose higher and higher, until before nightfall the whole work was finished. When the last stone had dropped into place, Apollo stopped his playing and returned to the bright halls of Olympus; while Neptune, shaking the salt spray from his shaggy eyebrows, stared hard at the walls that had risen by magic before his wondering eyes.

II

The story of Arachne's sad fate should have been warning enough to all mortals not to compare themselves with the gods; but such was the pride of a certain youth named Marsyas that he boasted openly of his skill in flute-playing, and dared to proclaim himself the equal of Apollo. Now Marsyas had not always been a musician, for he was by birth a shepherd— some even say a satyr—and had never seen a flute or heard it played until one day, as he sat tending his flock on the bank of a stream, he heard sounds of music coming from some spot near by. He was very curious to see who the musician might be, but he dared not move lest he startle the player and make the beautiful melody cease. So he sat still and waited; and presently there came floating down the stream a flute—something that

Marsyas had never seen before. He hurriedly snatched it out of the water, and, no longer hearing the wonderful music, he guessed that it had come from the strange thing he held in his hand. He put the flute to his lips, and lo, the same sweet melody greeted his ears, for the flute was not a common thing such as any man might use—it was a beautiful instrument that belonged to no less a person than Minerva. The goddess had hidden herself on the bank of the stream and had been trying her skill as a flute-player; but chancing to look down into the water, she saw her puffed-out cheeks and distorted features and angrily threw the flute into the stream. Thus it had come into Marsyas's possession; and the shepherd, having found such a treasure, never let it leave his hands. He neglected his work and left his flocks unguarded while he spent all his days in the delight of flute-playing.

It was not long before he believed himself to be the greatest musician in all Greece; and then it was only a step further to declare that even Apollo could not equal him in the sweetness of his playing. The god of music allowed this boasting to go for some time unpunished; but at last he grew angry at the presumption of the shepherd boy, and summoned Marsyas to a contest in which the nine Muses were to be judges. Nothing daunted, Marsyas accepted the challenge; and on the morning when the contest took place, a great silence fell over all the earth, as if every living thing had stopped to listen. The playing of Marsyas was wonderfully sweet, and as the soft tones of his flute greeted the listeners' ears they sat as if under a spell until the last sounds died away. Then Apollo took up his golden lyre, and when he struck the first chords, the air was filled with music far sweeter than any melody that had fallen from the lips of Marsyas. The judges, however, found it hard to give a verdict in favor of either musician; so a second time Marsyas began to play, and his music was so strangely wild and sweet that even Apollo listened in delight. But, charmed as he was by the youth's playing, the god of music had no intention of being outdone by a shepherd; so when he took up his golden lyre again, he began to sing, and added the wonder of his voice to the sweetness of his playing. When the singing ended there was no longer any doubt to whom the victory belonged; and Marsyas was forced to admit his defeat. As the price of failure was to be the terrible penalty of being flayed alive, the wretched Marsyas had to submit to this cruel death. Apollo bound him to a tree and slew him with his own hands.

III

When the news of Marsyas's dreadful fate spread abroad, people were careful for many years not to anger any of the deities by presuming to rival them; but in time the memory of that tragic event faded away, and the horror of it was forgotten.

In the halls of King Midas was the noise of great mirth and feasting, and the sound of music filled the spacious room where the king and his court sat at the banquet-table. Beside the king stood Pan, his favorite flute-player, who was no other than the famous sylvan god of shepherds; and as the wine went round and the king grew boastful of his possessions, he exclaimed loudly that not even Apollo himself could produce such exquisite music as fell from the flute of Pan. The guests, remembering the fate of Marsyas, grew pale and begged the king not to let his boast be heard; but Midas laughed scornfully and, raising his drinking cup above his head, called upon Apollo to appear.

To the surprise and dismay of all, the god of music suddenly stood before them, beautiful as the dawn and glowing with divine wrath. Though Pan was himself a deity, he had no desire to challenge Apollo, and looked fearfully at the sun-god's angry frown; but the king, drunk with pride, commanded him to play, and bade the god of music surpass the playing if he could. There was, of course, no question as to which was the better musician, and the guests loudly proclaimed Apollo the victor. One story tells that to prove further the superiority of Apollo's playing the company went to the old mountain-god Tmolus, and let him make the final decision. Tmolus had to clear the trees from his ears to listen; and having done this he bent his head, and all his trees leaned with him. He heard with delight both musicians play; and when the last soft notes fell from Apollo's lyre, the mountain-god awarded him the victory. But Midas at the beginning of the contest had demanded the right to decide on the merits of the players, and he would not accept this verdict. In his mad perversity and fondness for his favorite, he cried out that Pan was the better player, and would therefore be awarded the prize. Angered at this unfair decision, Apollo left the banquet-hall, but not before he had assured Midas that the injustice would be punished.

These words came true in a most unexpected way, for when the king looked into his mirror the next morning, he found a pair of large fuzzy ass's ears growing in the place of his own natural ones. Horrified at his absurd appearance, Midas did not dare show himself to his people; but sent in haste for a barber, and bade him make a wig large enough to cover the monstrous ears. For many hours the barber was closeted with the king, and when the wig was finished, he was allowed to leave the palace, after having sworn never to reveal the king's misfortune under pain of death. For some time the secret was safely kept; but the poor barber found life unbearable, since he lived in constant fear of letting out the truth about the king's ears in spite of his frantic efforts to be silent. Whenever Midas appeared in the city streets, the barber had to rush home and shut himself up lest he should scream out the story of the wig. One day he thought of a happy solution of his difficulty and one that broke his long seal of silence without endangering his life. He went out into the fields, dug a deep hole, and putting his head down as far as he could he shouted:—"King Midas has ass's ears, King Midas has ass's ears."

Then he went home again, much happier for having told some one of his secret, even though it was only Mother Earth. But the truth once told did not stay hidden even in the earth; for in time the hole was filled again and reeds grew over the spot, and as the wind swayed them back and forth they murmured: "King Midas has ass's ears. King Midas has ass's ears." It was not long before all the people in the countryside had gathered to hear the strange whispering of the reeds, and then the secret could be kept no longer. But though every one knew the truth King Midas continued to wear his wig, and no one ever saw the real size of his ears.

CHAPTER VII
THE LOVE OF APOLLO

I

LIKE his father, Jupiter, the young Apollo was not content to stay always in the shining halls of Olympus, but spent many days wandering over the broad lands of Greece in search of adventure, or for the sake of some maiden's love. There were many fair ones among the daughters of men, and they were wont to look with favor upon the beautiful young god who came down from the high heavens to woo them. Each morning as he drove across the sky the fiery horses that were harnessed to the chariot of the sun, some maiden gazed with longing at the splendor above her, and prayed that the radiant Apollo might look kindly upon her. Seldom did these prayers go unanswered; but sometimes the heart of the god was untouched by the devotion so freely offered, and the maiden pined away over her hopeless love.

Such a one was Clytie,11 who worshiped the glorious sun-god, and longed in secret for his love; but in spite of her tears and sighing she met with only coldness in return. Each day she rose before the dawn to greet Apollo as soon as his chariot appeared in the heavens, and all day long she watched him until the last rays of light were lost behind the hills. But the young god felt no sympathy for her sorrow, and the unhappy Clytie grew so pale and sick with longing that Jupiter in pity changed her into a sunflower, that she might always stand watching the course of the sun, and turn her face forever toward him, no matter where his beams might shine.

II

The great beauty of Apollo12 usually assured his success whenever he stooped from his high estate to love the maidens of the earth; but once he was repaid for his hard-heartedness to poor Clytie, and failed in his wooing when he sought the love of the beautiful wood-nymph Daphne. He was wandering one day in the forest when he came suddenly upon Daphne as she was gathering flowers, and her beauty and grace so charmed him that he desired her love above everything else in the world. Not wishing to frighten her, he stood still and softly spoke her name. When the nymph heard his voice, she turned quickly and looked at him with the startled eyes of some wild forest-creature. Surprise and fear held her for a moment while Apollo spoke again gently and begged her not to be afraid, for he was no hunter nor even a rude shepherd. But Daphne only shrank away, fearful of his eagerness; and when Apollo grew bolder and ventured to draw near, she turned and fled through the forest. Angered at this rebuff, the god followed her, and though the nymph ran swiftly she could not escape from her pursuer, who was now more than ever determined to win her.

Apollo and Daphne

In and out among the trees she darted, hoping to bewilder him into giving up the chase; but Apollo kept close behind, and little by little gained on her flying feet. Wearied but unyielding, Daphne now hurried her steps toward the stream at the edge of the forest, where she knew that she would find her father, the river-god Peneus. As she neared the stream she cried aloud to him for help; and just as Apollo had reached her side and his outstretched hand was on her shoulder, a rough bark began to enclose her soft body in its protecting sheath; green branches sprouted from the ends of her uplifted arms; and her floating hair became only waving leaves under the grasp of the god's eager fingers. Apollo stood dismayed at this transformation, and when he saw a laurel tree rooted in the spot where, but a moment ago, had stood a beautiful living maiden, he repented of his 47 folly in having pursued her and sat for many days beside the river, mourning her loss.

Thus it was that the laurel became the favorite tree of Apollo; and when the god returned sadly to Olympus, he decreed that whenever poet or musician or any victor in the games was to be crowned with a garland of leaves, those leaves were to be taken from the laurel tree in memory of Daphne.

III

In one of the flower-filled meadows of sunny Greece, there played all day a golden-haired boy named Phaëton,13 who was the pride and delight of his mother Clymene, a stately maiden whom Apollo had once wooed and won. The boy was willful and headstrong, but beautiful as a young god; and his mother, in her foolish pride, often reminded him how favored he was above all other children in being the son of Apollo. Each morning she led him to a place where he could see the sun rise, and told him that his father was just then harnessing the fiery steeds to his golden-wheeled car, and would soon be leaving his palace of burnished gold to drive across the heavens, bringing daylight to the darkened earth. She told him of Apollo's great beauty, and of his wonderful music, and of his high position among the gods, because his chariot was nothing less than the glorious sun. Phaëton never tired of hearing these stories, and it was no wonder that he became very proud of his divine parentage, and boasted of it among his playmates. The children only laughed at his wonderful tales, and to convince them he grew more arrogant in his bearing, until they, angered by his continued boasts, bade him give some proof of his claims or else be silent. This Phaëton could not do; so they taunted him with his godlike appearance, and sneered at his pretensions until the boy, roused to action by their repeated insults, ran to his mother, and begged her to tell him whether he might not speak to his wonderful, but unknown father, and obtain from him some proof to silence the children's tongues.

Clymene hesitated to send the child on the long necessary journey, but yielding at last to his entreaties, she showed him the way to his father's palace. It was night when Phaëton set out, and he was obliged to travel quickly if he wished to reach his journey's end before the sun-car left the golden portals of the east. The palace of the sun was marvelously wrought, and the light from its golden columns and glittering jeweled towers so dazzled the eyes of Phaëton that he was afraid to draw near. But remembering the taunts of his playmates, he grew bolder, and sought out his father to beg the boon for which he had traveled so far and wearily. When Apollo, from his ivory throne, saw the boy approaching, he welcomed him kindly and called him by the name of son. Hearing this, Phaëton lost all fear, and told his father how the children had refused to believe Clymene's stories, and had taunted him because he could not prove the truth of his mother's claim.

The lofty brow of Apollo grew cloudy as he listened to Phaëton's words, and he promised to give the boy the proof he desired by granting him any favor he might ask. Instantly Phaëton demanded that he be allowed that very day to drive the sun-chariot; for when those on the earth saw him in that exalted place, they could no longer refuse to believe that he was indeed the favored child of Apollo. Dismayed at this unexpected request, the sun-god sought to persuade Phaëton to ask some other boon, for he knew that no hand but his own could guide the four winged horses that were harnessed to the golden sun-car. But the boy was determined to carry out his plan; and with all the willfulness of a conceited child, he refused to heed his father's warnings. As Apollo had sworn by the river Styx—the most terrible of all oaths—to grant Phaëton's request whatever it might be, he was obliged to fulfill his promise; and very reluctantly he led the boy to the portals of the palace, where the impatient horses already stood pawing the ground.

Phaëton gazed at the sun-car in delight, for it was all of gold—except the spokes of the wheel, which were of silver—and the body of the chariot was studded with chrysolites and diamonds that reflected the sun's dazzling brightness. The impatient boy sprang into the chariot and seized the reins in his hands, while his father bound on his head the blazing sun rays; but before the journey was begun, Apollo poured over him a cooling essence, that his skin might not be shriveled by the burning heat of the sun, and gave him careful instructions how to handle the restless steeds. Phaëton but half listened to these words, and fretted to be off on his triumphant course; so Apollo ordered the gates to be thrown open, and the sun-car dashed out into the heavens.

For a while all went well, for the boy remembered his father's caution about using a whip on the fiery horses; but as the day wore on he became reckless, and forgot everything but his own proud triumph. Faster and faster he drove, flourishing his whip, and never heeding in what direction the maddened horses sped. Soon he lost his way and the chariot came so close to the earth that its fierce heat dried up the rivers and scorched the ground and shriveled up all vegetation, even turning the natives in that part of the country brown,—which color they are still to this very day. Smoke rose up from the charred and blackened earth, and it so clouded the eyes of the now terrified Phaëton that he could not find his way back to the path of the sun and drove wildly far away from the earth. This caused terrible disaster, for under the sudden cold all growing things withered, and the blight of frost settled over all the land.

Then a great cry arose from the people of the earth when they saw their country laid waste; and though Jupiter was fast asleep on his golden couch he heard the cry, and started up in surprise. What *could* be happening on the earth that the sound of human wailing should break in upon the silence of his dreams! One glance was sufficient for him to see the smoke rising from the burnt-up land and to realize the cause of all that useless destruction; for far across the heavens—like a vanishing comet—Phaëton was madly driving the flaming chariot of the sun. Angered at the sight of a mere boy presuming to take upon himself so great a task, Jupiter seized one of his deadliest thunderbolts and hurled it at the unhappy youth, whose scorched body was immediately dashed from its lofty seat and sank into the calm waters of the Eridanus River.

Clymene mourned her son's untimely death, and gathered his remains from the river that they might have honorable burial. Phaëton's dearest friend, Cycnus, continued to haunt the river's edge, looking for any relic of his favorite that might chance to rise to the surface of the water. In recognition of this devotion the gods changed him into a swan that might stay forever on the river and plunge his head fearlessly into the clear waters to search for some scattered fragments of his unfortunate friend.

Niobe

CHAPTER VIII
DIANA

I

DURING the childhood of Apollo and Diana the goddess Latona lived happily on the island of Delos, and forgot all her early misfortunes in the joy of her children. As they grew up she boasted of their strength and beauty to all who came to the shores of Delos, and no village or hamlet—however small—but had heard of Latona's children. When Grecian mothers put their little ones to bed at night, they told wonderful tales of an island far out at sea where a brother and sister lived who were fairer than all the flowers in the meadows; and maidens, sighing for a loveliness greater than their own, wove garlands to adorn the shrines of those two who walked the earth in all their immortal grace.

Latona was proud of her children's fame, and boasted of it far and wide. Few mothers cared to dispute her claim, and these spoke only in whispers; but there was one, bolder than the rest, who openly laughed at the goddess's boast and taunted her with having but *two* such children whom she could praise. This was Niobe, a Grecian princess and the mother of fourteen children,—seven sons and seven daughters,—all of them fair and strong and godlike in spite of their mortal birth. When Niobe learned that the people in her kingdom were loud in their praises of Latona's children, and were neglecting to honor her own splendid sons and daughters, she was very angry and ordered all the statues of Apollo and Diana to be destroyed; for the people, in their devotion to beauty, had set up many in the temples and the market place. Then she bade a messenger go tell the goddess what had been done, and show her in what contempt the mother of fourteen children held her who had but two.

When Latona received the message she was so enraged at the insult that her desire for revenge knew no bounds. She called Apollo and Diana to her side and commanded them to go forth and slay the children of Niobe. It was easy for Apollo to accomplish his part of the cruel task, for he met the seven sons of Niobe hunting, and slew them so quickly that not one of the brothers had time to ask what he had done to merit the god's wrath. The daughters of Niobe were in the palace with their mother; but this did not daunt the young Diana, who put seven sharp arrows in her quiver, and, bow in hand, went forth to complete Latona's revenge. She found the maidens seated at Niobe's side, weaving, and one by one the remorseless goddess shot them down in spite of their mother's heart-broken cries for mercy. Finding that her entreaties were in vain, and seeing six of her daughters lying dead beside her, the distracted Niobe sought to shield the remaining one with her own body while she prayed wildly to the gods to spare her this one child. But the gods were deaf to her cries, and Diana, fitting the last arrow to her bow, shot the maiden as she cowered in her mother's arms.

Over her fallen body the wretched Niobe wept so long that the gods at last felt pity for her grief, and changed her into stone. This statue was placed by a running stream, and ever afterward the waters were fed by the tears that continued to course down the cheeks of the stone image; and travelers came from foreign lands to gaze on this marvel of a devoted mother who could not cease from mourning for her children even when turned into stone.

II

Though the goddess Diana14 spent most of her daylight hours in hunting, it was not often that she exercised her skill to such cruel purpose as was shown in the case of poor Niobe. Wherever the wild deer roamed, and the pathless forest knew no touch of woodman's ax, there Diana, fleet-footed and tireless, followed the chase. As soon as the flaming chariot of the sun threw its first streak of light across the hills, the goddess donned her short tunic, and, armed with her golden bow and quiver, set out with her band of nymphs for the day's hunt. At noontide, wearied with the chase, she sought out some secluded spot where the mountain stream ran clear, and where the foliage hung round her like a curtain.

Diana of Versailles

On a certain day, when she and her maidens were enjoying the refreshing coolness of the water, they heard a slight rustle among the trees, and looking around, perceived a young hunter watching them. This was

Actæon, who had himself been following the deer since daybreak, and had been drawn to this spot by the noise of running water. As he neared the stream he heard sounds of girlish laughter, and this so roused his curiosity that he hastily put aside the branches to see who the merrymakers might be. Great was his dismay when he recognized Diana and her nymphs; but before he could disappear among the bushes the goddess saw him, and catching up some water in her hand, she threw it into his face, crying: "Go now, if you can, and say that you have seen Diana at her bath."

The moment these words were spoken Actæon felt a queer change coming over him, and he stared in horror at his hands and feet, which were becoming hoofs, and at his skin, which was rapidly changing into a deer's hide. Antlers grew out of his head, he dropped on all fours, and found himself turned into a stag. Before he quite realized what had befallen him he heard the baying of hounds, and knew that his only safety was in flight. He dashed off through the bushes, but the dogs were on his track. Before he had gone far the pack had overtaken him, since he knew no lore of the wild things by which they elude their enemies, and were snapping and snarling at his throat. Deprived of his human voice he could not cry for help, and in a moment the hounds had torn him into pieces. So was Diana avenged.

III

There was another young hunter who encountered Diana and her maidens in the woods, but he met with a kinder fate at the hands of the goddess than did poor Actæon, whose only fault had been a most natural curiosity.

The fleet-footed Diana was no more ardent in the chase than was the hunter Orion, who roamed the forest all day with his faithful dog, Sirius. One morning, as he rushed eagerly through the woods in pursuit of a deer, he came suddenly upon the seven Pleiades,—nymphs of Diana,—who were resting after a long and arduous hunt begun at daybreak. Charmed with their beauty, Orion drew nearer, but the maidens, terrified at his outstretched arms, fled away through the forest. Undaunted by the remembrance of Actæon's fate, the hunter pursued the flying nymphs, determined that so much beauty should not escape him. Seeing that he was gaining on them in spite of their swift feet, the maidens called upon Diana for help, and were at once changed into seven white pigeons which flew up into the heavens before Orion's astonished eyes. Sometime later these same Pleiades became seven bright stars, and were set as a constellation in the sky, where they have remained ever since.

Orion continued to hunt from early dawn until nightfall without any misfortune overtaking him on account of his impetuous love-making. On the contrary his ardor evidently found favor with the goddess Diana, for one day, when he unexpectedly met her alone in the forest, she smiled graciously upon him and offered to share the day's sport with him. Perhaps it was the beauty of the young hunter as well as his boldness that charmed the goddess; but however that may be, she continued to meet him in the forest, and they hunted together hour after hour until the twilight began to fall. Then Diana knew that she must leave her lover and mount her silver moon-car.

When Apollo learned of his sister's affection for the young hunter, he was very angry, for Diana had refused the love of the gods, and had begged of Jupiter the right to live unwed. The sun-god determined therefore to put an end to Orion's wooing. So he waited at the shadowy portals of the west until Diana, her nightly journey over, descended from her silver car and threw the reins on the necks of her wearied steeds. Then Apollo spoke to his sister of her hunting, and praised her skill with the bow. Presently he pointed to a tiny speck that was rising and falling on the crest of the waves a long distance away, and bidding her use this as a target, he challenged her to prove her skill. Diana, suspecting no treachery, fitted an arrow into her bow and let it fly with unerring aim. Great was her distress when she learned what her brother's trickery had led her to do; for it was no floating log or bit of seaweed that her arrow had pierced, but the body of Orion. Apollo had seen the hunter go each morning to the ocean to bathe, and he thought this an easy way to dispose of the unworthy lover.

Diana mourned Orion15 many days; and to keep his memory honored she placed him and his faithful dog, Sirius, in the sky as constellations.

CHAPTER IX
THE STORY OF ENDYMION

THE chaste Diana was not only a famous huntress, but she was goddess of the moon as well. By day she roamed the forest with her band of nymphs, and by night she sailed in her bright moon-car across the star-strewn sky, and looked down at the sleeping earth lying in the shadow except where her soft light fell. As soon as Apollo had driven his tired, foam-flecked horses within the western gates, and twilight had begun to creep over the hills, Diana mounted her silver car drawn by milk-white steeds, and started on her nightly journey. During the first hours of her ride, the friendly twilight kept a faint glow in the heavens, and the road lay plain before her; but as night came on and the blackness deepened, her horses might have wandered from their accustomed path had not the stars wakened from their day-dreaming and come out in great luminous clusters to light the goddess on her way. Though the journey was always the same, night after night, Diana never wearied of her course or found the sleeping earth less lovely, as it unfolded hour by hour before her eyes.

One evening as she looked down upon the quiet scene, she saw the form of a shepherd-boy lying upon a grassy hilltop, where the moonlight shone full upon his upturned face. Diana was not susceptible to love; but when she saw Endymion sleeping, she marveled at his beauty, and felt a strange longing to be near him. So she stepped softly from her silver car and floated down to the earth—to the spot where the unconscious shepherd lay dreaming. There was perfect stillness all around, and no whisper came but the soft murmur from the pine-trees, which sounded like some great creature sighing in its sleep. For some time the goddess watched the youth in silence, then, stooping, she gently kissed him. Endymion half wakened at her touch, and looked sleepily around, bewildered by the radiance that seemed to be enfolding him in its unearthly light. But in a moment the glory had faded away, and there was only the deep blueness of the night all about him; for Diana, frightened at her own boldness, had hurried back to her silver car and had sped away into the darkness. Endymion thought then that he had dreamed a dream of some beautiful form that had lingered by his side, and although he waited patiently and hopefully all through the night, he saw no other vision, and only the dawn came to greet his weary eyes.

The next night Diana drove her milk-white horses impatiently and often at random, until the quiet stars, as they watched her restless course, wondered and felt half afraid. When the clouds wrapped her closely in their white embrace, the goddess drove them angrily aside, lest they shut out from her eyes the sight of the sleeping earth. At last she drew near the hillside where Endymion lay, and, on seeing him there, Diana glided again from her silver car and stood beside his unconscious form. At her light touch he stirred, and tried to rouse himself from his heavy slumber; but some spell seemed to bind his eyelids, and through sleep-dimmed eyes he saw the radiance fade away. Night after night he felt the presence of that bright being whom his eyes so longed to behold; but only in his dreams could he see her face or touch her floating garments that passed by him like the rustle of the night wind.

Each night Diana left her restless horses to stand unwatched among the shifting clouds, while she lingered on the earth to gaze upon the sleeping shepherd-boy; and as she stood beside him she wished that he might always be as now—ever beautiful, ever young. So to keep him untouched by sickness or sorrow or death she took him to Mount Latmus, where there was a cave dedicated in her honor which no mortal foot had ever profaned. Here she placed Endymion, and caused an eternal sleep to fall upon him, so that his body in all its youth and beauty might never know decay. And every night when her long journey was ended, and the watchful stars had withdrawn their shining, Diana hastened to the lonely cave on Mount Latmus, there to linger beside Endymion16 sleeping, and touch him with a kiss that could not waken.

CHAPTER X
MERCURY

I

MERCURY was the son of Jupiter and Maia, goddess of the plains, and from the day of his birth he was a most remarkable infant, even for a god. When scarcely a day old, he sprang from his mother's arms, and ran some distance off to where a tortoise shell was lying on the ground. Picking this up, he bored holes in its side, stretched strings across it, and began to play. Thus it was that the first lyre was made.

Flying Mercury

Proud of this beginning to his day's adventures, Mercury ran away again toward evening, when his mother was asleep, and roamed about the fragrant meadows where Apollo kept his herd of cattle. The pasturage was rich and the oxen were fat, and the mischievous young god—only a day old—decided to have some of them for his dinner. He took fifty of the herd and tied branches of leaves to their feet—so that their hoofs might leave no print on the smooth turf—and drove them to a quiet spot far away from the meadow. Here he killed and ate two of the oxen, and kept the rest in hiding for another day's feast. Then he hurried back to his mother who had not yet wakened.

When Apollo found late that evening that fifty of his cattle were gone, he searched but could not find them. As he was about to give them up as lost, he remembered that a son had been lately born to Jupiter, whom that divine ruler had appointed to be the god of thieves. Suspecting that his stolen oxen were in the hands of this master-thief, Apollo hastened to where Maia and the babe were sleeping. Rousing the child angrily, the irate god accused him of the theft; but Mercury protested his innocence, and asked, "How could an infant but a day old ever do such an unheard-of thing?" Apollo was unconvinced, however, by this appearance of candor, and feeling sure of the boy's guilt, dragged him off to Olympus, where Mercury found it impossible to pretend any longer that he knew nothing of the missing oxen. He acknowledged his thieving, showed Apollo the hiding place of the stolen cattle, and in return for those that he had eaten gave the sun-god his wonderful new lyre. This gift so delighted Apollo that he presented the day-old prince of thieves with a magic wand, which, when held between any who were quarreling, would cause all anger and strife to cease. To test the value of the wand Mercury thrust it between two snakes which were struggling over the possession of a wounded bird; and immediately they twined themselves around the staff, and remained coiled together in perfect friendliness. This pleased Mercury so much that he bade them stay there forever as long as the wand should last.17

There were two other valuable gifts that the gods gave the young Mercury,—a winged cap and a pair of winged sandals,—so that, as the messenger of the gods, he might be fleet of foot on his many errands to and from Olympus.

"Hastily beneath his feet he bound
The fair ambrosial golden sandals, worn
To bear him over ocean like the wind
And o'er the boundless land."

—BRYANT'S Homer's *Odyssey*, Book V, line 56.

Among the varied duties assigned to Mercury was that of conducting the souls of the dead to Hades; but this did not occupy all the god's time, and he still had many hours in which to go on other missions. In spite of his rather doubtful reputation for honesty, the gods often sought his assistance in their difficulties; and in one very delicate commission he proved himself a competent ally. This was when Jupiter went wooing the maiden Io.

The jealous and vengeful Juno was always on the watch whenever her lord took a fancy to go wandering about the earth; so to woo the gentle Io unseen by his wife required some diplomacy on Jupiter's part. Accordingly he spread a thick cloud over the meadow where he was wont to meet the maiden, and trusted that its appearance would not arouse Juno's suspicions. He also took the precaution to visit Io at the time when the watchful queen of heaven was accustomed to sleep; but one day Juno awoke sooner than usual, and finding Jupiter absent, she at once surmised that he was adventuring again in some love-affair. When she looked down at the earth, she saw the thick cloud that hung over the meadow and noticed that it never altered its position, no matter how the winds blew. Feeling sure that this was some trick intended to deceive her, the wrathful goddess glided down to the earth and appeared at the astonished Jupiter's side—but not before he had had time to change Io into a heifer.

"Golden-sandaled" Juno walked about the meadow gathering flowers, then she asked her husband why he was lingering there, so far from bright Olympus. Jupiter answered that he was amusing himself by creating a heifer. This explanation did not deceive Juno; but she pretended to be satisfied, and praised the beautiful creature's glossy skin and large soft eyes. Then she demanded it of Jupiter as a gift, and the ruler of the gods, not knowing how to refuse, consented. The triumphant goddess led away the heifer and put her in charge of Argus. Now Argus had a hundred eyes, and though he often went to sleep, some of his eyes always kept awake; so Juno felt sure that no device of Jupiter's could enable Io to escape from the watchful guardian who never wholly slept.

Meanwhile Jupiter was in despair over this unhappy ending to his wooing, and sought the help of Mercury, who often lent his ready wits to gods and mortals in distress. Laying aside his cap and sandals and snake-entwined wand, by which he might easily be recognized, Mercury went down to the earth in the disguise of a shepherd. With his pipes in his hand he strolled through the country until he came to the mountain-side, where Argus sat watching the heifer; and when he began to play, the music was so sweet that Argus begged him to stop awhile that he might listen longer to the wonderful playing. The wily god consented, and as he piped on, some of the hundred eyes grew drowsy with sleep, but some of them stayed open and watchful.

The droning of the pipes kept on, and to add to the drowsiness of the music, Mercury began to tell stories in a low sing-song tone that cast a kind of spell over the eyes that were still watching. He told of Apollo's affection for the youth Hyacinthus,18 whom Zephyrus, god of the west wind, also loved; and how, when the sun-god was playing quoits with his friend, Zephyrus in a fit of jealous anger blew aside the missile hurled by Apollo so that it struck Hyacinthus and killed him. But the sun-god would not let the fair youth be forgotten, and changed each drop of his blood into delicate white flowers which were forever to bear his name.19 Then Mercury told of Æsculapius, son of Apollo and Coronis, who was entrusted to the care of Chiron,—most famous of the Centaurs,—and was also taught by his divine parent the art of healing. In this he became so skillful that he even restored the dead to life, and so incurred the wrath of Jupiter, who, fearing that Æsculapius20 would receive undue honor, killed him with a thunderbolt. To these stories Mercury added many more that told of the loves of the gods, and at last all the hundred eyes of Argus were closed. Then Mercury, drawing a sharp sword, cut off the great head as it drooped forward, and rolled it down the rocks.

When Juno heard of the death of her faithful servant she was terribly angry, and vowed that she would bring punishment on those who had been the cause of his slaying; but before doing this she commemorated the fidelity of Argus by taking his hundred eyes and putting them in the tail of her favorite bird, the peacock. Then she carried out her revenge by sending an enormous gadfly to torment poor Io, who was still in the form of a heifer. From one country to another the unhappy creature wandered; and once, in a desperate effort to escape her tormentor, she plunged into the sea, which was afterwards called Ionian in her honor. Across this she swam and reached the shore of Africa; but even here the gadfly followed her, and the vengeance of Juno never allowed her a moment's rest. Jupiter could do nothing to ease her sufferings by interceding for her to the remorseless queen of heaven; but at last Juno consented to send away the gadfly and to restore Io to her own form if Jupiter would promise never to visit her again. Reluctantly the ruler of the gods agreed to this demand, and Io became once more a beautiful maiden.

II

When Jupiter went wandering on the earth in search of adventures other than the wooing of some maiden, he often made Mercury his companion, for this slender young god was his favorite among all the dwellers of Olympus. One day both the gods, disguised as travelers, stopped at the hut of an aged couple named Philemon and Baucis; and pretending weariness, they asked to be allowed to rest. The old couple were delighted that strangers had honored their humble roof, and in order to extend the hospitality still further, Philemon decided to kill the one thing he had that could furnish meat for the guests. This was a large fat goose, who had no mind to be killed and eaten, even to supply a meal for gods; so when the old man tried to catch him, he sought refuge between Jupiter's knees. When the ruler of the gods learned that the couple intended to sacrifice their one possession, he was greatly touched by their kindness, but would not allow them to kill the trusting bird that had fled to him for protection.

Then the good wife Baucis set before her guests olives, and cornel berries preserved in vinegar, and cheese, with eggs cooked in the ashes. She laid earthen cups and dishes on the table, which she had already rubbed with sweet-smelling herbs, and placed beside them an earthen pitcher full of their best wine. While the simple meal was going on, and the guests were partaking of a dessert of apples and wild honey, Baucis was so fluttered over her duties as hostess that she did not observe the pitcher; but old Philemon looked on in astonishment at the wine which renewed itself in the pitcher as fast as it was poured out. He whispered to his wife to watch this miracle; and when she, too, saw the never-empty pitcher, she was filled with a vague terror, and looked fearfully at the smiling strangers. So Jupiter told the old man and his wife who their guests really were, and bade them ask of him some boon, swearing by the terrible river Styx to grant whatever they might desire. Then Philemon and Baucis begged that they might be allowed to serve the gods as long as they lived; and that when their time of service was over, they might die together. Pleased with the simplicity of this request, Jupiter gladly promised that all should be as they wished; and he transformed their humble cottage into a beautiful temple, where they might worship the gods all their days. And when after years of faithful service Philemon and Baucis died, Jupiter changed them into lordly oaks, which stood before the pillars of the temple as a monument to their fidelity.

Juno

CHAPTER XI
VENUS

I

ONCE the stately Juno looked down from high-peaked Olympus and saw Jupiter walking in a meadow with a maiden so exquisitely fair that the flowers at her feet looked dull and faded beside her dazzling whiteness. This was Callisto, so famous for her beauty that suitors came from distant lands to woo her; but she cared nothing for their rich gifts, nor would she listen to any vows of love. Then Jupiter sought her as she wandered alone in the meadow; and the maiden gladly yielded to the great ruler of the gods the love that no mortal man had been able to win. When white-armed Juno learned how many hours Jupiter spent by the side of Callisto, she determined to punish the helpless maiden, and accordingly turned her into a bear. For a long time Jupiter sought her in the familiar meadow, but she never came again to meet him. Then one day he found her in the forest with her little son Arcas—both turned into bears by the jealous hate of Juno. Grieved as he was at this misfortune, the ruler of Olympus could not restore them to their human form; but he took them to the heavens, that they might suffer no further harm, and placed them in the sky as the constellations of the Great and Little Bear.

Jupiter often assumed the form of a bird or animal so as to escape Juno's watchful eyes. As a swan he won the love of Leda, and their child was the fair-haired Helen whose beauty cost the men of Troy so dear. As a white bull he wooed the gentle maid Europa, who was frightened at his sudden appearance in the meadow where she was playing; but as soon as she saw how tame the beautiful animal was and how anxious to be petted, she lost all her fear. She made a wreath of flowers to hang about his neck, and grew so accustomed to her new playmate that she got upon his back as he bent his lordly head to receive her garlands. The bull then galloped away toward the sea, and before the terrified girl could realize what had happened he plunged with her into the waves. As soon as they were far from the land, the white bull spoke gently to Europa and told her who he really was and how, for love of her, he had assumed this strange disguise. So the maiden was no longer afraid, but allowed herself to be carried to an unknown land that was afterward called Europe in her honor.

It was no wonder that Juno kept watch over the earth as no other goddess needed to do, for she knew that the loveliness that belonged to the daughters of men could easily lure great Jupiter from his golden throne.

She was therefore very reasonably angry when she looked one day through the white clouds around Olympus and saw—not on the earth, but in the lap of the ever-tossing sea—the most beautiful being that could exist outside of a dream. So wonderfully fair was this maiden upon whom Juno fixed her resentful gaze, that she seemed too perfect to be made of flesh and blood, and the jealous watcher was almost persuaded that it was no real living thing which rested softly on the crest of the waves, but some creature made from the rainbow colors and white mist of the sea. The ocean rocked her lightly on its breast, and Zephyrus, the west wind, bore her gently toward the shore. The sunlight shone on her rosy flesh, and her long hair lay out upon the waves, glistening like spun gold. The sky above her was not more soft or deep than the blueness of her eyes, and the smile upon her perfect lips was of a subtle sweetness more alluring than the breath of spring. As she lay pillowed in the arms of the slow-swinging sea, the west wind bore her to the island of Cyprus; and when her foot touched the warm sand, the goddess rose from the waves, which were so loth to yield her to the waiting earth, and stepped lightly upon the shore. She flung the wet ringlets from her forehead, shook the foam from her breast and shoulders—white as the purest marble—and stood upright in the warm sunshine—the most perfect thing that the wondering old earth had ever looked upon. This was Venus,21 goddess of love and beauty, born of the foam of the sea, and destined to be the most far-famed of all the dwellers in Olympus.

It was not long before others than the watchful Juno had seen this vision of loveliness, and she was eagerly welcomed by the gods as soon as she appeared among them. The beauty and grace of the new goddess so charmed them that all were eager to yield her homage, and she was immediately sought in marriage—even Jupiter himself becoming an enamored suitor. But "laughter-loving" Venus refused to be wed, and would not listen to any wooing. Then the ruler of the gods, finding his proffered love scorned by the proud goddess, determined to punish her by compelling her to marry Vulcan, the ugliest and most ill-favored of deities; and as Jupiter's word was law in all the universe, Venus was obliged to obey. But though married, she was by no means a devoted or faithful wife, and she caused poor Vulcan many unhappy moments; for he saw how his misshapen form repelled her, and he knew that she would soon seek for happiness elsewhere.

The first to win the love of "golden" Venus was Mars, the handsome god of war, who, though delighted at being honored as the chosen one of beauty, was careful that the goddess's preference should not be known. When he and Venus met in some lover's bower, they placed Alectryon—the attendant of Mars—on guard, so that no one, not even prying Juno, would come upon them unawares. Things went on happily for some time; but one day Alectryon fell asleep at his post, and slept so soundly that he did not see Apollo, in his golden chariot, driving close to the trysting place of the lovers. When the sun-god realized what was happening, he went straightway to Vulcan and told him how much his wife was enjoying the society of Mars.

Vulcan, angry and ashamed, set to work to forge a net of linked steel; and when it was finished, he hurried with it to the spot where Venus and the god of war were still conversing together. Stepping up softly behind them, Vulcan drew the net over their heads, and thus held them fast. Then he hastened back to Olympus, where he told his story and bade all the gods go look upon the ridiculous and humiliating plight of the imprisoned lovers. When the captured pair were at last set free, Mars rushed off to find Alectryon and to learn why they had not been warned of Apollo's approach. Finding his sentinel peacefully sleeping, unmindful of the disaster that had occurred through his neglect of duty, Mars was so enraged that he changed Alectryon into a cock, and commanded him to rise early every morning and crow to announce the coming of the sun.

II

The next fancy of Venus was for Adonis,22 a handsome young hunter, who was so fearless in his pursuit of game that the goddess often felt anxious for his safety. She urged him to give up the chase and spend all his day with her; but however much Adonis enjoyed the society of Venus, he also loved to roam the forests, and no entreaties could induce him to give up his favorite sport. One day Adonis was following a wild boar, and believing that the creature was wounded, he boldly drew near, when the boar turned suddenly upon him and drove his long tusks into the youth's side. As he lay dying in the forest, Venus heard of the tragic ending of the day's hunt and hurried to save him. So careless was she of her own hurt that she rushed heedlessly through the rough briers, which tore her soft skin and scattered drops of blood on the white wood flowers. When she reached Adonis, he was already past her help and could not respond to her caresses. Holding his lifeless body in her arms, Venus wept and mourned for her beloved; and her tears, as they fell upon the sympathizing earth, were changed into anemones. Then to hide from her eyes the painful sight of the young hunter's mangled body, the kindly earth again took pity on her grief and turned the drops of blood that came from Adonis's side into red roses. Still the goddess would not be comforted, but sat mourning alone with her dead.

Then Mercury came to lead the soul of Adonis to gloomy Hades; and when the messenger of the gods had departed with his slight burden, Venus went back to Olympus, and throwing herself on the ground before Jupiter's throne, she besought him to give Adonis back to her, or else to allow her to stay with him in Hades. Since the world could not well spare the goddess of beauty, Jupiter refused to let her go to the sunless realm of Pluto; but neither would that dread ruler consent to give up Adonis to her longing arms. Then the gods, touched by the depth of Venus's grief, interceded in her behalf, and reluctantly Pluto agreed to allow Adonis to spend six months with the goddess in the warmth and joy of the sunlight if for the rest of the year he would be content to dwell in Hades.

III

Another of the fortunate ones who gained the love of Venus was Anchises, prince of Troy; but though the goddess lavished much affection upon him, she was rather ashamed of her attachment, for Anchises was of only mortal birth. She therefore bade him to keep the matter secret, and for a time Anchises obeyed; but being proud of his relation to the goddess he forgot her instructions, and boasted of his good fortune. This so angered the willful Venus that she never bestowed her favors on him again; but transferred all her affection to her son Æneas, who fared better at her hands than his father Anchises. In the many adventures that befell this famous hero, Venus was always a ready protectress, and whenever Æneas was involved in some apparently hopeless situation, his goddess mother would immediately hide him in a thick mist which was sure to baffle his enemies. Sometimes, as in the Trojan war, she wrapped him in her shining robe and bore him from the battle-field; and if the hero *was* constantly in tears, as the poet Virgil says, it was certainly not the fault of Venus.

As to the ultimate fate of Anchises, some authorities say that the offended goddess borrowed one of Jupiter's thunderbolts and disposed of her talkative lover in this fashion; but the most probable story is that he lived to see Æneas become a famous prince of Troy, and was himself carried from the ruins of that burning city on the shoulders of his devoted son.

CHAPTER XII
THE STORY OF CUPID AND PSYCHE

CUPID,23 god of love, was the son of Mars and Venus; and though he was always the happiest of children, his mother was distressed because he never grew up, but remained year after year a chubby, dimpled child. When she consulted Themis, the goddess of Justice, to find out why Cupid was never any older, she was told that "Love cannot grow without Passion." This explanation was at first very mystifying; but later, when Anteros was born, Venus understood the meaning of the strange words. Cupid then developed into a tall slender youth who did not revert to his childish form except in his brother's absence, when he again became a rosy, mischievous child. Though grown larger in stature, the god of love still kept his gauzy wings, and always carried a bow and a quiver full of arrows. No mortal ever saw him, though many knew when he had come and gone; but should any one be touched by a shaft sent carelessly from Cupid's golden bow, he was henceforth a slave to the slender winged god who bore lightly in his hand so much of human happiness and misery.

There was once a king who had three daughters whose beauty was famed far and wide; but the loveliness of the youngest was so great that people called her the goddess of Beauty and worshiped her with offerings of flowers. The maiden, Psyche, was troubled over all this adoration, and begged her followers to cease from their mad worship; for she knew that Venus would be sure to punish the one who usurped her title and received the homage due only to an immortal. The people continued, however, to call Psyche the goddess of beauty; and when Venus saw her own temple forsaken and her shrines ungarlanded, she was so incensed at the insult that she vowed to punish poor Psyche, who had been a most unwilling object of all this mistaken devotion. The goddess summoned her son Cupid to her presence and bade him go slay the maiden who had presumed to be her rival in beauty.

Believing that his mother's anger was justified, Cupid was quite willing to kill the offending mortal with one of his poisoned arrows; and accordingly he went in search of Psyche, whom he found asleep in one of the rooms of her father's palace. It was night, and the moonlight shone through the open window, falling softly upon the couch where the maiden, unconscious of her doom, lay sleeping. One bright beam had lightly touched her forehead just as Cupid entered, and he saw with delight the loveliness that his mother had been eager to destroy. As he leaned nearer to the sleeping maiden one of his own arrows grazed his side, and all unknowingly he was wounded. Not wishing to harm the beauty that he was now beginning to love, Cupid softly left the room and went back to Olympus.

When Venus found that her rival was not dead, and that Cupid refused to hurt a thing so fair, she began to persecute poor Psyche until life grew unbearable for the helpless maiden, and she determined to kill herself. So she stole secretly from the palace and climbed up a high mountain, where there was a ledge of rock overhanging a steep cliff. It was rather fearful to look down into the valley from the rocky ledge, and for a moment Psyche's heart failed her; but then she remembered the daily annoyances that Venus inflicted upon her, and she remembered also the words of the oracle which said that her future husband was to be "no mortal, but a monster whom neither gods nor men can resist." So, summoning all her courage, she threw herself over the cliff, expecting to be dashed to pieces upon the rocks below. But Cupid had been watching over her, ever since she began her weary journey up the mountain; and when he realized what she meant to do, he commanded Zephyrus to keep very near and to catch her lightly when she fell. So it was not upon the cruel rocks that Psyche's soft body lay, but in the friendly arms of the west wind who bore her to a distant island, where Cupid had already made preparations for her coming.

Psyche

On the thick grass in the midst of a beautiful garden, Zephyrus laid his slight burden; and when Psyche opened her eyes, she found herself unhurt, though bewildered by her strange journey through the air and by its unexpected ending. She rose from the grass and began to wander about the garden, wondering where she might be and what land lay beyond the blue water whose waves rolled lazily upon the beach that stretched away for miles at the foot of the garden. Then she strolled further inland among the flowers, and soon came to a beautiful palace whose doors were opened wide as if to welcome her. Timidly she entered the stately hall, and saw before her a richly-laden table and a chair placed in readiness for the coming guest. Soon she heard voices speaking to her gently, and they bade her eat and drink, for the feast was spread in her honor. Seeing no one, but reassured by the kindly voices, she ate of the food so generously provided. Then she went again into the garden, but left it soon and hurried down to the sea; for when evening came on, she began to be lonely, and the silence of the garden grew oppressive. On the beach she heard the sound of lapping water and felt herself a part of the life that beats forever in the restless changing sea.

At night she sought the palace where the unseen servitors again ministered to her wants; and in the darkness, Cupid came to woo her. He did not reveal his name, but he told how he had rescued her from death and brought her to this island, that she might never again be persecuted by jealous Venus. Everything that she wished for would be hers for the mere asking, and the invisible attendants would always be on hand to do her bidding. He himself would ever be her loyal lover; and would come each night to cheer her solitude. The only thing that he asked in return was that she should never seek to know his name or try to see his face. Psyche listened to the words of Cupid, and was won by the soft pleading of his voice. She was content to stay on the unknown island, and to be with her unseen lover, whose name and face must remain forever a mystery. Many happy weeks passed, and Psyche never wished to leave her new home, for though she was often lonely as she walked each day in the rose-garden, she forgot the long hours of solitude when Cupid came at night to gladden her with his love and to tell her of his wanderings.

As time went on Psyche began to wonder how things were faring at her father's palace; and she wished very much to see her sisters who must have long since believed her dead. Cupid had told her she might ask for anything that she wished save the two forbidden things, so she summoned the west wind and bade him bring her sisters to her. Zephyrus gladly obeyed, and soon Psyche saw her two sisters standing beside her, more astonished than she to find themselves there. For hours they talked together, and Psyche told them of her adventure on the mountain and how she had been rescued by the friendly west wind. She told them of her mysterious lover, of his riches and his great kindness, and regretted that she could not describe his appearance; but, she explained, this was impossible since she herself had never seen him. As the sisters listened to

Psyche's story, their hearts were filled with bitter envy that she should be thus favored above all other maidens; and they planned to rob her of her happiness. They reminded her of the words of the oracle that she should marry a monster; and under the pretense of a loving interest in her welfare, they urged her to break her promise to her lover and to find out whether he was in truth a monster that was only waiting his time to devour her. Psyche at first scorned these malicious suggestions, but by and by they began to make an impression on her troubled mind, and she found herself ready to listen and to believe. Finally she agreed to carry out the plan that her sisters arranged, which was to secrete a sharp knife in her room and use it to kill the monster as he slept.

When Zephyrus had taken the sisters back to their own home, and Psyche was once more alone, she felt ashamed of the promise that she had made them; but at the same time she could not forget the words of the oracle nor cast off the suspicions that now filled her mind. She was anxious, too, to see her lover's face and to be able to confront her sisters with the truth when they should taunt her again. So that night when Cupid was fast asleep, she rose softly, and by the light of a tiny lamp which she noiselessly lit, she groped for the knife with which she intended to slay the creature who—her sisters assured her—was so frightful that he dared not show his face. Cautiously she stepped to Cupid's side, and held over him the flickering lamp; but how astonished she was to behold—not an ugly monster as she had expected—but a slender youth whose beauty was so great that she felt her heart beat fast with joy. Breathless she gazed at the unconscious form, and dared not move for fear of waking him; but as she bent adoringly over him a drop of oil fell from her lamp on Cupid's shoulder, and he awoke.

For a moment he stared with startled eyes at the knife and the lamp held in her trembling hands; then he understood the meaning of it all, and his beautiful face grew sad. In a voice full of pity he spoke to the now remorseful Psyche, and told her that, as she had broken her promise, he must go away from her and never come again. In vain Psyche wept and begged him to forgive her rash deed, confessing that it was her sisters who had tempted her to betray her trust. But Cupid gently freed himself from her clinging arms, and spreading his gauzy wings flew out into the night. Psyche, still weeping, went down into the garden, hoping that Love might relent and return in spite of his parting words; but as the hours passed she was still waiting alone, and when the morning came it found her fast asleep, lying wet-eyed among the dew-laden flowers.

When at last Psyche awoke, it was midday; and looking around she found to her surprise that she was in a deep valley with mountains on all sides, and that the palace with its rose-garden had vanished. All day she wandered in the valley, meeting no one who might direct her to her home; and when at length she came to a stately marble temple, she was glad to enter it and rest. Though she did not know to whom the temple was dedicated, Psyche prayed to the gods for help; and Ceres, at whose altar she was kneeling, heard her, and in pity answered her prayers. She told the disheartened maiden that her lover was no other than Cupid, the god of Love, "whom neither gods nor man can resist," and that if she wished to gain favor in the eyes of his mother,—and thereby win her lover back,—she would do well to seek the temple of Venus and offer her services to the offended goddess.

Psyche listened to these friendly words, and thanked Ceres for taking pity on her suffering. When she left the temple she walked many miles through the valley, until she came to a shrine on which were hung flowers, fruit, and jewels, which the suppliants of Venus had brought as votive offerings. Before this shrine Psyche knelt very humbly, and implored the goddess of Beauty to accept her service and set her some task by which she could prove her fidelity. Venus was still angry at the memory of Psyche's former honors, and she was not to be placated by any prayers, however sincere. She accepted the maiden's service, but determined to torment her by setting impossible tasks.

She brought Psyche into a granary, where there were thousands of different kinds of seeds all thrown in bewildering and unsorted heaps. Pointing to these, the goddess bade her separate them all, and pile them together so that by nightfall each seed should be in its proper place. Poor Psyche was in despair at ever being able to tell one kind of seed from another; but Cupid, hearing her sighs, sent an army of ants who worked silently and swiftly at the enormous heap of seeds, and before twilight came the work was done.

Charon and Psyche

When Venus saw this almost impossible task accomplished, she knew that Psyche had never done the work unaided; so reproving her angrily for her incompetence, she gave the maiden another commission, which was to gather some golden fleece from the sheep that were browsing in a meadow not far from Venus's shrine. Next morning Psyche set about her task, but as she neared the river that must be crossed before she could reach the meadow, the kindly reeds on the water's edge spoke to her, and warned her of the danger of her undertaking. They told her that the rams in the flock were so fierce that they would surely destroy her if she ventured at this hour among them; but that if she waited until noontide, when they grew drowsy and lay down on the grass beside the river, then she could cross in safety, and gather the bits of golden fleece which she would find caught on the bushes. Psyche listened gratefully to this advice; and when the sun was high overhead, and the panting sheep were gathered by the river, lulled to sleep by the drowsy murmur of the reeds, she crossed the water fearlessly, and gathered an armful of golden fleece from the bushes among which the flock had wandered. That night she delivered her precious burden to Venus, who again reproved her angrily, knowing well that it was through Cupid's intervention that she had escaped the dangerous rams.

Then the goddess gave her a third errand, and bade her go down to gruesome Hades to beg of Proserpina, Pluto's queen, a box of her magic ointment, which could restore all fading beauty to its former perfection. In the early morning Psyche set out on her journey, fearful of the dangers that lurked by the way, but eager to gain the favor of her hard-hearted mistress, so that she might thereby win her lover back. When she had walked many hours, not knowing where to find the entrance to remote and unsought Hades, a voice whispered softly in her ear, telling her of a certain cave through which she might enter the dreaded region of the dead. Then the voice directed her how to go unharmed past Cerberus, the three-headed dog, and how to persuade Charon, the silent ferryman, to row her across the black and swiftly-flowing river. Encouraged by this timely help, Psyche was able to secure the desired box, and to come safely out of that dark country from which only the gods are privileged to return.

As she trod wearily up the valley back to the shrine of Venus, it occurred to her to take a little of the magic ointment for herself, for she knew that these days of waiting and working had dimmed the beauty that once charmed Cupid's eyes. So she opened the box and out sprang the invincible Spirit of Sleep, who seized upon poor unresisting Psyche and laid her, apparently lifeless, by the roadside. But Cupid was watching over his beloved through all the stages of her journey; and when he saw her unconscious on the ground, he flew quickly to her assistance, and fought with the masterful Spirit of Sleep until he conquered it, and compelled it to return to the box from which it had been set free. Then he roused Psyche from her sudden sleep and told her that her troubles were at an end, for henceforth he would always stay beside her. Together they went up to bright Olympus and stood before Jupiter's throne, where Cupid besought the gods to look with favor upon their love and to grant to Psyche the gift of immortal life. To this great Jupiter gladly consented; and Venus, who was now ready to forgive her one-time rival, welcomed her as the fitting wife of Cupid,—for Psyche is but another name for Soul, and the Soul, to find its true happiness, must dwell forever with Love.24

Cupid and Psyche

CHAPTER XIII
FAMOUS LOVERS

I. Echo and Narcissus

ECHO was a wood-nymph and a follower of Diana; and she had the one fault of wanting to talk all the time, especially if she found some one who was willing to listen. One day Juno went down in great haste to the earth, suspecting that Jupiter was spending too much time in the society of the nymphs; but before she had gone very far into the forest she met Echo and stopped to speak to her. Now Echo knew that the ruler of the gods was happily engaged with the nymphs, and would not be pleased at his wife's sudden appearance; so she began to talk rapidly to Juno, and to tell her such entertaining stories that the unsuspicious goddess waited to listen. While Echo was thus keeping the jealous queen from seeking for her husband, Jupiter—warned of her coming—left the nymphs and returned in haste to Olympus. When, later on, Juno learned that Echo had intentionally kept her listening so that Jupiter could make his retreat unseen, she was so angry with the officious nymph that she forbade her ever to speak again, except to repeat the last word of any conversation she might hear. Thus she could never more tell beguiling stories, or interfere in behalf of Jupiter.

At first Echo was very miserable over this misfortune; but in spite of it she managed to spend her time happily in the forest, and to hunt with the other nymphs of Diana. One evening as she stopped at a brookside to drink, she met a handsome youth named Narcissus, and at once fell in love with him; but unfortunately she could not tell him of her affection except by languishing looks and sighs. Narcissus was not at all pleased by her evident interest in him, for many maidens had loved him, and he had turned coldly from their advances, preferring to roam the forest alone. Sometime later Narcissus was hunting with a companion, and, having rushed away in pursuit of a stag, he found that his friend was no longer in sight. He called to him, but no one answered except the devoted Echo who was always dogging his footsteps. When Narcissus called "Are you here?" Echo replied, "Here." "Come!" cried the youth, and Echo answered, "Come." Then she appeared before the young hunter and mutely begged for his love; but Narcissus scornfully turned from her, exclaiming, "You shall never have me." "Have me," cried the unhappy maiden; but her frank offer was repulsed, and the hard-hearted youth turned away. Echo made no further attempt to win his love, but went into the mountains to live out her sad life alone. No one ever saw her again, and in time she pined away and died; but her voice remained to whisper among the hills, and to give back the last word to any one who sought to call her.

As for Narcissus, his scorn of love brought its just punishment, for Venus decreed that he should suffer even as poor Echo had done. One day when he was hunting in a remote part of the forest, he came upon a beautiful deep pool in which all objects were reflected as clearly as in a mirror. No wild things had ever come to drink of the cool stream; no feet of beasts had ever trampled the grass on its margin or muddied its pure waters; not even a floating leaf had ruffled its calm surface.

When Narcissus knelt on the lush grass at the pool's edge and looked down into the clear water, he was surprised to see a beautiful face gazing up at him from the depth of the pool. He leaned nearer, and the face did not withdraw, but seemed to approach his own. Then he put out his arms to the water-nymph who, he believed, was returning his advances, and he was delighted to see two white arms stretched out as if to clasp him in their embrace. But as soon as he attempted to grasp them, there was only the cool water in his hands, and the nymph had vanished. When the surface of the pool had grown clear again, and Narcissus leaned anxiously over it to see what had become of this baffling maiden, there she was still, gazing at him with her beautiful eyes. Again and again Narcissus strove to embrace her, but she eluded his eager arms, and each time he clasped only the unsubstantial water. Maddened by these repeated defeats, he spoke reproachfully to the water-nymph, and asked her why she thus tormented him; but though the lovely mouth so near his own seemed to move as if framing words, no answer came to his appeal.

Each day Narcissus sought the forest pool, and each day he found the nymph ready to return his smiles and fond looks, but always escaping from his touch. By and by he spent all his time beside her, and cared for nothing else than to gaze beseechingly into the lovely eyes that looked into his own with the same fever of longing. Absorbed in the adoration of this strange being who seemed so responsive to his passion and yet so unwilling to allow him near, he forgot to eat or sleep, and became only a wan shadow of his former self. The nymph, too, was pining away with hopeless love, for her face grew pale and thin, and the deep-shadowed eyes were full of sadness. Sometimes Narcissus slept from sheer exhaustion; but when the moonlight fell on the calm water, he would wake with a start and look anxiously to see whether the nymph was sharing his weary vigil. And always he found her waiting there in the cool depths of the pool. Finally he grew so sick with longing that he died of his hopeless love without ever knowing that it was no water-nymph whom he adored, but only his own reflection. The gods, believing that such devotion should not go unrecognized, changed him into a white flower which bears his name; and this is usually found blooming beside some clear lake or tiny crystal pool.

II. Pyramus and Thisbe

In far-off Babylon there dwelt a youth and maiden whose families lived in adjoining houses with a party-wall between the two estates. As the heads of these households were sworn enemies, in spite of their proximity, the wall was made so high that no one could climb over it, much less see what was on the other side. The maiden Thisbe, as she walked in her garden, often wondered who it was whose feet she could hear pacing up and down along the wall; and one day she was delighted to find a small crack in the masonry which enabled her to peep into the adjoining garden. About this time young Pyramus was planning some way to scale the wall, when he, too, discovered the same chink; and when he peered cautiously through it, he found to his great joy that there was a sweet-faced maiden standing near, who hastened to assure him that she did not share in the family feud. This acquaintance soon ripened into friendship, and Pyramus and Thisbe spent many hours standing patiently by the chink in the wall, which was the only way in which they could exchange confidences. Soon they grew dissatisfied with this meager allowance of space in which to see each other, for by this time they had become so much in love that the tender whispers breathed through the broken wall only made them long to be together without this cruel barrier between them.

So they planned to steal away from their watchful parents on a certain night, and meet just outside the city walls at Ninus's tomb, where a great white mulberry tree would hide them in its protecting shadow. Accordingly, at the appointed hour, the trembling Thisbe wrapped herself closely in her veil and crept out of the house. Finding that she had come first to the trysting-place, she waited under the mulberry tree, and idly watched the moonlight shining on a broad pool that lay close to Ninus's tomb. Suddenly a lioness stole out of the bushes, her mouth bloody with the recent gorging of oxen, and slunk down to the pool to drink. Thisbe, terrified at the sight of the creature's dripping jaws, fled into a near-by cave for refuge; but in her fright she let fall her silken veil, and it dropped on the ground near the tree.

The lioness having drunk her fill walked over to the tree and sniffed curiously at the bit of silk, then worried at it with her bloody teeth, as a dog plays with a rag. Just as the lioness departed, Pyramus came hurrying to the trysting-place, and seeing Thisbe's torn and blood-stained veil and the print of the lioness's feet on the ground, he was beside himself with remorse and horror. Being certain that his beloved had been torn to pieces by some wild beast, he cursed his own carelessness in letting her come first to a spot so full of dangers. Then he drew his sword, exclaiming that he no longer wished to live now that Thisbe was dead. He called upon the mulberry tree to bear witness to his oath of undying devotion, and then fell heroically upon his sword, uttering the name of Thisbe with his last breath. As his blood gushed out upon the ground at the foot of the tree, the earth absorbed it so quickly that the white fruit of the tree turned a deep purple, and its juice became like drops of crimson blood.

All this time Thisbe was hiding safely in the cave, and when she at length ventured out, she gazed fearfully around to be sure that no lioness was lying in wait to devour her. When she reached the spot where she hoped to meet her lover, what was her terror and dismay to find him stretched dead upon the ground with her veil held close to his parted lips. Realizing what had happened, and that it was too late now to convince him of his terrible mistake, Thisbe knelt down beside him and vainly strove to bring him back to life. Finding this useless, she seized Pyramus's sword and plunged it into her heart determined to die with him. As she sank forward on her lover's lifeless body, she prayed the gods to have pity on her great love and to allow her to be buried in the same tomb with her beloved Pyramus. The gods heard her dying prayer and answered it by making the hard hearts of the parents relent so far that they consented to bury the lovers together. A costly tomb was erected over them as a fitting monument to these two unfortunates whom life so cruelly divided.25

III. Hero and Leander

In the town of Sestus on the Hellespont lived a beautiful maiden named Hero, who was a priestess in the temple of Venus. Most of her time was spent in the service of the goddess; but when these hours of attendance were over, and she was free to leave the temple, Hero was glad to seek her own dwelling-place, which was a lonely tower on the cliffs overlooking the sea. Here the maiden loved to sit, watching the white-winged gulls as they skimmed over the waves, or listening to the breakers as they dashed angrily against the rocks at the foot of her tower. The beauty of Hero was famed throughout the country-side; and many a youth sought the temple of Venus at festival time under the pretext of honoring the goddess, but really to gaze upon the lovely young priestess. Among those most eager to see the maiden was Leander, a youth who lived in a town just across the Hellespont and within sight of Hero's tower. When he joined the solemn procession that came to do homage to Venus, he saw the beautiful priestess and determined to win her in spite of the many restrictions that forbade even an acquaintance with one dedicated to the temple. Ignoring the thought of the inevitable punishment that would be meted out to him if his rash presumption were known, Leander managed to find an opportunity to speak with Hero and to tell her of his love.

At first she would not listen to his pleading; but at last she was won by the sincerity of his words, and consented to disregard her sacred vows by receiving him in her tower. Leander did not dare to visit her until nightfall; and as he would have to swim across the Hellespont in the darkness, Hero promised to put a light in her tower so that he might have some beacon to guide him as he breasted the uncertain sea. When night came and Leander stood impatiently on the shore, waiting for the promised signal, suddenly a torch blazed in the distance, and he knew that Hero was awaiting him in her lonely tower. He plunged fearlessly into the waves; and though the current was swift, he struck out boldly and was carried out of its dangerous grip. Now and then he looked up to where the light was still burning, and his heart beat fast with hope when he saw it grow larger and brighter as he neared the land. At last he reached the rocks at the foot of the tower and was soon standing beside the trembling Hero, who had feared each moment to see him sink beneath the waves.

The lovers were so happy in being together that each night Leander swam across the treacherous sea, and Hero placed her torch in the tower to light him on his perilous journey. All summer they lived in this idyllic happiness, but when winter came with its storms and its icy hand, Hero feared for her lover's safety and begged him not to venture into the sea. Leander laughed however at her fears and continued to brave the narrow stretch of water that lay between his home and Hero's tower. The wind often beat him out of his path, and the icy water numbed his limbs; but he kept bravely on, with his eyes fixed on the welcoming light. One morning a fierce storm broke over the sea, and increased in fury through the day, so that by night the waves were lashing themselves madly against the rocks, and the wind beat the sea-gulls back to land. Hero dreaded the approach of that hour when Leander would start on his nightly journey, for she knew that he would not hesitate to risk his life in the maddened sea for the sake of being beside her.

When the time came for her to light the torch, she did so reluctantly, hoping that Leander would not come. On the opposite shore stood the impatient lover, waiting for the accustomed signal, and when it blazed out into the night, he plunged boldly into the waves. But now the sea was too strong even for his experienced arms, and the huge waves tossed him about as though he were so much foam. The wind and rain beat upon his defenseless body, and the cold sea gripped him in its deadly embrace. He struggled bravely to make some headway, and called upon the gods for help; but his cries were drowned in the howling of the storm. His strength began to fail as he fought desperately with the current,—grown terrible in its swiftness,—but now and then he lifted his head weakly above the waves to see whether Hero's torch was still burning. Just as he was making a last heroic effort to reach the land, a sudden gust of wind blew out the light; and seeing this, Leander with a despairing cry, gave up his unequal battle and sank down into the sea. The next morning when Hero, anxious and fearful, stood on the rocks at the foot of the tower, she saw Leander's body, which had been tossed there in wanton cruelty by the waves. Unable to endure this sight, and not wishing to live any longer now that her lover had perished, Hero threw herself into the sea; and when the tardy fishermen came to launch their boats on the furious waves, they found the white-robed body of the young priestess lying dead beside her faithful Leander.26

Hero and Leander

IV. Pygmalion and Galatea

Pygmalion, king of Cyprus, was a sworn bachelor, and had shunned the society of women for many years. He was also a famous sculptor, and spent all his leisure hours carving wonderful things out of marble and ivory. Though he would not deign to admire any living woman, he had lofty ideals of feminine beauty, and loved to carve statues whose perfection of form and exquisite grace surpassed any charms that could be claimed for a flesh-and-blood maiden. Once Pygmalion made a beautiful ivory statue that was such a marvel of loveliness that even the sculptor himself became enamored of it, and lavished upon it a devotion that was hardly consistent with his supposed indifference to love. This perfect creation he called Galatea, and he treated her with all the extravagant fondness that a lover bestows upon his mistress. He brought her presents of quaint seashells and delicately perfumed flowers, beads, pearls, and the rarest of jewels, and even gayly colored birds. Sometimes he hung a string of precious stones about her neck, and draped her white body in softest silks, treating her in every way as a maiden reluctant to be wooed.

When the festival of Venus was being celebrated, Pygmalion joined in the procession and placed a rich offering on the goddess's shrine. As he did so he looked up toward high Olympus and prayed Venus to grant him a wife like his peerless Galatea. The goddess heard his prayer, and as the patroness of all true lovers, she inclined with favor to his wish; so when Pygmalion returned to his home and hastened into the presence of his adored statue, he was bewildered at the change that seemed to be coming over it. A beam of sunset light that was streaming in through the open window had touched the ivory coldness of the statue and warmed it with a rosy glow that made it look wonderfully soft and yielding. But this was not all, for as the astonished sculptor stood wondering at this unexpected answer to his prayer, the beautiful face of Galatea turned toward him, and the perfect lips parted as if to speak. Breathlessly Pygmalion watched the statue gradually warming into life, and when he was at last assured that it was no longer a piece of unresponsive ivory, but a breathing, blushing maiden, he knelt adoringly at her feet and besought her to be his queen.27

CHAPTER XIV
THE STORY OF ORPHEUS AND EURYDICE

THE deeds of the immortal gods were told and sung at every fireside in Greece; and among these hero-tales there was none more popular than the story of how Apollo built for Neptune the famous wall of Troy. Many musicians would have been glad to perform a similar service for the mere fame that it would bring them, but they feared that the attempt to imitate Apollo would only result in failure and ridicule. So no mortal ever presumed to say that he could make rocks and stones obedient to the spell of his music. There was, however, one musician, Amphion, king of Thebes, who was anxious to prove that his playing was equal to Apollo's, but knowing how unwise it was to vie with an immortal, he determined not to test his skill publicly, but to carry out his cherished plan at night, when men were dreaming in their beds. He was eager to build a high wall around Thebes, and to build it as Apollo did the wall of Troy; so when the sun set, and darkness crept over the earth, Amphion stood just outside the city gates and began to play on his lyre. Immediately the stones rose from the ground and moved rhythmically into their places in the wall, which soon rose strong and high—a firmer defense than any that could be built by men's hands.28

Another famous musician was Arion, who won not only praise for his great skill in playing, but also much wealth. Whenever a contest was held in which a prize of money was given, Arion was usually a competitor; and, as his music was really finer than that of most players, he easily won the reward. Once he was returning from a festival in Sicily whither many musicians had gone on account of the rich prize; and as he had come off victor, he was leaving the foreign shores well-laden with gold. Unfortunately he happened to embark on a ship owned by pirates who had heard of his great wealth, and were plotting to seize whatever part of it he had on board. As the easiest way to do this was to kill him, the pirates began to bind him with ropes that he might not be able to struggle when thrown over-board. Arion calmly accepted his fate, but begged the brutal crew to allow him to play once upon his lyre before going to his death. To this the pirates consented, and when the wonderful music filled the air, a school of dolphins swam toward the ship and kept close beside it, charmed by Arion's playing. Feeling sure that there was some magic in the music, the pirates hastened to throw the player and his lyre into the sea without waiting to bind him; but Arion did not drown as they had expected, for a friendly dolphin caught him on its back and swam with him to the shore, where he landed in safety. When in the course of time Arion died, the gods placed him, together with his lyre and the kindly dolphin, in the sky as constellations.

The most famous of all musicians, except the one who played in the shining halls of Olympus, was Orpheus, son of Apollo and of the muse Calliope.29 When he was a mere child, his father gave him a lyre and taught him to play upon it; but Orpheus needed very little instruction, for as soon as he laid his hand upon the strings the wild beasts crept out of their lairs to crouch beside him; the trees on the mountain-side moved nearer so that they might listen; and the flowers sprang up in clusters all around him, unwilling to remain any longer asleep in the earth.

When Orpheus sought in marriage the golden-haired Eurydice, there were other suitors for her hand, but though they brought rich gifts, gathered out of many lands, they could not win the maiden's love, and she turned from them to bestow her hand upon Orpheus who had no way to woo her but with his music. On the wedding day there was the usual mirth and feasting, but one event occurred that cast a gloom over the happiness of the newly-married pair. When Hymen, god of marriage, came with his torch to bless the nuptial feast, the light that should have burned clear and pure began to smoke ominously, as if predicting future disaster.

This evil omen was fulfilled all too soon, for one day when Eurydice was walking in the meadow, she met the youth Aristæus, who was so charmed with her beauty that he insisted upon staying beside her to pour his ardent speeches into her unwilling ears. To escape from these troublesome attentions, Eurydice started to run away, and as she ran she stepped on a poisonous snake, which quickly turned and bit her. She had barely time to reach her home before the poison had done its work, and Orpheus heard the sad story from her dying lips. As soon as Mercury had led away the soul of Eurydice, the bereaved husband hastened to the shining halls of Olympus, and throwing himself down before Jupiter's golden throne, he implored that great ruler of gods and men to give him back his wife. There was always pity in the hearts of the gods for those who die in flowering time, so Jupiter gave permission to Orpheus to go down into Hades, and beg of Pluto the boon he craved.

It was a steep and perilous journey to the kingdom of the dead, and the road was one that no mortal foot had ever trod; but through his love for Eurydice Orpheus forgot the dangers of the way, and when he spoke her name, the terrors of the darkness vanished. In his hand he held his lyre, and when he arrived at the gate of Hades, where the fierce three-headed dog Cerberus refused to let him pass, Orpheus stood still in the uncertain darkness and began to play. And as he played the snarling of the dog ceased and the noise of its harsh breathing grew faint. Then Orpheus went on his way undisturbed, but still he played softly on his lyre, and the sounds floated far into the dismal interior of Hades, where the souls of the condemned labor forever at their tasks. Tantalus heard the music, and ceased to strive for a drop of the forbidden water; Ixion rested a moment beside his ever-revolving wheel; and Sisyphus stood listening, while the rock which he must roll through all eternity fell from his wearied arms. The daughters of Danaüs laid down their urns beside the sieve into which they were forever pouring water, and as the mournful wailing of Orpheus's lyre told the story of his lost love, they wept then for a sorrow not their own. So plaintive, indeed, was the music, that all the shadowy forms that flitted endlessly by shed tears of sympathy for the player's grief, and even the cheeks of the Furies were wet.

When Orpheus came before the throne of Pluto, that relentless monarch repulsed him angrily as he attempted to plead his cause, and commanded him to depart. Then the son of Apollo began to play upon his lyre, and through his music he told the story of his loss, and besought the ruler of these myriad souls to give him the single one he craved. So wonderfully did Orpheus play that the hard heart of Pluto was touched with pity, and he consented to restore Eurydice to her husband on condition that as they went out together from the loathed country of the dead he should not once turn his head to look upon her. To this strange decree Orpheus gladly promised obedience; so Eurydice was summoned from among the million shadow-shapes that throng the silent halls of death. Pluto told her the condition on which her freedom was to be won, and then bade her follow her husband.

Orpheus and Eurydice

During all the wearisome journey back to earth, Orpheus never forgot the promise he had made, though he often longed to give just a hurried glance at the face of Eurydice to see whether it had lost its sadness. As they neared the spot where the first faint glimmerings of light filtered down into the impenetrable darkness, Orpheus thought he heard his wife calling, and he looked quickly around to find whether she was still following him. At that moment the slight form close behind him began to fade away, and a mournful voice—seemingly far in the distance—called to him a sad farewell.

He knew that no second chance would be given him to win his wife from Pluto's hold, even if he could again charm the three-headed Cerberus or persuade Charon, the grim ferryman, to take him across the river. So he went forlornly back to earth and lived in a forest cave far from the companionship of men. At first there was only his lyre to share his solitude, but soon the forest creatures came to live beside him, and often sat listening to his music, looking exceedingly wise and sorrowful. Even in his sleepless hours, when he fancied he heard Eurydice calling, he was never quite alone, for the bat and owl and the things that love the darkness flitted about him, and he saw the glow-worms creep toward him out of the night-cold grass.

One day a party of Bacchantes found him seated outside the cave, playing the mournful music that told of his lost love, and they bade him change the sad notes to something gay so that they might dance. But Orpheus was too wrapped up in his sorrow to play any strain of cheerful music, and he refused to do as they asked. The Bacchantes were half maddened by their festival days of drinking, and this refusal so enraged them that they fell upon the luckless musician and tore him to pieces. Then they threw his mangled body into the river, and as the head of Orpheus drifted down the stream, his lips murmured again and again "Eurydice," until the hills echoed the beloved name, and the rocks and trees and rivers repeated it in mournful chorus. Later on, the Muses gathered up his remains to give them honorable burial; and it is said that over Orpheus's grave the nightingale sings more sweetly than in any other spot in Greece.30

CHAPTER XV
MARS AND VULCAN

I

THE three children of Jupiter and Juno were Hebe, Mars, and Vulcan. Hebe, goddess of youth, was cupbearer at the feasts of Olympus and poured from golden flagons the sparkling, ruby-tinted nectar. Many times were the brimming cups emptied and filled again, for the gods loved long draughts of the life-giving nectar that kept off all sickness and decay. No wine of earth's yielding ever appeared at these royal banquets, nor were there seen here the heaped-up platters of food such as mortals crave; for the gods ate only of the divine ambrosia which insured to them eternal youth and beauty.

For so long a time had fair-haired Hebe served at the feasts of Olympus that the gods never thought that she could be deprived of her office; but once, as she was handing Jupiter a well-filled cup, she stumbled and fell, and the ruler of gods and men was so angry that he vowed that she should never again be cupbearer. Since no one among the gods was willing to fill this humble position, Jupiter was obliged to seek over the earth for some mortal to take the place of poor disgraced Hebe. To make the journey as speedily as possible he assumed the form of an eagle, and spent many days soaring over the land before he found the youth whose slender grace made him feel assured that its possessor would be able to serve the gods less awkwardly than Hebe. On the sunny slopes of Mount Ida he saw a group of youths playing games, and among them was one whom Jupiter determined to bear away at once to Olympus. This was Ganymede, a prince of Troy; and the fact that he was no common mortal, but a king's son, did not deter Jupiter from swooping down upon the astonished youth, and carrying him aloft on his wings. Whether Ganymede was happy in Olympus we do not know; but the story goes that he remained forever at Jupiter's side, and the city of Troy never saw him again, nor did the king his father ever know the reason for his strange disappearance.

II

Mars31 was the god of war; and though he was the least loved of all the deities in Olympus, he was the one most feared by the people of every land. As he was always a hater of peace, and would stir up strife among men for the mere delight of fighting and bloodshed, the poet Homer calls him "the slayer of men, one steeped in blood, the destroyer of walled towns." His shrines were never wreathed with flowers, nor were children often found among the people grouped about his altars. Instead of the yearling ox with gilded horns, men sacrificed a savage bull to the god who took no pleasure in the tame shedding of blood. Sometimes Bellona, goddess of war, accompanied Mars in his chariot to watch over his safety; and since she was equally eager to urge men on to bloody fighting, their appearance together on the battle-field brought terror to the bravest heart. Seldom were prayers addressed to these two deities, except those of vengeance upon enemies; and there was little hope of peace for the nation when men thronged the temples where Mars and Bellona were jointly worshiped. The fiercest passions were kindled at their shrines, and their altars were the only ones that were ever defiled by human sacrifices.

Though so fierce in warfare, Mars was as susceptible to love as were all the immortals; for he was not only the chosen one of golden-haired Venus, but was also the devoted lover of the vestal Rhea Silvia.32 This maiden, being dedicated to the goddess Vesta, did not dare to listen to any words of love until her time of service in the temple was over; for the penalty of breaking her solemn vows would be the terrible one of being buried alive. But Mars was not to be denied; so at last the vestal yielded, but kept her marriage secret and continued to live in the temple until the birth of her twin sons Romulus and Remus. When her parents learned that she had failed to keep the sacred promise made at the altar fire of Vesta, they demanded that she should suffer the prescribed punishment. She was therefore taken at night into an underground room of the temple and inclosed in the wall which had been built to allow for just such a tragic event. As her children were declared outcasts, they were taken into the forest and left to perish by the teeth of wild beasts. Romulus and Remus did not die, however; for a she-wolf carried them to her lair and reared them with her own cubs. Later on they were found by a kindly shepherd who took care of them until they grew to manhood. Then they left him, and went out into the world to seek adventures, which soon ended in Romulus killing his brother Remus and himself becoming the founder of Rome.

When this new city was well established, Mars was made its patron deity and protector; and before an army set out on any military campaign the leader would first go into the temple where the sacred shield—the Ancile—hung; and touching it fearfully would pray, "Oh, Mars, watch over us." This shield was carefully guarded in Rome, for upon it depended the safety of the city. It was a special token sent by the god of war to show that the people of Rome were under his protection; for once when a plague was raging among them and the dead were numbered by thousands, the Romans fled to the temple of Mars and begged him to help them. As they were praying, a shield fell from the skies into their midst, and a voice told them that as long as this—the sacred Ancile—was with them, no harm could come to Rome. That day the plague ceased, and ever afterward the shield was jealously guarded. To insure its safety, eleven other shields were made so like the Ancile that no one but the Salii, the priests of the temple, knew which it was. These were carried in the streets during the festivals in honor of Mars which were held in March—the month that bears his name; and as the priests bore aloft the shields they sang war-songs and performed rude war dances. Sometimes the shields were displayed on the broad grounds where the soldiers and youths of the city held their exercises. This place was dedicated to the god of war, and was called the Campus Martius, or Field of Mars.

During the war between the gods and giants, Mars was so eager to prove his skill in warfare that he engaged in a fierce battle with Otus and Ephialtes. These two giants were only nine years old; but they were already of immense size, as they increased in height at the rate of nine inches every month. The young giants were very proud of having conquered the god of war, and carried him off the battle-field in triumph. They bound Mars with iron chains, and kept a careful guard over him so that none of the gods could set him free. Whenever Mars attempted to escape at night, believing that the giants were asleep, the rattle of the chains woke his guardians, and all hope of rescuing him was over. In this disgraceful bondage the unhappy Mars lingered for fifteen months until Mercury, the prince of thieves, unfastened the chains and restored the god to freedom.

When Cadmus went on his search for his sister Europa, whom Jupiter, in the form of a white bull, had carried off to a distant land,33 the devoted brother was at last bidden to give up his hopeless quest, to settle in the country, later called Bœotia, and to found a city there. Cadmus was glad to rest after his long march, and he sent some of his men in search of a spring. When they did not come back, he sent others to look for them, and when these did not return, he went himself to see what had caused all this delay. He carried his sword in his hand, and also a long spear, for he guessed that some disaster had overtaken his men. He wandered some time before he discovered any trace of them, and then at the edge of a forest he came upon the lifeless body of one of those who had first set out to find the spring. As he went farther into the forest he found others of his men, all of them lifeless, and soon he came to a large cave, at the entrance of which bubbled a fountain of purest water.

Not knowing that this was a grove sacred to Mars, and a fountain that had never been polluted by mortal touch, Cadmus stooped to drink, when suddenly, out of the deep shadows of the cave, rushed a huge dragon with crested head and glittering scales and a triple tongue vibrating between triple rows of teeth. This monster, twisting his body into a huge coil, darted toward Cadmus with gleaming fangs; but the young prince dealt his assailant a terrific blow that pierced the dragon in a vital spot, and it rolled over dead upon the floor of the cave. Then Cadmus heard a voice telling him to take out the dragon's teeth and to sow them in the ground where he wished to build his future city of Thebes. As soon as the teeth were sown, a crop of giants in glittering armor sprang up out of the ground, and when they were about to turn their spears upon Cadmus, he again heard the voice—this time bidding him throw a stone into the midst of the armed men. This caused a terrific battle to begin among the giants themselves, and soon they were all killed except five who laid down their weapons and offered their services to Cadmus.

As a punishment for the desecration of his grove and the slaying of its sacred guardian, Mars compelled Cadmus to serve him for eight years. At the end of this time the prince was made ruler of the new city of Thebes, and Mars so far forgave the sacrilege of his grove as to give Cadmus his daughter Harmonia in marriage. The career of the new king was very prosperous at first, and Cadmus was supposed to have contributed a great boon to his people by the invention of the alphabet. Later on he incurred the wrath of the gods by forgetting to offer them suitable sacrifices, and both he and his wife Harmonia were changed into serpents.

Just above the city of Athens was a hill called the Areopagus (from the Greek word meaning Mars Hill), which received its name from a famous trial that took place there. Neptune's son had carried off the daughter of Mars; and when the god of war learned of the abduction, he hurried after the daring youth and killed him. Then Neptune demanded that Mars should be punished for his deed of blood; and to decide the matter, both were summoned to appear before a court of justice, which was held on the hill above Athens. As it was the custom for all important cases to be tried at night, so that the judges might not be prejudiced by the favorable appearance of either party, the court assembled in the darkness, and Mars told the story of his daughter's capture and his own subsequent revenge. In spite of Neptune's objections to what he considered an unfair verdict, the judges decided in favor of Mars, and he was therefore acquitted. The hill was afterwards called by his name, and the judges of the principal court of justice were always termed *areopagitæ*.

III

Vulcan,34 god of fire and the forge, was not often seen in the halls of Olympus, for he knew that the gods despised him for his ungainly appearance, and he preferred to stay in his own sooty workshop. He had also no desire for the society of his divine parents, since his mother had never shown anything but indifference toward him, and his father had been the cause of his deformity. Jupiter was once so angry with Juno for interfering in his love affairs that he fastened her to the end of a strong chain, and hung her out of heaven. Vulcan, seeing his mother in this sad plight, dragged at the chain and finally succeeded in drawing Juno into safety. Full of wrath at this defiance of his wishes, Jupiter kicked his son out of heaven; and as the distance of the fall was so great, it was a whole day and night before Vulcan reached the earth. Had he been a mortal, there would have been nothing left to tell the story of his meteorlike descent; but being a god, he still lived and had only a slight deformity and lameness as the result of his fall. When he learned that Juno was so unconcerned over his fate that she had never even inquired whether he was badly hurt, he would not go back to Olympus, but shut himself up in the heart of Mount Etna, where he established a mighty forge that poured out fire and smoke for many years after.

Vulcan did not forget about his mother's heartless indifference; but none of the gods suspected him of harboring any revenge, until one day a beautiful golden throne arrived in Olympus as a present to Juno from her son. The goddess admired the exquisite designs carved on its polished surface, and seated herself in it proudly. Now Vulcan had contrived to hide some springs in the interior of the throne, and these were so skillfully arranged that the moment a person was seated, the entire structure quickly contracted and held the occupant prisoner. So in a moment proud Juno found herself securely caught, and no assistance that the gods could render her was of the least avail. Then Jupiter sent Mercury to the grimy abode of Vulcan to beg politely that the god of fire would honor, with his presence, the feast that was that day to be held in Olympus; but Vulcan was not to be moved by any flattery, for he well knew why he was so much desired at this particular time. So Mercury returned alone to Olympus, and Jupiter was obliged to think of some other device for luring Vulcan from his forge. This time he sent Bacchus, god of wine; and when the scowling deity of Etna saw Bacchus's jolly red face and heard his hearty laugh, he welcomed the jovial visitor and drank freely of the wine that Bacchus poured. The roisterous god of revels, who dearly loved to see good wine flowing, beguiled Vulcan into taking draught after draught of the choice vintage that he had purposely brought, until the sullen master of the forge was unable to tell what was happening, and allowed himself to be led unresistingly to Olympus. Once there the gods persuaded him to release the repentant Juno, and to allow himself to be reinstated in Jupiter's favor.

Though Vulcan grudgingly complied with these requests, he would not consent to live in Olympus, but returned to his workshop in Mount Etna. There he made many things out of gold and precious stones and gave them to the gods as an evidence that he no longer bore them any ill will. Their golden thrones were made by Vulcan's crafty hands, and the wonderful palaces, with all their costly furnishings, were the best result of his skill. He also forged Jupiter's thunderbolts and fashioned the weapons that the gods used in battle. He made Apollo's marvelous sun-chariot, and even deigned to use his skill in shaping the arrows that Cupid used in his golden bow.

When Jupiter decreed35 that laughter-loving Venus should wed his misshapen son, Vulcan took his reluctant wife to the smoky workshop in Mount Etna, and for a while Venus was amused at the unusual sights and sounds that greeted her in her new home; but she soon wearied of the dirt and darkness, and left the society of her surly husband to return to Olympus, where there was plenty to delight her pleasure-loving soul.

The Abduction of Proserpina

CHAPTER XVI
THE STORY OF PROSERPINA

WHEN Jupiter made himself ruler of the world, he imprisoned some of the warring giants under Mount Etna in Sicily, much to the disgust of Pluto, who was always fearing that when the giants got restless and turned over and over underground (thus causing earthquakes), they would some day make such a large crack in the earth that daylight would be let into Hades. So Pluto often went up out of his sunless land to look carefully over the island, and to be sure that no new fissure was being made in the earth's surface. One day, as he was driving his four coal-black horses through the vale of Enna, he saw a group of maidens gathering violets on the hillside; and among them was one so exquisitely fair that Pluto determined to take her for his wife. This was Proserpina,36 daughter of Ceres, the goddess of agriculture, a maiden who had ever shunned the thought of marriage and preferred to spend her life playing games, and dancing in the beautiful plain of Enna, where there is never any frost or snow, but springtime lasts through all the year.

Pluto had often tried to gain a wife by gentle means, but no one would consent to share his grewsome home; so, knowing that this maiden he desired would never listen to soft words of love, he determined to take her by force. Driving his fiery horses at full speed, he rushed toward the group of laughing girls, who scattered and fled at his approach. Proserpina alone stood still, and stared, frightened and wondering, at the grim figure confronting her, while the flowers she had gathered dropped from her trembling hands. In a moment Pluto had seized her in his strong arms; and, trampling all her violets under his ruthless feet, he sprang into the chariot and urged his horses to their full speed, hoping to reach Hades before the maiden's cries brought Ceres to the rescue.

As he neared the Cyane River the waters, wishing to befriend Proserpina, began to rise higher and higher, and with tossing waves opposed the madly-rushing steeds. Fearing to risk the chariot in the angry waters, Pluto struck the ground with his terrible two-pronged fork, and a great chasm opened before him, into which the ruler of Hades hurriedly plunged. Then the earth closed again over him and the captured maiden. During the dreadful moments when Proserpina felt herself held a prisoner in the arms of this bold wooer, she called wildly to her mother for help; but soon she realized that her cries would never reach Ceres's ears, and that she must find some other way to let the goddess know of her unhappy fate. So she summoned enough strength to struggle in her captor's embrace until she freed one arm from his hold, and with it loosened her girdle, which she flung into the Cyane River just before the yawning earth hid her so completely that no traces were left to tell where she had gone.

When Ceres37 came that evening into the vale of Enna and found that her daughter was not playing as usual with the other maidens, she questioned them, and learned their tearful story of the chariot with its four black horses and terrible driver. Just what had become of Proserpina no one could tell her; so the distracted mother began her search, not knowing whether she might at any moment come upon her daughter's body mangled by the chariot wheels. For days and days she wandered, never stopping to rest except for a few hours at night when it was too dark for her to see her way. Rosy-fingered Aurora, when she left her soft couch to open the gates of the morning, and Hesperus, when he led out the stars at evening, saw her still searching for the lost Proserpina. Sometimes she was so weary that she sank down by the roadside and let the night-dew drench her aching limbs. Sometimes she rested under the trees when a storm broke over her head; but even here the rain beat down upon her, and the wind blew its cold breath in her face. Kindly people gave her food whenever she stopped to ask for it, and though none knew that she was a goddess, they sympathized with her grief when she told them that she was seeking her lost child. Only once did she meet with unkindness. She was sitting at a cottage door eating gruel from a bowl, and a lad—Stellio by name—laughed insolently at her enjoyment of the meal. To punish him for his rudeness the goddess threw some of the gruel in his face, and immediately he was changed into a lizard.

One day Ceres found herself near the city of Eleusis, and to avoid being recognized as a goddess, she disguised herself as an old beggar woman. She sat for a long time on a stone by the roadside, mourning her lost Proserpina, until a little girl came by, driving some goats. Seeing the old woman's tearful face, the child stopped to ask her her trouble, but before Ceres could answer, the girl's father joined her and together they begged the stranger to come to their cottage and rest. The goddess yielded at last to their kindly insistence, and as she walked beside the old man, whose name was Celeus, he told her that at home he had a sick boy who had lately grown so ill that to-day they believed he would surely die. Ceres listened to his pathetic story, and for a moment forgot her own grief. Seeing a chance to return the old man's kindness, she followed him into the cottage; but first stopped by the meadow to gather a handful of poppies. When the parents led her to the sick child's bedside, she stooped and kissed the pale little face and immediately it became rosy with health. The boy sprang up well and strong again, to the great astonishment of his delighted family.

As they sat at the simple evening meal, the goddess put some poppy-juice in the glass of milk set out for the boy; and that night, when he was in a heavy sleep, she rubbed his body with oil, murmured over him a solemn charm, and was about to lay him on the red-hot ashes in the fire—that his mortal parts might be consumed and he himself be made immortal—when his mother chanced to enter the room, and springing forward with a cry of horror, snatched the boy from the fire. Before the excited mother could vent her wrath on the old woman, Ceres assumed her goddess form and quietly reproved the intruder; for her interference had not averted a harm, but had prevented a great gift from being conferred upon the unconscious child.

When Ceres left the cottage of Celeus, she continued her wanderings over the earth, and finally returned, discouraged and heartbroken, to Sicily. Chancing to be near the river Cyane, she went down to the water's edge to drink, and happily discovered the girdle that Proserpina had dropped there in her flight. This made her hopeful of finding further traces of her lost daughter, so she lingered by the river bank, eagerly scanning the overflowing stream. As she stood there holding the recovered girdle in her hand, she heard a low murmuring sound as if some one were speaking in whispers. The goddess listened, wondering from what place the voice came; and soon she found that the soft tones proceeded from a fountain which was so close to her that its lightly-tossed spray fell on her hand. The murmur was often indistinct, but Ceres understood enough to realize that the words were addressed to her, and that the fountain was trying to tell her how Pluto had come up from Hades and carried off Proserpina to be his wife.

While the goddess was musing over this painful revelation, the fountain went on to say that it had not always been a stream in sunny Sicily, but was once a maiden named Arethusa38 and a native of the country of Elis. As a follower of Diana she had roamed the wooded hills; and one day, being wearied from the chase, she sought refreshment in the forest stream. The drooping willows hung protectingly over the water, and here the nymph bathed fearlessly, believing herself alone. But Alpheus, the river-god, heard the splashing of the water, and rose from his grassy bed to see who was disturbing his noon-day rest. At the sight of Arethusa he was so delighted that he ventured to approach her; but she fled terrified through the forest, calling on Diana for help. The goddess, hearing her cries, changed her into a fountain; and to further baffle the pursuing Alpheus, she wrapped it in a thick mist. As the river-god could no longer see the nymph, he was about to give up the chase, when Zephyrus maliciously blew away the cloud, and Alpheus saw the bubbling fountain. Suspecting that this was Arethusa, the god changed himself into a rushing torrent, and was preparing to mingle his impetuous waves with the waters of the fountain, when the nymph again called on Diana to protect her. The goddess came to her rescue by opening a crevice in the earth, and here the shivering waters of the fountain found a speedy refuge. To keep far out of the reach of Alpheus it continued to flow underground for many miles, and even crept beneath the sea until it reached Sicily, where Diana again cleft the earth and allowed the fountain to come up into the sunlight. During her journey through the dark underworld, Arethusa said that she had seen Proserpina sitting, tearful and sad, on a throne beside the grim ruler of the dead.

When she heard this story, Ceres was no longer in doubt where her lost daughter could be found; but the knowledge gave her little comfort, for she was aware how useless it would be to ask Pluto to give up the wife he had so daringly won. Seeing no hope of regaining her child, Ceres retired to a cave in the hills, and paid no heed to the waiting earth that had suffered so long from her neglect. There was drought in the land, and the crops were failing for want of water. The fruit trees were drying up, and the flowers were withering on the parched hillsides. Everything cried out for the protecting care of Ceres; but the goddess stayed her hand, and in the solitude of the cave mourned unceasingly for Proserpina. Famine spread over the land, but the people, in spite of their dire need of food, burned sacrifices of sheep and oxen on the altars of Ceres, while they importuned her with their prayers. Jupiter heard their cries and besought the goddess to take the earth again under her wise care; but Ceres refused to listen, for she was indifferent now to the welfare of men, and no longer delighted in the ripening harvest.

When sickness and death followed hard upon the famine, Jupiter saw that he must save the sorely-stricken land, so he promised the goddess that her daughter should be restored to her if she had eaten nothing during all her sojourn in Pluto's realm. Mercury was sent to lead Proserpina out of Hades; but when he reached there, he found that Pluto had already given his wife some pomegranate seeds, hoping that she would thereby stay forever in his keeping. Dismayed at this unexpected downfall of her hopes, Ceres was about to shut herself up again in the cave, when Jupiter, in behalf of the suffering earth, made a compromise with Pluto whereby Proserpina was to spend half her time with her mother in the land of sunshine and flowers, and the rest with her husband in cold and cheerless Hades. Each spring Mercury was sent to lead Proserpina up from the underworld lest her eyes, grown accustomed only to shadows, should be dazzled by the blinding sunlight, and she herself should lose the way. All things awaited her coming; and as soon as her foot touched the winter-saddened earth the flowers bloomed to delight her eyes, the grass sprang up to carpet her way with greenness, the birds sang to cheer her long-depressed spirit, and above her the sun shone brilliantly in the blue Sicilian sky.

Ceres no longer mourned, nor did she again suffer a great famine to afflict the land. The patient old earth smiled again on Proserpina's return, for then her mother gave the blighted vegetation a redoubled care. But her happiness did not make the goddess forget the kindly old man who had given her food and shelter at Eleusis, for she returned there and taught the boy Triptolemus all the secrets of agriculture. She also gave him her chariot, and bade him journey everywhere, teaching the people how to plow and sow and reap, and care for their harvests. Triptolemus carried out all her instructions; and as he traveled over the country he was eagerly welcomed alike by prince and peasant until he came to Scythia, where the cruel King Lyncus would have killed him, in a fit of jealous wrath, had not Ceres interfered with timely aid and changed the treacherous monarch into a lynx.

CHAPTER XVII
PLUTO AND THE UNDERWORLD

IN the beginning of the world, before the gods came to dwell in Olympus, all the universe was in the hands of the Titans; and among these the greatest was Saturn,—or Cronos,39—who wedded his sister Rhea (also called Cybele) and became the father of three sons and three daughters, Jupiter, Pluto, Neptune, Ceres, Vesta, and Juno. For many ages Saturn and Rhea, having subdued all the opposing Titans, ruled over heaven and earth; but when the cruelty of Saturn drove his children into rebellion, there arose a mighty war in the universe, in which the sons and daughters of Saturn leagued against their father, who had called upon the other Titans for aid. After years of combat the six brothers and sisters, helped by the Cyclops,40 defeated the allied Titans and imprisoned them in the black abyss of Tartarus—all except a few who had not joined in the war against the children of Saturn. Among those who were wise enough to accept the new sovereignty were Mnemosyne (Memory) and Themis, goddess of justice. Those descendants of the Titans who refused to acknowledge the supremacy of Jupiter were consigned to the center of Mount Etna, and were the giants who constantly turned over and over, making Pluto fear for the safety of his realm. A few of the giants were spared: Atlas, whose punishment was to hold the heavens on his shoulders, and Prometheus and Epimetheus who had espoused the cause of Jupiter and so escaped the fate of the conquered Titans. When the children of Saturn found themselves masters of the world, they agreed to accept Jupiter as their ruler, on condition that the two other brothers be given a share in the universe. So a division was made whereby Pluto became king of the underworld—or Hades; Neptune took the dominion of the sea; and Jupiter, having married his sister, Juno, established his dwelling in Olympus as lord of heaven and earth.

The kingdom of Pluto41 was dreaded by all mortals, and its ruler inspired men with great fear. Though Pluto was known to visit the earth from time to time, no one wished to see his face, and each man dreaded the moment when he should be obliged to appear before the grim monarch of Hades, and be assigned a place among the innumerable dead. No temples were dedicated to Pluto, though altars were sometimes erected on which men burned sacrifices to this inexorable god while petitioning him to be merciful to the souls of the departed. The festivals held in his honor were celebrated only once in a hundred years, and on these occasions none but black animals were killed for the sacrifice.

The underworld, over which Pluto reigned, was deep in the heart of the earth; but there were several entrances to it, one being near Lake Avernus, where the mist rising from the waters was so foul that no bird could fly over it. The lake itself was in an extinct volcano near Vesuvius. It was very deep, and was surrounded by high banks covered with a thick forest. The first descent into Hades could be easily accomplished (*facilis descensus Averno*, says the poet Virgil); but no mortal was daring enough to venture far into the black depths, lest he should never again see the light of day.

At the portals of Hades sits the fierce three-headed dog Cerberus, who keeps all living things from entering the gate, and allows no spirit that has once been admitted to pass out again. From here a long dark pathway leads deeper into Hades, and is finally lost in the rivers that flow around Pluto's throne. The waters of the river Cocytus are salt, as they are made of the tears that stream forever from the eyes of those unhappy souls who are condemned to labor in Tartarus—that part of Hades that is the exclusive abode of the wicked. The Phlegethon River, which is always on fire, separates Tartarus from the rest of Hades, and wretched indeed is the soul that is forced to cross its seething waters. On the banks of the Acheron, a black and turbid river, stand the souls who come fresh from the sunlit earth; for all must pass this river and be brought before the judgment-throne of Pluto. There is no bridge over the murky stream, and the current is so swift that the boldest swimmer would not trust himself to its treacherous waters. The only way to cross is by the leaky, worm-eaten boat rowed by Charon, an aged ferryman who has plied his oar ever since the day that the curse of death first came upon the earth.

No spirit is allowed to enter the leaky craft until he has first paid Charon the fee of a small coin called the obolus. (During the funeral services, before the body is committed for burial, this coin is laid on the tongue of the dead, that the soul may have no trouble in passing to the throne of Pluto.) If any spirits cannot furnish the necessary money, they are ruthlessly pushed aside by the mercenary boatman and are required to wait a hundred years. At the end of this time Charon grudgingly ferries them over the river free of charge. As the unstable boat can hold but few, there is always an eager group of spirits on the further bank, clamoring to be taken across the river; but Charon is never in a hurry, and repulses, sometimes with his oar, the pitiful crowd that waits his grim pleasure.

There is also in Hades the river Styx, by whose sacred waters the gods swear the most terrible of all oaths, and on the other side of Pluto's throne is the softly flowing Lethe, of which only those souls can drink who are to spend endless days of happiness in the Elysian Fields. As soon as those blessed spirits have tasted of the waters of Lethe, all regrets for friends that mourn completely vanish, and the joy and grief, and pleasure and pain of the soul's life on earth are forgotten. In the Elysian Fields there is no darkness such as fills the rest of Hades with its thick gloom; but a soft light spreads over the meadows where the spirits of the thrice-blessed wander. There are willows here, and stately silver poplars, and the "meads of Asphodel" breathe out a faint perfume from their pale flowers.

"There do men lead easiest lives.
No snow, no bitter cold, no beating rains are there."

—BRYANT'S *Odyssey*, Book IV, line 722.

The sighs and groans that rise by night and day from the black abyss of Tartarus do not reach the ears of those who dwell at peace in the Elysian Fields, and the sight of its painful torments is hid forever from their eyes.

Beside Pluto's throne sit the three Fates (also called Parcæ), those deathless sisters who hold the threads of life and death in their hands. Clotho, the youngest, spins the thread; Lachesis, the second, twines into it the joys and sorrows, hopes and fears that make up human experience; and Atropos, the eldest sister, sits by with huge shears in her hand, waiting for the time when she may cut the slender thread.

The Three Fates

Pluto and his queen Proserpina are seated side by side on a sable throne, ruling over the myriad souls that compose the vast kingdom of the dead. Perched on the back of the throne is the blinking owl, who loves this eternal darkness, and the black-winged raven that was once a bird of snowy plumage and the favorite messenger of Apollo. The raven fell from his high estate on account of some unwelcome tidings that he once brought to Apollo when that god was an ardent lover of the fair-haired Coronis. Believing that no one could supplant him in the maiden's affections, Apollo was happy in the thought of being beloved by so beautiful a mortal; but one day his snow-white raven flew in haste to Olympus to tell him that the maiden was listening to the wooing of another lover. Enraged at this duplicity, Apollo seized his bow and shot the faithless Coronis; but the moment that he saw her lying dead, he repented of his rash deed and vainly sought to restore her to life. Though skilled in the art of healing, Apollo could not save the maiden; and in his frenzied grief he cursed the unfortunate raven that had brought the evil tidings, and banished it forever from his sight.

"Then he turned upon the Raven,
'Wanton babbler! see thy fate!
Messenger of mine no longer,
Go to Hades with thy prate!

'Weary Pluto with thy tattle!
Hither, monster, come not back;
And—to match thy disposition—
Henceforth be thy plumage black.'"

—SAXE.

Near Pluto's throne are seated the three judges of Hades (Minos, Rhadamanthus, and Æacus) who question all souls that are brought across the river. When they have learned every detail of the newcomer's past life, they deliver the cowering spirit into the hands of Themis, the blindfolded goddess of justice, who weighs impartially the good and bad deeds in her unerring scales. If the good outweighs the evil, the soul is led gently to the Elysian Fields; but if the bad overbalances the good, then the wretched spirit is driven to Tartarus, there to suffer for all its wrongdoings in the fires that burn forever and ever behind the brazen gates. To these gates the guilty one is urged by the three Furies,42 whose snaky hair shakes hideously as they ply their lashes to goad the shrinking soul to its place of torment. Sometimes they are joined by Nemesis, goddess of revenge, who hurries the doomed spirit over the fiery waters of the Phlegethon with her merciless whip, and sees that it follows no path but the one leading to the brazen gates of Tartarus.

As soon as the gates close on the newly-admitted soul, there is a renewed clamor of voices, while heart-breaking sighs and groans mingle with the curses of those who in their misery dare to defy the gods. And beneath all the awful sounds that greet the listener's ears, there is an undertone of pitiful wailing like the sea's "melancholy, long-withdrawing roar" that seems to come from millions of throats too feeble to utter a loud cry. The deepest sighs proceed from the Danaïdes,—the beautiful daughters of Danaüs, king of Argos,—who must forever strive to fill a bottomless cask with water. They form a sad procession as, with their urns on their arms, they go down to the stream to begin their hopeless task, and then climb wearily up the steep bank to pour the water into the ever-empty cask. If they pause a moment, exhausted with fatigue, the whips of some avenging attendants of Pluto lash them again into action. Their punishment is severe, but the crime for which they are suffering was a dreadful one. The fifty daughters of Danaüs were once pledged in marriage to the fifty sons of Ægyptus, brother of Danaüs; but when the wedding was being celebrated, their father remembered the words of an ancient prophecy that said that he would die by the hand of his son-in-law. Fearing for his life, he confided to his daughters what the oracle had foretold, and gave them each a dagger, bidding them slay their husbands. On the evening of the wedding, when the sons of Ægyptus were heavy with wine, the new-made wives stole in upon them and killed them as they slept. Danaüs then believed himself safe, until he learned that one of his daughters had spared her husband out of love for him. This son-in-law was eager to avenge his brothers' murder, and having sought out the wicked Danaüs, fulfilled the prophecy by killing the king with the very dagger intended for his own death. The gods punished the cruel daughters—except Hypermnestra, who had saved her husband—by condemning them to labor in Tartarus at their impossible task.

Near the Danaïdes stands Tantalus, the father of Niobe, who on earth was a most inhuman and brutal king. He ill-treated his subjects, defied the gods, and dared to make his own will the religion of his kingdom. He boasted that the gods were not so omniscient as people were led to believe; and insulted the immortals by offering them at a banquet the flesh of his own son Pelops, believing that they would never learn the truth of this loathsome feast. But the gods were not deceived, and left the meal untouched,—all except poor Ceres, who, still mourning over her daughter's detention in Hades, did not realize what was happening and bit off some of the lad's shoulder. When the gods restored Pelops to life, Ceres was very sorry for her carelessness and gave him a shoulder of ivory. The inhuman Tantalus was condemned to the torments of Tartarus, where he stands up to his chin in a clear stream. Though frenzied with thirst he can never drink of the water, for whenever he bends his head the stream recedes from his parched lips. Above him hangs a branch of delicious fruit; but when, tormented with hunger, he strives to grasp it, the branch eludes his eager fingers. Thus he stays, always "tantalized" by the sight of food and drink he never can secure.

Not far from Tantalus is Salmoneus, also a king, who dared to challenge the gods by impersonating Jupiter. He made a huge bridge of brass, and drove heavily over it while he threw lighted torches among the people who were waiting below, hoping thus to frighten them into believing that he was the very ruler of the heavens who hurls the mighty thunderbolts. This insult to his divinity so angered Jupiter that he seized a real thunderbolt and soon dispatched the arrogant king. When Salmoneus came before the throne of Pluto, his fate was quickly decided, and he was driven to terrible Tartarus, where he sits under a huge rock that threatens every moment to fall and crush him beneath its weight.

Another unhappy king is Sisyphus, who, when ruler of Corinth, became a famous robber, and in the pride of his great wealth dared to set the gods at naught. Therefore he was consigned to Tartarus, and his punishment is to roll an immense stone to the top of a steep hill. As soon as he reaches the summit, the rock slips from his aching arms and tumbles to the foot of the hill, and he must at once start on the hopeless task of pushing it up the long ascent again.

"With many a weary step, and many a groan,
Up the high hill he heaves a huge round stone."

—HOMER—Pope's translation.

Beyond Sisyphus lies Tityus, a giant whose huge body covers nine acres of ground. He was condemned to the blackness of Tartarus because he dared to affront a goddess with his addresses, and so was doomed to suffer, like Prometheus, by being chained to a rock, while a vulture tears at his liver. Near him is Ixion, who was promised the hand of a certain maiden in marriage, on condition that he would give her father a large sum of money. Ixion agreed, but when the maiden became his wife, he refused to give the stipulated sum, in spite of her father's clamorous demands. At length, wearied by the old man's insistence, Ixion slew him; but the deed did not go unpunished, for the gods summoned him to appear before them and answer for his cruelty. Ixion pleaded his cause so well that Jupiter was about to dismiss him, when he saw the presumptuous mortal making love to Juno. This offense could not be overlooked, so Ixion was sent to Tartarus, where he was bound to an ever-revolving wheel of fire.

If any one could follow the course of the gentle Lethe River, it would lead beyond the sunless realm of Pluto to a quiet and far-distant valley, where, in a soundless cave, live Somnus, the god of sleep, and his twin brother Mors, god of death. "Here the sun, whether rising or in his mid course, or setting, can never come; and fogs, mingled with the dimness, form a strange twilight. No wakeful bird calls forth the morn, nor do watchful dogs disturb the brooding silence. No sound of wild beast or cattle, nor any noise of creaking bough, nor human voice, breaks in upon the perfect stillness, where mute Rest has her abode. Before the cave bloom abundant poppies and other sleep-producing herbs, which Night gathers, that she may distil their juice and scatter slumbers on the darkened earth. Within the cave is no door that could creak on rusty hinges, and no porter stands at the entrance of that inner room where, on a downy couch made of black ebony and draped with sable curtains, over which black plumes wave, lies Somnus, the god of sleep,—Sleep, the repose of all things, gentlest of the deities from whom all care flies, the peace of mind who can sooth the hearts of men wearied with the toils of the day, and can refit them for labor."43

Near Somnus sits Morpheus, one of his many sons, who watches over his slumbers and sees that no one shall break in upon his sleep. This god holds a vase in one hand, and with the other he shakes the nodding poppies that bring drowsiness and sleep. Sometimes he assumes varied forms in which he appears to men at night, and always he flies through the darkness with wings that make no noise. Around the couch of Somnus hover shadowy forms, the Dreams,44 which are as numerous as the forest leaves or the sands upon the seashore. In a distant corner of the room lurk the horrid Nightmares, which creep out of the cave to visit sleeping mortals, but are never led to earth by Mercury, as are the welcomed Dreams. Two gates lead out of the valley of sleep, one of horn and one of ivory.

"Of dreams, O stranger, some are meaningless
And idle, and can never be fulfilled.
Two portals are there for their shadowy shapes,
Of ivory one, and one of horn. The dreams
That come through the carved ivory deceive
With promises that never are made good;
But those which pass the doors of polished horn,
And are beheld of men, are ever true."

—BRYANT'S Homer's *Odyssey*, Book XIX, line 679.

"Sunt geminæ Somni portæ, quarumaltera fertur
Cornea, qua veris facilis datur exitus Umbris;
Altera candenti perfecta nitens elephanto,
Sed falsa ad cælum mittunt insomnia Manes."45

—VIRGIL, *Æneid*, Book VI, line 893.

Mors, god of death, occupies one of the rooms in the cave of sleep. He is a fearful-looking deity, cadaverous as a skeleton, and wrapped in a winding sheet. He holds an hourglass in one hand, and a sharp scythe in the other; and stands watching the sand run out of his glass that he may know when a human life is nearing its end. Then, as the last grains fall, he glides from the valley of sleep and stalks silently and unseen upon the earth, where he cuts down the unhappy mortal, who cannot even hear the rustle of his garments as he approaches. It is nothing to him whether the life he takes belongs to childhood or youth, for he mows them down as relentlessly as he does tottering old age. And to the rich he is as unsparing as to the poor.

"Pallida Mors æquo pulsat pede pauperum tabernas regumque turres."46

—HORACE, *Carminum*, Book I, § IV, line 13.

The divinities who dwelt in the Cave of Sleep were distrusted by the ancients, and Mors was held in universal dread. No homage was ever offered to him, and no temples were dedicated in his honor; though sacrifices were sometimes made to ward off his dreaded coming. He was never represented in art except in a pleasing aspect, for although they believed him to have in reality the fearful appearance that tradition ascribed to him, yet the beauty-loving Greeks refused to have this kind of horror embodied in marble. So when Death appears in sculpture, it is usually with his brother Sleep, and both are represented as sleeping youths, whose heads are crowned with poppies or amaranths, and who hold inverted torches in their listless hands.

CHAPTER XVIII
NEPTUNE AND THE SEA-GODS

I

IN the days when the Titans ruled the universe, Oceanus, with his wife Tethys, controlled all the lakes, rivers, and seas; but when the Titans were overthrown, Neptune took possession of this great kingdom, and old Oceanus reluctantly gave up his dominion over the waters of the earth. Though anxious to assert his supreme authority, Neptune allowed some of the descendants of the Titans to keep their small kingdoms, on condition that they own allegiance to him as their ruler. Among these was Nereus, son of Oceanus, who was celebrated for his vast knowledge, his gift of prophecy, and his love of truth and justice. He and his wife Doris (also a child of Oceanus) had fifty daughters called Nereids,47 and they were so beautiful that Neptune chose one of them, named Amphitrite, for his wife. There were two others of the Nereids who became famous: Galatea, beloved by the Cyclops Polyphemus,48 and Thetis, the mother of Achilles; but none of them equaled Amphitrite in beauty.

Fountain of Neptune

When Neptune first went wooing the Nereid, she was frightened by his formidable appearance, for he drove in a chariot drawn by huge sea-horses with brazen hoofs and golden manes; and the god himself carried his terrible trident, or three-pronged spear, with which he shatters rocks, and commands the storms, and shakes the shores of earth. None knew better than Amphitrite the extent of Neptune's power, for she had often watched him, when a storm was at its height, raise his all-compelling trident, and immediately the waves would cease raging and there would be a great calm. Sometimes she saw a ship, doomed by the sea-god to disaster, gliding confidently in quiet waters, when all at once a fierce storm would break over its head; and the hapless sailors, as they breasted the angry waves, would pray vainly to Neptune for the help that would never come. Many a good ship had nearly gained her port when

"He spake and round about him called the clouds
And roused the ocean—wielding in his hand
The trident—summoned all the hurricanes
Of all the winds, and covered earth and sky
At once with mists, while from above the night
Fell suddenly."

Odyssey, Book V, line 348, Bryant's trans.

When Amphitrite saw this imposing-looking god driving toward her, she was frightened by so much splendor, though she could not help admiring Neptune himself with his sea-green beard, and his long flowing hair crowned with shells and seaweed. Since the enamored god could never come near enough to plead his suit, he sent one of his dolphins to do the wooing; and this was so successful that the fair Nereid was persuaded to become Neptune's wife, and share his golden throne in the heart of the sea. To reward the dolphin for its skill in having won for him his much-desired bride, Neptune placed it in the sky, where it forms a well-known constellation.

Though Neptune had undisputed control over all the waters of the earth, and over all that moves through the paths of the sea, he once aspired to greater power, and even plotted to dethrone Jupiter. But the ruler of gods and men discovered his wicked plans, and to punish him deprived him of his kingdom for some years, during which time he was obliged to submit to the humiliation of serving Laomedon, king of Troy. It was while he was in service here that he sought Apollo's help in building the wall of Troy, whose stones fell into place under the spell of the sun-god's music.49 Laomedon had promised Neptune a large reward if the wall was built within a certain time; but when it was finished, he refused to pay the sum agreed upon. Though angered at this treachery, Neptune had to endure the king's injustice until his years of service were over; but as soon as he was restored to his former power, he created a terrible sea-monster, which spread terror and death over all the land. Not knowing how to meet this calamity, the Trojans consulted an oracle, and were advised to sacrifice to the monster a beautiful maiden each year; and so prevent the wrath of Neptune from overwhelming the whole country in disaster.

Reluctantly the sorrowing people prepared to obey the oracle; and a victim was chosen by lot, and led by the priest to a large rock on the seashore, where she was securely chained. Then the hideous sea-beast glided out of its cave in the slimy rocks and devoured her. Each year this terrible ceremony was repeated, and at last the lot fell upon Hesione, the king's only daughter. Laomedon tried in vain to save her, but the lot was cast, and nothing could avert the appointed sacrifice. In despair, the wretched father saw the fatal hour approaching; and when the day drew near when Hesione was to be led down to the sea, he forgot his avarice and proclaimed throughout the land that a great reward would be given to any one who could slay the monster. Hercules appeared just in time to save the doomed maiden, and killed the monster with his oaken club as it was dragging Hesione into its cave. The king was overjoyed at his daughter's rescue, and told Hercules that he might claim the reward; but even when he saw the hero come with the beast's head as a proof that he had slain it, he refused to part with his much-loved gold. So Hercules returned home, but he did not forget Laomedon's perfidy; and when later on he came again to Troy, he killed the king and took his children captive to Greece.50

Neptune, like all the immortals, loved more than once; and among those who shared his affections was a maiden named Theophane, who had so many suitors that it kept the jealous sea-god in constant fear lest she should prefer some earthly lover. So he took her to the island of Crumissa, and there changed her into a sheep, while he carried on his wooing in the form of a ram. The offspring of this marriage was the famous golden-fleeced ram, whose pelt was the object of that ill-fated expedition made by Jason and his fellow Argonauts.

Neptune also loved the goddess Ceres, and followed her during the long time that she spent in search of her daughter Proserpina. Ceres was angered by the sea-god's persistent wooing, and hoping to escape from him, she took the form of a mare; but Neptune was not so easily discouraged, for he changed himself into a horse and contentedly trotted after her. The child of this strange pair was Arion,51 a wonderful winged steed that had the power of speech, and was of such incredible swiftness that nothing could ever equal it in speed.

The most famous children of Neptune and Amphitrite were Triton and Proteus. Triton was his father's trumpeter, and at Neptune's command he blew upon his conch-shell to calm the restless sea. His body was half man and half fish, and he gave the name of Tritons to all his male descendants, who, with the Nereids and Oceanides (daughters of Oceanus), followed the chariot of Neptune when he went abroad to view his kingdom. Proteus had charge of the great flock of sea-calves which fed on the soft seaweed and basked in the warm sands near his cave. He was celebrated for his wisdom and for the truth of the answers that he gave to those fortunate enough to make him speak. Homer calls him "the Ancient of the Deep whose words are ever true"; but his knowledge was not easy to obtain, for he had the extraordinary power of assuming any shape he pleased, and only those mortals gained his advice who persistently clung to him through his many bewildering changes.

"When the climbing sun has reached
The middle heaven, the Ancient of the Deep,
Who ne'er deceives, emerges from the waves,
And, covered with the dark scum of the sea,
Walks forth, and in a cavern vault lies down.
The sea-calves from the hoary ocean throng,
Rank with the bitter odor of the brine,
And slumber near him. Then ye must exert
Your utmost strength to hold him there, although
He strive and struggle to escape your hands;
For he will try all stratagems, and take
The form of every reptile on the earth,
And turn to water and to raging flame.

But hold him fast, until the aged seer
Is wearied out in spite of all his wiles,
Then question him."

—BRYANT'S Homer's *Odyssey*, Book IV, line 518.

II

Aristæus was the son of Apollo, and the water-nymph, Cyrene. Beside tending his flocks and herds, he took care of the olive trees and vineyards, and was a famous keeper of bees. He was very proud of his hives, and the swarm of bees increased each year under the guidance of his skillful hands; but one day he found hundreds of the bees lying lifeless beside the hives, and on the morrow there were still more among the dead. Not knowing how to account for this disaster, Aristæus hurried to his mother to ask her help in saving the few bees that remained. Cyrene lived under a mountain stream; and, hearing that her son wished to speak to her, she commanded the river to divide and form a wall on either side, so that Aristæus might walk in dry places. When the youth told her of the tragedy befalling his hives, she could not help him, but bade him go to old Proteus, for he alone could tell what the trouble was and find a remedy. She warned Aristæus of the difficulty in holding the Ancient of the Deep when he tried to bewilder and terrify the stranger by rapidly assuming different forms; and she bade him remember that he must keep the sea-god fast bound if he would receive the wished-for answers. Then she led him to the cave of Proteus and hid him there, exhorting him to be bold and fearless.

At noon the Wizard of the Deep came up out of the sea, followed by his herd of sea-calves; and while they lay stretched out on the warm sands, the god sought the retreat of his cave and soon was in a deep slumber. When Aristæus saw Proteus fast asleep, he stepped cautiously up to him and bound him with strong fetters. The god woke with a start, and tried to shake himself free of his chains; but on finding that he was a prisoner, he resorted to all the trickery that he could command. He became a fire, a flood, a wild beast, a horrible serpent, and many other forms calculated to terrify the beholder. But Aristæus was not afraid, and soon the old wizard realized that he must submit; so he assumed his own shape, and asked the youth what it was that he wished to know. The son of Cyrene told him of the death of his bees, and begged for some remedy. Then Proteus reminded him of how he had been the real cause of Eurydice's death, by making her flee from him in such haste that she did not see the snake at her feet.52 The wood-nymphs, who were Eurydice's companions, had therefore wished to punish Aristæus, and had sent this destruction to his hives. It was necessary to appease the wrath of the nymphs; and to do this Proteus bade the youth build four altars, and sacrifice on them four bulls and four cows of perfect form and size. This burnt-offering was to placate the nymphs, and when it was made, he must pay funeral honors to Orpheus and Eurydice to pacify their anger against him. At the end of nine days he was to return to the grove where he had made the sacrifices.

Aristæus thanked the Ancient of the Deep for his wise words, and after releasing him from the fetters, hurried away to do as Proteus had advised. The sacrifices were made, and suitable honors paid to the dead; and then, after waiting impatiently for nine days, Aristæus went back to the grove. To his great joy he found that a swarm of bees had taken possession of the carcasses, and that he was now the owner of a much larger number than he had ever had before.

III

One of the many sea-gods who ruled under Neptune was Glaucus, who was once a poor fisherman, and earned his living by selling the fish that he caught each day. One morning he had an extra large haul; and when he threw the fish on the ground beside him, he noticed that they were eagerly nibbling the grass that grew very thickly in the spot where he had flung his net. As he stood watching them, the fish suddenly leaped up from the ground; and having flopped back into the water, swam away. Curious to see whether it was the grass that gave them this extraordinary power,

Glaucus chewed a bit of it himself, and immediately he felt an irresistible desire to plunge into the sea. Fearlessly he dived beneath the waves, and soon found no difficulty in keeping under water, for the ocean seemed now to be his native element. He saw his beard turning a lovely sea-green; and he found that his hair, grown suddenly long and green, was trailing out behind him. His arms were azure-colored, and his legs became a fish's tail; but he felt no regrets over losing his human form, and stayed contentedly in the ocean. In time Neptune made him one of the lesser gods, and took him into the friendly fraternity of the sea.

As Glaucus was swimming one day near the shore, he saw a beautiful maiden named Scylla; and fell so much in love with her that he forgot he was half fish, and begged her to be his wife. Scylla stared at his green hair and blue skin, but this did not frighten her, nor did she wonder at his fish's tail; for she had often played with the sea-nymphs, and was accustomed to their strange appearance. Glaucus felt encouraged by her behavior, and begged her to listen to the story of his life. He told her how he had suffered a sea change, and now occupied the lofty position of a god. The maiden was interested in this recital, but she had no desire to marry a merman, even if he were a god; so when Glaucus ventured to come nearer to her, she turned and fled. Discouraged but still determined, the young god sought the aid of the enchantress Circe, and begged her to give him some love-potion by which he might win the unwilling Scylla. Circe was so well pleased with the handsome sea-god that she urged him to accept her love, and forget the maiden who scorned him; but Glaucus would not yield to the persuasions of the enchantress, and kept pleading for the desired love-potion.

Seeing that she could not gain his affections, Circe determined that at least no one else should enjoy his love; so she refused to make the potion, and sent Glaucus angrily away. When she saw him go sorrowfully from her palace, she mixed a magic liquid, brewed from poisonous plants and deadly weeds, and this she poured over the waters where Scylla was wont to bathe. The maiden, suspecting no treachery, sought the ocean at her accustomed hour, and as soon as the poisoned waves touched her body she became a horrible monster with six heads—each having three rows of sharp teeth. She saw all around her serpents and barking dogs that were part of her own body, which had suddenly become rooted to the spot where she stood. She never regained her human form, but stayed in this place forever to terrify all mariners, and to devour the hapless sailors that came within her reach. Opposite her was the den of Charybdis, who three times a day swallowed the waters of the sea, and three times threw them up again. On the rock above the den was an immense fir-tree, and all ships that passed that way watched eagerly for this signal of danger, and prayed that they might safely steer between the double horrors of Scylla and Charybdis.

"There Scylla dwells,
And fills the air with fearful yells; her voice
The cry of whelps just littered, but herself
A frightful prodigy—a sight which none
Would care to look on, though he were a god.
Twelve feet are hers, all shapeless, six long necks,
A hideous head on each, and triple rows
Of teeth, close set and many, threatening death.
And forth from the dark gulf her heads are thrust,
To look abroad upon the rocks for prey,—
.... No mariner can boast
That he has passed by Scylla with a crew
Unharmed."

—BRYANT'S Homer's *Odyssey*, Book XII, line 100.

IV

Two other minor deities of the sea were Leucothea and Palæmon. They were not born of the ocean-nymphs or any water-god, but were once mortals, named Ino and Melicertes. Ino was the wife of King Athamas, whom cruel Juno goaded into madness; and through fear of him Ino fled from the palace with her little son, Melicertes, in her arms. She hoped to reach some place of safety; but imagining herself pursued, in her frenzy she plunged from a cliff's edge into the sea. Neither she nor her son perished, however, for the gods, in pity for her sufferings, changed them both into ocean deities under the names of Leucothea and Palæmon. They were widely worshiped by all who had business in great waters, and their protection was invoked against the danger of shipwreck. A famous altar to Palæmon was built on the shores of Corinth, and in his honor were instituted the celebrated Isthmian games.53

V

Neptune was not only willing to befriend a goddess in distress, as he did when he raised the island out of the sea for Latona, but was equally ready to assist mortals—especially in their love affairs. Once he lent his chariot to a youth named Idas when he wished to elope with the maiden Marpessa, whose father had refused to allow the lovers to wed. They were overjoyed at Neptune's kindly offer of assistance; and on the day arranged for their flight, the happy pair mounted the chariot, and the swift steeds carried them far out of reach of Marpessa's angry father. When he discovered that his daughter had eloped with her lover, he started in pursuit; but finding it impossible to overtake Neptune's splendid horses, he flew into such a rage that he flung himself into a river and drowned. (The river was afterwards called by his name—Evenus.) Knowing themselves out of reach of the irate father, the lovers continued their journey very happily, and believed that no misfortune could overtake them, when suddenly Apollo appeared before them, and, declaring himself in love with Marpessa, offered to fight Idas then and there for the possession of the maiden. Poor Idas felt that his chances for happiness were indeed ended, for how could a mortal contend with an omnipotent god? Suddenly a thunderbolt fell from the blue sky, and a voice declared that Marpessa herself should choose between her two suitors. The maiden looked at the glorious sun-god, and her heart beat fast at the thought of being loved by one so beautiful and young; but when she turned to Idas, she remembered that he was a mortal like herself, who would grow old as she grew old, and would, therefore, not cast her aside when her youthful charm was gone, as Apollo would be sure to do as soon as her beauty waned. So she held out her hand to Idas, and refused the sun-god's love. This choice was approved by Jupiter, and the lovers, happy once more, urged Neptune's swift horses over the mirror-like sea, which the kindly god had made calm as a forest pool on the softest summer day. In time they reached a pleasant land far from their native country, and here they lived happily ever afterward. The chariot, no longer needed, was sent back to Neptune with many thanks for his timely aid; and each year Idas and Marpessa burned as sacrifices to their protector a white bull, a white ram, and a white boar, which was the kind of offering most pleasing to Neptune.

CHAPTER XIX
BACCHUS

AMONG all the maidens whom Jupiter honored with his love, none was more beautiful than Semele, daughter of Cadmus and Harmonia. Cadmus was the brother of Europa, whom Jupiter, in the form of a white bull, carried on his back across the sea. The maiden's three brothers had been with her in the meadow, and had witnessed her strange departure, but knowing that it would be useless to attempt to catch the fleet animal, they hurried to their father, Agenor, and told him of the manner in which his favorite daughter had been spirited away. The old man was frenzied with grief, and bade his three sons to go in search of Europa and not return until they had found her. The youths set out, accompanied by their mother, Telephassa, and spent many weary days in a fruitless search for the stolen maiden. At last Phœnix refused to go any farther, and, not daring to return to his father, he remained in a land that was afterwards called in his honor—Phœnicia. Cilix, the second brother, grew weary of the hopeless quest and settled in a country named from him—Cilicia; and finally Telephassa, exhausted by fatigue and grief, died, and Cadmus was left to continue the search alone. He kept doggedly on for many days, and when he reached the town of Delphi, he consulted the oracle, hoping to find some clew to help him. To his surprise the oracle gave this ambiguous answer: "Follow the cow and settle where she rests." Cadmus left the temple, and before he had journeyed far he saw a cow walking leisurely in front of him. Judging this to be the animal intended to guide him, he followed her, and on the way was joined by a curious crowd who were eager to see where the absurd procession would finally stop. Some hoped that by accompanying the hero on his march they might meet with new adventures. The cow at last lay down in Bœotia, and here Cadmus founded the city of Thebes.54

To reward Cadmus for his loving search for Europa, Jupiter gave him in marriage the fair Harmonia, daughter of Mars and Venus. The child of this union was Semele, whom Jupiter wooed in the disguise of a mortal; but such was the maiden's pride that she would not listen to his pleading until he told her who he really was. Then her love was easily won, for no pride could be above yielding to the ruler of Olympus. Jupiter was very happy in the society of Semele, and went down to earth many times to visit her, but it was inevitable that Juno should notice his frequent absences, and should set about finding out where the charm lay that lured him so often to the earth. When she discovered her beautiful rival, she decided upon an ingenious method of punishing her, and accordingly took the form of Semele's old nurse, Beroë. By feigning a loving solicitude for her charge's welfare, she soon won the confidence of the unsuspecting maiden, and listened with well-concealed anger while Semele talked of her lover and showed her pride in having won the affections of the greatest of gods.

The nurse was evidently delighted at Semele's happiness, but seemed worried over the new suitor's identity, and now and then expressed a doubt as to whether he really was the great Jupiter. On questioning the maiden more closely, she assumed a virtuous indignation when Semele admitted that her lover always visited her in the disguise of a mortal, and that she had only his word as proof of his divinity. Hearing this, the old woman urged Semele to make sure that it was no impostor who was playing on her credulity, and pricked the girl's pride by asking her why it was that Jupiter—if it were indeed he—should not honor her as he did the stately Juno by appearing before her in all his splendid majesty. Then the pretended nurse described the glory of Jupiter as it was seen by the dwellers in Olympus, and finally so worked upon Semele's pride and curiosity that the unsuspicious maiden promised to put her lover to the test. So when Jupiter came again, she begged him to grant her a favor, and the ruler of the gods, not knowing of Juno's wiles, readily promised to grant any request Semele might make. To further bind himself, he swore by the river Styx—the most terrible of all oaths. Then the maiden bade him return to Olympus, clothe himself in all his regal apparel—omitting no part of his terrible splendor, not even the dreaded thunderbolts—and having done this, return to her, that she might know he was indeed the awful Thunderer.

Jupiter was dismayed at this request, for he knew that no mortal could endure the greatness of his glory. He begged Semele to ask another boon; but the maiden was obstinate, and insisted upon her request being granted. Sorrowfully Jupiter returned to Olympus, and after robing himself in his fearful majesty, he dimmed the radiance wherever he could, wrapped about him the mildest lightning, and took in his hand the feeblest thunderbolt.

"To keep his promise he ascends, and shrouds
His awful brow in whirlwinds and in clouds;
Whilst all around, in terrible array,
His thunders rattle, and his lightnings play.

* * * * *

Thus dreadfully adorned with horror bright
The illustrous god, descending from his height,
Came rushing on her in a storm of light."

—ADDISON'S Ovid, *Metamorphoses*, Book III, line 302.

But in spite of his attempt to lessen his splendor, even this mild glory so overwhelmed poor Semele that when Jupiter appeared before her, she dropped dead at his feet. In trying vainly to bring her back to life, Jupiter did not notice what havoc the lightning, that played about his head, was making in the palace. In a short time the whole place was reduced to ashes, and in the smouldering ruins the body of Semele was consumed. The only person who escaped uninjured was the infant son of Jupiter and Semele, the golden-haired Bacchus.55

Having rescued his son from the burning palace, Jupiter first intrusted him to his aunt Ino, who cared for him as tenderly as if he were her own child. But the jealous hatred of Juno was not satisfied with the death of Semele, and she tried to extend her vengeance to Bacchus by sending the fury Tisiphone to goad Athamas, the husband of Ino, into madness. As king of Thebes, Athamas had always been a kind ruler, but when the frenzy, inspired by cruel Juno, took possession of him, he imagined that his wife and children were wild beasts, and attempted to kill them. He did succeed in slaying Learchus, but Ino and her other son, Melicertes, escaped from his murderous fury, and afterwards became deities of the ocean.56

Faun

Not daring to leave the infant Bacchus in such a household, and fearing the further persecutions of Juno, Jupiter took the boy to Mount Nysa, where the nymphs—the Nysiades—guarded him faithfully. During his youth, Bacchus was made god of wine and revels, and was intrusted to the tutorship of Silenus, one of the most famous of the satyrs. This jovial old man had a bald head, pointed ears, a fat red face, and a body that was half man and half goat. As he carried a wine bag with him wherever he went, he was generally tipsy, and would have broken his neck long before reaching old age if he had tried to walk unsupported; but some of Bacchus's chosen band of followers always held him up on either side; or, when they themselves were unsteady, set him on an ass's back. Thus protected, he roamed about with Bacchus, and taught him all the craft of wine-growing and the making of choicest wine. The young god soon became a master of revels, and had a large train of followers composed of men and women, nymphs, fauns, and satyrs. They were usually crowned with ivy leaves, and were always drinking wine, eating grapes, singing, and dancing. The most unruly among them were the Bacchantes, who, though women, were often so crazed with wine and the excitement of their dancing that they committed such inhuman crimes as tearing the musician Orpheus to pieces.57 Wherever Bacchus traveled—and it was far and wide—he taught the people the art of cultivating grapes and making wine. He was always welcomed, and when they knew he was approaching, men, women, and children flocked to meet him and his merry company.

Juno tried hard to check his triumphant progress, but she did not dare take his life for fear of Jupiter's wrath; so she afflicted him with a kind of madness that drove him forth a wanderer alone over the earth. He had many adventures during this unhappy period, and finally landed in Phrygia, where the goddess Rhea cured him and taught him her religious rites. After this he wandered in Asia and India, teaching the people the wonderful new art of making wine. When he returned to Greece, he was welcomed everywhere, until he reached his native city of Thebes, where his cousin Pentheus was king. When Pentheus heard that the people were flocking out of the gates to meet Bacchus and his revelers, he tried to stop the excited crowds and force them to return. In vain he pleaded, commanded, threatened. Men and women, and even children, were eager to join in the revels, and would not turn back. Then Pentheus sent some of his servants to seize Bacchus and bring him a prisoner to the city. Soon the messengers returned, but they had not succeeded in getting near the god—so great was the crowd that pressed eagerly around him. They had, however, captured one of his followers; and when they dragged their prisoner before the king, he stood in the presence of the angry monarch without any sign of fear in his calm face. Pentheus commanded the man to tell what sort of revelry and rites were performed under the leadership of Bacchus; and threatened to put him instantly to death if he did not tell the truth. The prisoner smiled at the king's anger, and seemed quite undisturbed by the threats against his life. He refused to tell anything of the ceremonies attending the worship of Bacchus, but began calmly to relate his own story.

He said that his name was Acetes of Mæonia, and that he was a poor fisherman by birth, but had himself learned the pilot's art of steering by the stars. He had thus become master of a cruising vessel; and once, when he was near the island of Dia,58 he sent some of his men to shore for fresh water. They soon returned, bringing with them a youth whom they had found asleep in the forest, and had captured, hoping to obtain a large ransom for him, as the lad was surely some king's son—so haughty and regal was his bearing. When Acetes saw the youth, he begged his men not to force him on board the ship, for the pilot felt convinced that it was no mere mortal who stood so proudly before them. But the sailors would not listen to his advice, and thrust the youth roughly on board. Then Acetes refused to steer the ship; but the men only laughed and declared that they could pilot the craft as well as he. An angry discussion took place on the decks, and soon the quarreling grew so loud that the captured youth, who had been gazing listlessly over the sea, turned to the wrangling crew and asked in what direction the ship was sailing.

"We will steer wherever you wish to go," replied one of the men with a wink at his companions.

"Then sail back to Naxos, for that is my home," said the youth. The sailors promised to do so, but turned the ship toward Egypt, where they hoped to sell their prize for a large sum in gold. Acetes made several brave attempts to get possession of the helm and steer for Naxos, but the sailors struck him down, and threatened to throw him overboard if he interfered in their plans.

Soon the lad seemed to notice that the familiar shores were receding, and anxiously inquired if they were really sailing toward Naxos. He begged them not to ill-treat a friendless boy; but to let him return home in safety. Then the crew, weary of their pretense, told him brutally that he was being taken to Egypt to be sold as a slave; and that he could try his pretty speeches on his future master. The youth did not reply to these taunts, but looked calmly at the jeering sailors, and raised his hand above his head. Immediately the ship stopped as if it had been suddenly rooted to the sea; and though the men pulled frantically at the oars, not an inch could the vessel move. Then, as in a dream, they saw ivy twining rapidly about the sails, and wrapping the oars in its strong tendrils. A vine with its heavy clusters of grapes clung to the mast and the sides of the ship. There was the delicious smell of crushed fruit in the air, and the fragrance of new-made wine.

The sailors stared at the transformed ship and at the captured youth, who now shook off his mask of simplicity and appeared before them in all his godlike beauty—for it was no other than the divine Bacchus whom they had derided and had hoped to sell as a slave. The sound of flutes was heard all around him, and the shrill notes of the pipes. At the feet of Bacchus crouched tigers, lynxes, and panthers, and the god himself bore in his hand a staff wreathed with ivy. Then terror seized the trembling sailors, and they sprang madly over the side of the ship; but as soon as they touched the water they were changed into dolphins. Only Acetes was left standing on the deck before the smiling Bacchus, who bade him have no fear, but take the helm and steer straight for Naxos. The pilot gladly obeyed, and soon reached the desired port, where he left his ship and became a follower of the god of wine.

When Acetes finished this remarkable story, King Pentheus swore that not a word of it was true, and ordered his prisoner to be taken away at once and executed. The soldiers threw Acetes into a dungeon; but while the preparations for his execution were being made, his chains suddenly dropped off and his prison doors flew open. When the jailers came to lead him to his death, he was nowhere to be found. Meanwhile the king had learned that the people were thronging around Bacchus on the Cithæron mountain, just outside the city, and were eagerly joining in all the joyous rites that attended the worship of the god of wine. The shouts of the Bacchanals filled the air, and in spite of his anger against them, Pentheus was curious to see what these ceremonies were that occasioned such roisterous mirth. So he disguised himself as a beggar, and joined the shouting crowd that surrounded Bacchus and his followers. The noisiest of the revelers were the Bacchantes, who danced and sang in a very frenzy of excitement as they tossed their ivy wreaths into the air and poured the red wine recklessly upon the ground. When this group, flushed with wine and half clad, whirled madly toward him, the king was astonished to see among them his own mother Agave. As he leaned nearer to the shouting dancers, wondering how his mother came to join in such orgies, she suddenly saw him, and pointing a finger at his shrinking figure cried:—

"There is the monster who prowls in our woods. Come on, sisters. I will be the first to strike the wild boar." Blinded by the madness that Bacchus had purposely inspired, she rushed upon the terrified king, followed by the crowd of half-crazed Bacchantes. In vain did Pentheus cry out that he was her son. Agave and her companions trampled him down in their fierce onslaught, and in a moment tore him to pieces. Thus was the worship of Bacchus established in Greece.

The spot that the god of wine loved best was the island of Naxos; and here he spent much of his time when he was not wandering over the earth to teach the art of making wine. One day Bacchus was walking on the seashore with his ivy-crowned company, who followed him singing and dancing to the music of their shrill pipes. As they neared a spot where the rocks rise like a cliff above the water's edge, they discovered a maiden sitting on the white sand. This was Ariadne, who had been deserted by her lover, Theseus,59 and left to pine away alone on the island. For days Ariadne had sat looking mournfully out over the sea; and now when Bacchus, with his joyous group of revelers, suddenly broke in upon the silence of her solitude, she was frightened by the sight of so many strangers. Bacchus soothed her fears, and in a short time so won the maiden's confidence that he persuaded her to become his wife. Ariadne was quite content to stay on the island with such a merry company, and if she ever felt any regret over the faithless Theseus, it was soon forgotten in the joy of the wedding celebrations, which lasted for several days. As a marriage gift, Bacchus placed on Ariadne's white forehead a crown adorned with seven glittering stars; but wonderful as it was, it did not eclipse the beauty of the wearer. The happiness of the newly-wedded pair did not last long, however, for in a few months Ariadne sickened and died. After her death Bacchus left the island, and did not return there for many years; but before he set sail he took Ariadne's crown and threw it up into the sky, where it forms a brilliant constellation known as Corona.

One day Silenus fell asleep in the forest, and his companions, believing him safe for a while, went away and left him propped up against a tree with his wine-bag at his side. Here he was found by some peasants, who were subjects of Midas, king of Lydia. The rustics watched the sleeping Silenus for a long time, wondering who he might be. At length the old man woke up, and after rubbing his eyes, asked the staring peasants where he was. As he received no answer to his question, Silenus motioned to the rustics to help him up, and then started to hunt for Bacchus and his lost companions. Seeing him unable to walk the men led him to the court of King Midas who, as soon as he saw the wanderer's jolly red face and his body—half goat and half man—knew at once that it was Silenus, the tutor of Bacchus. This Midas was the same king who had challenged Apollo to compete in the musical contest with Pan; and, because of his unfair decision, had been cursed with ass's ears by the offended god.60 The fact that Silenus had ears unlike the average mortal may have made King Midas feel a bit more sympathy for the old man's distress; but whatever the reason might be, he entertained Silenus royally for ten days, and then led him back to his pupil, who had been wondering at his long absence.61

Delighted to have Silenus returned to him unharmed, Bacchus promised to give the king any reward he might name; and Midas, being very avaricious, asked the god to grant that all that he touched should turn into gold. Bacchus had hoped that Midas would desire a better gift than this; but having made a promise, the god was ready to fulfill it, and he therefore assured the king that his wish was granted. Midas, overjoyed at his good fortune, hastened back to his palace, and on the way he hesitatingly tried his new power. He touched some leaves that hung from the trees near by, and immediately they became golden. He took up a stone from the roadway, and it turned into gold in his hand. He plucked an apple, and in a moment it looked like one of the golden fruit from the garden of the Hesperides. Midas was almost beside himself with joy; and as soon as he reached his palace he began at once to turn all its furnishings into gold. He was so delighted with his wonderful gift that he felt no desire to eat or drink or rest; but at last he grew a little weary of turning things into gold, and, being hungry, sat down at his well-filled table.

He took great pleasure in seeing the cloth and the cups and the plates change as everything else had done at his touch; but to his great amazement and horror, he also found that the bread he took in his hand, the food that touched his lips, turned into hard, unyielding gold. He tried to drink from the shining cups, but the wine in his mouth became melted gold. Then Midas knew the real meaning of his magic touch, and realized sorrowfully that until it was taken away, he would slowly starve in the midst of his great wealth. Already he hated his gift, and longed for some way to divest himself of his ill-fated power. He cried aloud to Bacchus for help, but no answer came to his prayers. Again he besought the god, and this time acknowledged his avarice, and lamented the greed that had led him to ask for the gift of the golden touch. Bacchus heard his prayers, and, believing him truly repentant, commanded him to go to the river Pactolus, trace the stream to its source, and plunge his head and body into the purifying water. In this way he could cleanse himself of his fault and its punishment. Midas did as he was instructed, and came away from the river a wiser and happier, though a poorer man. If at any time he was ever tempted to regret his lost gift, he had only to look into the river at the glittering golden sand on the bed of the stream; for where the king had stood, the sand was changed into gold, and so it has remained to this very day.62

CHAPTER XX
PAN AND THE NYMPHS

PAN,63 the god of woods and fields, god of the flocks and herds, and patron deity of all shepherds, was said to be the son of Mercury. It is apparently not known who his mother was, but she must have had some sylvan blood in her veins, for the youthful Pan showed every evidence of having been born of woodland creatures, as he had the pointed ears of the fauns, and the horns and goat's legs of the satyrs. The story goes that his mother—whichever nymph it was of the many reputed to have borne him—was disgusted with his absurd appearance, and refused to own him for her child; but Mercury was delighted with his son's grotesque figure, and took him to Olympus to amuse the gods.

Pan's favorite dwelling place was Arcadia; and here he wandered over the hills and among the rocks, or roamed through the fertile valleys. He delighted in hunting, and amused himself with various pastimes—his especial pleasure being to lead in the dances with the nymphs. He was devoted to music, and was usually seen playing on the syrinx,—or shepherd's pipes,—which he himself invented and named from a nymph whom he unsuccessfully wooed. The maiden Syrinx was a follower of Diana; and one day, as she was returning from the chase, she met Pan, who immediately fell in love with her beauty, and begged her to be his wife. The nymph had always scorned to listen to any lover, and Pan's appearance did not tend to soften her objections; so while he was praising her many charms and pleading for her love, she turned and ran away. The woodland god was not to be put off so lightly, however; and he promptly gave chase to the fleeing maiden, who, finding that her pursuer was gaining on her, called wildly on the river-nymphs for help. She had by this time reached the water's edge; and just as Pan's arms were about to enfold her, the kindly nymphs changed her into a cluster of reeds. The god was much chagrined at the failure of his hopes; but since he could not have the living maiden, he determined to take whatever remained of the beautiful thing that had charmed him. So he gathered a bunch of the reeds, and after cutting them into unequal lengths, bound them together into a sort of shepherd's pipes. When he put the reeds to his lips, they gave forth the softest and most plaintive tones, and Pan called them the syrinx in honor of the nymph.

Before inventing this new instrument, Pan had played upon the flute, and it was his skill in this direction that made King Midas dare to affront Apollo by declaring Pan to be the better musician. The god of woods and fields was not, however, a frequenter of palaces, but made his home in grottoes and piped to the murmuring trees. He loved to prowl by night in lonesome places, and lurk among the shadows where some belated traveler, startled by the weird hoot of an owl, would see his grotesque form and rush away, filled with that unreasoning terror called a "panic." Pan's partners in the sylvan dance were the wood-nymphs, who always welcomed him and his followers. When his days were spent among the mountain solitudes, the Oreads, or mountain nymphs, danced with him in the moonlight; and when he preferred to live in the valleys, the Dryads, or nymphs of vegetation, joined in the revels led by Pan and his company of fauns and satyrs.64 The Naides, the beautiful water-nymphs who dwelt in the clear depths of the fountains, did not come out of their quiet haunts to take part in the merriment; nor did the shy Hamadryads leave the safe shelter of their trees to mingle in the joyous dance. Among these latter nymphs each had her particular tree, and lived and died with the one intrusted to her care. It was held, therefore, to be an act of wanton cruelty to destroy or even mar a tree, lest the Hamadryad who inhabited it should be hurt and possibly killed. It was unwise to break off a flower recklessly, or to pull it rudely from the earth, for in this humble form might be lodged the spirit of some woodland creature.

Such a sad mistake did Dryope once make, and suffered for her carelessness by being changed from a mortal into a Hamadryad. Dryope was a beautiful young princess, the wife of Andræmon, and the mother of a golden-haired boy. Every day she carried her child to a small lake near the palace, and let him gather the gayly-colored flowers that grew on the water's edge. One day, as she wandered by the lake, Dryope saw a lotus blossom and pointed it out to her little son, who immediately tried to pluck it. As it was much beyond his reach, his mother leaned over the water and broke it off the stem. To her surprise, she saw drops of blood slowly oozing from the stem; and as the boy eagerly grasped the lovely flower in his chubby hand, a crimson stream trickled through his clasped fingers. He dropped the blossom with a frightened cry, and ran screaming to the palace, while Dryope stood looking down, bewildered, at the bleeding flower. Just then she heard a voice telling her that she had killed the nymph Lotis, who, to escape from the arms of the hateful god Priapus, had taken the form of a lotus.

When Dryope realized the dreadful thing that she had unknowingly done, she turned pale with fright, and would have hurried away from the unlucky spot; but when she tried to turn from the sight of the dying flower, she found that she could not move. Her feet seemed rooted to the ground; and, as she looked down, she was horrified to see that a rough bark was beginning to inclose her limbs. With dreadful rapidity it spread upward, and soon encircled her whole body, while her arms changed into twisted branches and her hands into green leaves. In vain she called to her husband and her friends for help. When they arrived, there was nothing left of the fair Dryope but her tear-stained face, which was covered all too soon by the cruel bark. Just before she disappeared completely from their sight, she begged that her little son might be taught to play beneath her branches; and when, in all the after days, the boy sat willingly beside the tree and listened to the soft rustling of its leaves, the passers-by would say: "Dryope is whispering to her child."65

The danger of recklessly destroying any tree is shown by the story of Erysichthon, who dared to defy the goddess Ceres, and so received a fitting punishment. There was a certain grove of trees sacred to Ceres, and among them was a lofty oak on which votive tablets were often hung, and around which the nymphs and Dryads danced hand in hand. Erysichthon ordered his servants to cut down this venerable oak; and when they hesitated, telling him that it was a tree beloved by Ceres and should not suffer such a sacrilege, he seized the ax himself and made a deep gash in the trunk. To the great horror of those who stood by, blood began to flow from the wound; and as Erysichthon was about to deal the tree another blow, one of his servants caught at his arm, imploring him not to touch the oak again, for the blood showed that a Hamadryad was being wounded. Maddened at this interference, and determined to carry out his brutal will, Erysichthon declared that he would cut down the tree if by so doing he killed a dozen Dryads. He lifted his ax for a mighty stroke, and as the servant again sought to stay his arm, he turned fiercely and killed the man with one swift blow. Then he proceeded to fell the tree, and soon it was lying, bruised and bleeding, on the ground.

The nymphs rushed to Ceres, and begged her to punish this wicked violation of her grove. The goddess promised that Erysichthon's deed should not go unpunished, and sent an Oread to the remote part of Scythia, where the ice lies thick on the dreary soil and the land is always desolate. "Here dwell drowsy Cold and Paleness and Shuddering and dreadful Famine." When the Oread drew near this barren country, she saw far off the gaunt form of Famine pulling up with her teeth and claws the scant bits of vegetation that could be found here and there in the frozen earth. The nymph did not want to linger near the dreadful form of Famine, lest the hag should reach out her lean finger and touch the maiden's robes; so she hurriedly delivered the message of Ceres, and sped quickly back to her own fair land of Thessaly.

Not daring to disobey the goddess's command, Famine left her dreary country and sought out the home of Erysichthon. She found him asleep; and as he slept she enfolded him with her wings, and breathed into his nostrils her deadly breath. Then she returned to her frantic digging in the unyielding soil. When Erysichthon awoke, he was at once consumed with a fierce desire for food; but, however much he ate, the terrible craving never ceased. All day long he devoured things greedily, but at night his hunger was still unsatisfied. His servants piled up food in enormous quantities before him, but the gnawing pangs of hunger never left him. He spent all his wealth in a vain attempt to buy enough food to appease the insatiable monster within him; but, though he at last sold all that he had, even to his house and his clothing, it was not enough to buy him the food he craved. There was nothing left him now but his daughter; and frenzied by his hunger, he offered to sell her to a slave-dealer.

The girl pitied her father's sufferings and would have done anything to help him; but she resented his baseness in selling her, for she came of a noble race. While her purchaser was disputing with her father over the price, the maiden, who was standing on the seashore, a short distance away from her new master, implored Neptune to save her from the disgrace of being sold as a slave. The kindly sea-god heard her cry, and changed her into an old fisherwoman. When the bargain between Erysichthon and the dealer was settled, the man looked around for his new purchase, but she was nowhere to be seen. The only person on the seashore, beside the brutal bargainers, was an old woman who sat mending her net. The irate owner searched in vain for his slave and even asked the fisherwoman if she had seen a weeping maiden. Unable to find the girl, he at last went away, concluding that Erysichthon's daughter had tried to escape and so had been drowned in the sea. The maiden was rejoiced at her deliverance; but her cruel father, on seeing her regain her own form, decided that this was an easy way of making the money he desperately needed. So he sold his daughter again and again, and each time she sought the help of Neptune, who obligingly turned her into many different shapes. At last even this device failed to bring to Erysichthon enough money to meet the ever increasing demands of his hunger. In despair over the lack of food he began to eat his own flesh; and in a short time he had devoured so much of his body that death came to end his torment. So was Ceres avenged.

The Hamadryads were seldom seen by men, but people knew them to be both gentle and beautiful. That they could repay a kindness is well shown by the story of Rhœcus, who gained the love of one of the shyest of these nymphs. One day the youth happened to see an oak-tree bent so far down by the wind that some of its branches were already broken. He propped up the tree, and gently bound up the broken limbs; then as he turned to go, he heard a soft voice calling him. It was the Hamadryad who had expected to die with her stricken tree, and was now so grateful to Rhœcus that she bade him ask of her any reward he wished. The youth boldly asked for her love, and the nymph reluctantly yielded to his wish, promising to meet him at the oak-tree each day just before sunset. To keep him mindful of the hour set for the tryst, she told him that she would send him a messenger—a bee—which would also guide him to the spot where she was waiting.

Rhœcus was very happy with the Hamadryad; and never failed to follow the flight of the bee that came each day at sunset to lead him to the trysting-place. One morning, however, he began to play at dice with his friends, and the game continued through the long summer afternoon. As it drew toward sunset, Rhœcus forgot that it was his hour to meet the Dryad, and continued his game, even though he noticed vaguely that a bee was buzzing near him. Soon the bee came close to his face, and buzzed so persistently that Rhœcus brushed it angrily away. Each time he tried to shake it off it came buzzing back, and at last he struck at it so viciously that it fell to the ground. Then in a flash Rhœcus remembered his promise to the Dryad, and throwing away his dice, he hurried to the trysting-place. He called to the nymph and begged her to come to him once more; but no sweet face appeared though a voice spoke from the heart of the oak-tree bidding him a sad farewell. Rhœcus had already repented bitterly of his forgetfulness; but nothing could restore him to favor. He sat all night beside the oak-tree, but the Dryad never came to him again.66

Vestals

CHAPTER XXI
THE VESTALS

VESTA was the oldest child of Saturn and Rhea, and was the goddess of the family hearth. As the hearth was the basis of all domestic ties, Vesta was considered the guardian of family happiness, and her worship was an essential part of the family life. The hearth in ancient days had a much greater significance than in modern times, for it was the center of the household, around which the family gathered for their common meal and common worship. On the hearth, as an altar-fire, the head of the household offered prayers and sacrifices; and it made a bond of union so generally recognized that he who partook of food there, or who shared in the family worship, could ever afterward lay claim to the master's hospitality. If a suppliant was seeking protection from any danger, it was to a man's hearth that he came as a sure place of refuge. The flames that burned on this family altar were sacred to the goddess Vesta, and prayers for domestic happiness and the household's welfare were usually offered to her. Thus the fire burning on the hearth of each dwelling was a perpetual worship of the beneficent Vesta, and even the sacrifices made to other gods were partly in her honor; for whenever the flames were rekindled, a prayer was offered to the goddess of the family fireside.

Every dwelling was, therefore, in some sense, a temple of Vesta; but there was also in each city a stately edifice where all the citizens worshiped at her sacred fire, and were thus bound together in one great family. In Rome, where the worship of Vesta was most celebrated, a beautiful circular temple, dedicated to the goddess, stood in the Forum. It was not necessary to place a statue of Vesta here, for the eternal fire that glowed on her altar was her living symbol, and through this she was worshiped. This fire was supposed to have been brought to Italy by Æneas when he fled from burning Troy and carried with him out of the city two valuable possessions, *i.e.* the fire of Vesta and his own household gods—or Penates. When a colony was sent out from any city, the emigrants took some of the fire from the temple of Vesta in the mother town, and guarded it during their voyages, that they might use its flames to light the fires that were to burn on the hearths of the new homes. Each city cherished carefully the fire that was sacred to Vesta, and never allowed it to burn out, for that was an evil omen sure to presage disaster. If by any chance it was allowed to become extinct, it was never relit from any ordinary fire, but was kindled with a spark produced by friction, or by drawing fire from the sun's rays through a glass. The temple at Rome was the most famous of those dedicated to Vesta, for here was the school of the Vestal Virgins whose duty it was to tend her ever-living fire. As any neglect on their part might bring some public calamity upon Rome, this altar was jealously guarded; and when, as it sometimes happened, enemies threatened the city, the Vestals carried the fire of Vesta down the Tiber and kept it in concealment until the danger was over. Since so much depended on the watchfulness and fidelity of the Vestals, the office of priestess to the temple was held in high honor, and the maidens were chosen from the noblest families of Rome. They entered the service at the very youthful age of six, and spent thirty years in the temple. The first ten years were devoted to learning their important duties; the next decade was the period for filling the office of priestess, and performing all the solemn rites that belonged to the worship of Vesta; the last ten years were given to instructing the novices. When the thirty years of service were over, the Vestals could continue in the temple, or leave it and marry if they desired; but so holy were the Virgins thought to become through their long residence in the temple, that it was held a sort of sacrilege for any man to marry them. Therefore the priestesses usually died, as they had lived, in the service of the goddess. The chief duty of the Vestals was to watch in turns, by night and day, the sacred fire of Vesta, and to see that the flames never grew dim. During their entire period of service, they were obliged to keep the strictest vows of chastity, under penalty of being buried alive in a vaulted room, built especially for this purpose by the king, Numa Pompilius. The Vestals, were, however, so true to all the vows made at the great altar-fire, that in a thousand years only eighteen failed in their promises and thus suffered punishment. The story is told that the Vestal Tuccia was accused of having broken her vow, but was able to prove her purity, by being given the miraculous power to carry water in a sieve from the Tiber to the temple.

Tuccia

Though the restrictions placed upon the Vestals were severe, and the rules of their order were pitilessly enforced, yet the privileges that they enjoyed were such as to raise them in dignity above the other women of Rome. They were entirely released from all parental authority; they had conspicuous places at the theaters and gladiatorial shows, and occupied seats of honor at all public festivals. Treaties and important state documents were intrusted to their care as in a place inviolable; and their persons were held so holy that, when they died, they were buried within the city limits—a privilege granted to but few. When they went abroad, each was preceded by a lictor; and consuls, prætors, and even tribunes made way for them, while if any one passed under their litter, he was put to death. If they chanced to meet a criminal on his way to punishment, they could demand his release, provided that it could be proved that the meeting was accidental. The Vestals wore a robe of pure white linen with a wide purple border, and over their shoulders was a purple mantle. When the festivals of Vesta, the Vestalia, were held, the priestesses marched in a procession through the streets, carrying their sacred fire, while the Roman matrons followed them barefooted, chanting hymns in praise of Vesta. During these ceremonies all work was suspended in the city, the houses were decked with flowers, and the beasts used in the procession were wreathed in garlands; banquets were set out before the houses, and the people gave themselves up to a gala-day.

II

When Æneas fled from burning Troy, and took with him some of the fire from the temple of Vesta, as the thing most necessary in the founding of a new city, he also brought to the shores of Italy his own household gods— or Penates—who presided over the daily affairs of the household, and were the guardians of each member of the family on whose hearth they held the place of honor. The statues of the Penates were of clay, wax, ivory, silver, or gold according to the master's wealth, and were always carried to the new home when the family changed its dwelling place. When the common meal was served, a small portion of it was set aside for the Penates, and a libation of wine was poured to them on the hearth. In return for this daily deference, the Penates blessed the household with happiness and prosperity.

The Lares were also worshiped by the Roman family, though they were quite unknown to the Greeks. They were the divinities that preserved the family unity, and often were a sort of embodiment of the spirit of its head and founder. The Lares also guarded the welfare of the city, and presided over the fortunes of those great groups of families that were the probable foundation of every Roman town. Tradition tells us that the Lares were the two children of Mercury and a beautiful Naiad named Lara. This nymph was so loquacious that she talked from morning to night, and was very fond of prying into other people's affairs, that she might thereby have some new subjects for conversation. One day she heard Jupiter making love to a beautiful wood-nymph, and instead of keeping the matter discreetly to herself, she hurried off to tell the whole affair to Juno. This impertinence so angered Jupiter that he determined to punish her severely and also to prevent her from doing any more talebearing; so he had poor Lara's tongue cut off. Then he summoned Mercury and bade him take the nymph to Hades, where the sight of her sad face could never offend his eyes. On the way down to Pluto's kingdom, Mercury fell in love with his fair companion; and instead of leading her into Hades, he took her to a kindlier place, where he soon won her love and persuaded her to be his wife. The two children of Mercury and Lara were called Lares, and to them the Romans paid many honors, reserving for them a place of honor on the family hearth.

CHAPTER XXII
MINOR DEITIES

I. Æolus

NOT far from sunny Sicily and the deep crater of Etna, in which Vulcan built his glowing forge, were the Æolian Islands—now called Lipari Islands—where Æolus, god of the winds and storms, kept his turbulent children. He never allowed them to roam at will, but held them securely bound in a great cave, and let them loose one at a time when they needed exercise or when the gods demanded their release. Only once were they allowed to give free play to their boisterous feelings, and rush over the waters, making havoc everywhere, and this was when Jupiter sent a deluge upon the impious earth. Since that time the winds have never roamed at large, though they always chafe at being restrained in their narrow prison and long to break free.

"Hic vasto rex Æolus antro
Luctantes ventos—tempestatesque sonoras
Imperio premit ac vinclis et carcere frenat.
Illi indignantes magno cum murmure montis
Circum claustra fremunt; celsa sedet Æolus arce,
Sceptratenens, mollitque animos et temperatiras;
Ni faciat, maria ac terras cælumque profundum
Quippe ferant rapidi secum verrantque per auras."67

—VIRGIL, *Æneid*, Book I, line 52.

Æolus wooed and married the dainty Aurora, goddess of the morning, who bore him his sons, *i.e.* Boreas, the north wind; Notus, the south wind; Eurus, the east wind; and Zephyrus, the soft and gentle west wind. Sometimes Aurora sought the services of her children, but they were entirely under the control of their father Æolus who ruled them with a strict hand. Sometimes when the stately Juno sought his assistance, he let the winds sweep over the calm sea until the waves rose mountain high, for he was reputed to have received his royal status as god from Juno's hands, and so was ever anxious to serve her. Once, at her request, he let loose the fiercest winds to destroy the ships of Æneas—that unfortunate hero who was always being pursued by "cruel Juno's unrelenting hate." The goddess was so eager for his destruction that she went herself to the cave of the winds, and begged Æolus to shatter the Trojan ships. So a terrible storm broke over the sea, and the winds drove the vessels of Æneas far out of their course, scattering them here and there, until no two could see each other amid the fury of the tempest. When Neptune realized what was happening, he lifted his head above the white-capped waves and saw the Trojan ships tossed about and beaten out of their course. As he himself had given no commands for such a storm, he knew it was the never-ending hatred of Juno for the Trojans that had brought about the disaster. But the sea, and all that therein is, was Neptune's to control, and he was justly angry with Juno's interference; so he recalled the winds from their mad race and bade the storm cease.

Quite differently did Æolus treat another famous hero, Ulysses, whose ships, on the long homeward journey, touched at the Lipari Islands. Here the wanderer was hospitably entertained by Æolus, and when he set sail again, the kindly god sent the west wind to blow the ships gently over the sea, while he shut up the blustering winds in a leather bag and tied it with a silver string. This bag he gave to Ulysses, "the sagacious," and bade him keep it closed until the journey was over. For nine days and nights the hero stood at the helm watching, while the west wind bore the ships along without the help of oars. At last, exhausted by his long vigil, Ulysses fell asleep; and the sailors, believing that the bag contained treasure that King Æolus had generously given, untied the string and freed the roistering winds. The ships were now driven hither and thither by the madly-rushing winds, and were tossed over the sea far away from the longed-for Ithaca. Finally they were blown back to the Lipari Islands, where Æolus received them but coldly, and refused to help them further. So they turned their prows once more toward home, and worked wearily against wind and weather by the slow pull of the oars.

The Athenians built a temple to Æolus, which is still extant, and is generally known as the Tower of the Winds, or the Temple of Æolus. The structure is hexagonal, and on each side there is a flying figure of one of the winds. Notus (or Auster), the south wind, was usually represented by an old man with dusky wings. He is clad in a black robe, and his head is covered with clouds, for he sends the rains and sudden showers. Eurus, the east wind, was a young man full of impetuous and lively motion. Corus, the northwest wind, drove clouds of snow before him, and Boreas was a figure rough and shivering. Zephyrus had a lapful of flowers, and was the one wind sent to play among children. Boreas was the bringer of hail and tempests, and when he wooed the nymph Orithyia, he sought in vain to approach her gently, and to breathe his love softly. But he could not sigh, and his lightest whisper frightened the maiden by its harshness; so Boreas gave up attempting to win her by gentle means and boldly carried her off to his home in the midst of snow and ice. Their children were Zetes and Calais—winged warriors who accompanied the Argonauts on their famous expedition, and performed a valuable service in driving away the Harpies.68

II. Janus

Janus,69—god of the past, present, and future; of gates and entrances; of war and peace,—was said to be the son of Apollo; but as he is a Roman god, and entirely unknown to Greek mythology, his ancestry is a matter of doubt. He presided over the beginning of everything, and was therefore invoked first in every undertaking—even before Jupiter. He opened the year and the seasons, and the first month of the year was called after him. He was the porter of heaven, and in this capacity he was represented as holding a key in his left hand and a staff or scepter in his right. On earth he was the guardian deity of gates, and as such he had always two faces turned in opposite directions, because every door looks both ways. Another explanation of his physical duality is that as god of the past and future he sees what is behind and what is before. Janus was also considered an emblem of the sun, and had therefore two faces, one to look at its rising and one to see its setting. Sometimes these faces were alike, but more often they were represented by a white-haired and white-bearded old man on the one side, and a smooth-cheeked youth on the other.

At Rome Numa Pompilius is said to have dedicated to Janus the covered passage—erroneously called a temple—that stood close by the Forum. This was kept open in times of war and closed in times of peace; but such was the belligerent nature of the Romans that the gates were closed but three times in seven hundred years, and then only for a short period.

As he was god of all beginnings, the first of every new year, month, and day was held sacred to Janus, and special prayers and sacrifices were then offered at his shrines. When he presides over the year, he is represented as holding the number three hundred in one hand and sixty-five in the other. Festivals in honor of Janus were celebrated on the first day of the new year, and on this day people exchanged visits, good wishes, and gifts, which usually consisted of sweetmeats and copper coins showing on one side the double head of Janus. The sacrifices offered to Janus on New Year's day and at other times of beginnings were barley, incense, cakes, and wine.

III. Iris and Aurora

Iris was the special attendant of Juno, and was often employed as a messenger by both Juno and Jupiter. In the Iliad she is the swift servant of the gods; but in the Odyssey it is Mercury who is the messenger to and from Olympus, and Iris is never mentioned. Sometimes Iris is described as the rainbow itself; sometimes the rainbow is only the road over which she travels, and which therefore vanishes when it is no longer needed. When Juno sends Iris to the Cave of Sleep "she assumes her garments of a thousand colors, and spans the heavens with her curving arch." As the personification of the rainbow—that brilliant phenomenon that vanishes as quickly as it appears—Iris might easily be considered the swift messenger of the gods.

* * * * *

Aurora

Aurora, rosy-fingered goddess of the dawn, opened the gates of the morning for the impatient horses of the sun, who chafed at being held behind the golden bars until Apollo was ready to start forth on his daily course, attended by the faithful Hours. Though Aurora was the wife of Æolus and mother of the winds, she had the usual weakness of the deities of Olympus for falling in love with mortals who won her favor. Thus she became enamored of the young hunter Cephalus, but was unable to gain his love, as he himself had already wedded the fair Procris, one of Diana's nymphs. The happiness of these lovers was a maddening sight to the jealous Aurora, and she determined to find some way to end it. Procris had brought to her husband as a dowry a hunting dog named Lelaps, who could outrun the swiftest deer, and a javelin that never missed its mark. So all day long Cephalus hunted in the forest, and his long absences gave the malicious Aurora an excuse for whispering to the young wife that her husband spend his time in the society of a wood-nymph. For some time Procris resisted these suggestions of the goddess; but at last, overcome by jealousy, she followed Cephalus to the forest to see who the maiden was that charmed him. At noonday the weary hunter sought his accustomed resting place; and as he lay beneath a wide-spreading tree, he called to the breeze to come and refresh him. Believing that he referred to some wood-nymph, Procris sank down among the bushes in a swoon; and her husband, hearing the leaves rustle suddenly behind him, hurled his javelin into the thicket, supposing that some wild beast was crouching near him ready to spring. To his horror he discovered the body of Procris; and though he did all that he could to stanch the wound made by his unerring spear, his wife died in his arms—but not before an explanation had been given.70

Though Aurora had succeeded in separating the lovers forever, she did not thereby gain the affections of Cephalus, but was obliged to console herself with the Trojan prince, Tithonus. She begged Jupiter to confer upon him the boon of immortal life; but forgetting that he would sometime grow old, she neglected to ask for him the greater gift of eternal youth. For a while she was very happy with her lover, but as soon as he lost the attractions of youth she wearied of his company and wished to get rid of him. She shut him up in a room of her palace, where his feeble voice could often be heard; and then, knowing that he would never die, she cruelly changed him into a grasshopper.71

The son of Aurora and Tithonus was Memnon, who became king of the Ethiopians, and went with a band of warriors to help his kindred in the Trojan war. He fought bravely, but at length met his death at the hands of Achilles. When he fell on the battle-field, Aurora commanded her sons, the winds, to carry his body to the banks of the river Æsepus in Asia Minor, where a tomb was erected to his memory. To honor him further, Jupiter caused the sparks and cinders from his funeral pyre to be changed into birds, which divided into two flocks and fought until they fell into the flames. Every year, on the anniversary of Memnon's death, the birds returned to celebrate the funeral rites in this same strange way. When the flames from the funeral pyre had burned out, Aurora sat by the ashes of her son, weeping and mourning his loss; and the many tears that she shed turned into glistening dewdrops. In Egypt there were two colossal statues, one of which was said to be the statue of Memnon; and tradition tells that when the first rays of morning fell upon it, it gave forth a sound like the snapping of harp strings.

IV. Flora, Vertumnus, and Pomona

Flora, goddess of flowers and of spring, was not among the deities worshiped in Greece, but was everywhere honored among the Romans. She was reputed to have married Zephyrus, the balmy west wind, and with him she wandered happily over town and country, distributing her favors with lavish hand. Though the gentle goddess was universally beloved, her principal devotees were young girls, who delighted in keeping her altars decorated with fruits and garlands of flowers. Her festivals were held during the month of May and were called the Floralia.

Vertumnus and Pomona were also Roman deities and presided over orchards and gardens. Pomona was a Hamadryad, and was so devoted to the care of her trees that she scorned the idea of love. Fauns and satyrs sought to woo her, and Sylvanus—a woodland deity—tried in vain to approach her. Even the wily Pan was never able to come near enough to her to urge his suit, but the youthful god Vertumnus was not to be discouraged by the nymph's coldness, and determined to win her for his wife. Hoping to catch her eyes and so get speech with her, he assumed various disguises. "How often did he carry the ears of corn in a basket under the guise of a hardy reaper. How often he bore a whip in his sturdy hand so that you would have sworn he had that instant been unyoking the wearied oxen. Now he was carrying a ladder, and you would suppose he was going to gather fruit. Sometimes he was a soldier with a sword, and sometimes a fisherman, taking up the rod."72 But no attractions in the form of man could induce Pomona to leave her orchard, or to admit one of the hated beings. At last the resourceful Vertumnus hit upon the plan that brought him well-earned success. "Having bound his brows with a colored cap, leaning on a stick and with white hair falling around his temples, he assumed the shape of an old woman and entered the well-cultivated gardens."73 After praising the fruit and flowers, the pretended old woman began to ask Pomona why she had persistently remained unwed, and told her how foolish it was to fly from love. Much to the surprise of Vertumnus, the maiden seemed to receive this advice very kindly; and when he went on to speak of a certain youthful god who had long sought her love, he was delighted at gaining the confession from Pomona that she might be willing to listen to Vertumnus if he came to woo. At this admission the bold lover threw off his disguise, and claimed the fulfillment of the maiden's promise.

CHAPTER XXIII
HERCULES

Part I

HERCULES was the son of Jupiter and Alcmene—a lovely princess, the granddaughter of Perseus and Andromeda. Juno hated her as she did all her mortal rivals, and sought to bring misery and suffering on the unoffending maiden. When she learned that Hercules, the son of Alcmene, was born, she sent two immense serpents with poisonous fangs to attack the child while he slept. The baby happened to waken just as the creatures were twining themselves about him; and grasping their necks in each of his tiny hands, he strangled them, thus showing from his birth the wonderful strength that was later to make him a famous hero. The education of Hercules was intrusted to Chiron, the most renowned of the centaurs, who had himself been instructed by Apollo and Diana in hunting, medicine, music, and the art of prophecy. The idea of a creature half man and half horse was not repulsive to the ancients, who were too fond of a horse to consider man's union with him degrading. When Hercules left the kindly tutelage of Chiron, he set out on his own adventures, and before he had traveled far he met two beautiful women, each of whom offered to guide him on his journey. Kakia (Vice) told him that if he followed her, he would gain love, riches, and ease; and Arete (Virtue) promised him honor, bought at the price of hardship, poverty, and endless toil. For a while the youthful hero deliberated over the two very different rewards offered him, and at last he gave his choice to Arete, who henceforth led him through many perils, and into labors such as no man had ever yet performed.74

The Infant Hercules

Like most heroes, Hercules was a great wanderer; and on one of his journeys he came to the city of Thebes, where Creon, the king, entertained him and showed him so much favor that when Hercules asked for the hand of Creon's daughter Megara in marriage, the king gladly gave his consent. The hero then rested from his wanderings, and spent many happy years in the society of his wife and children; but Juno had not forgotten her old hatred of Alcmene's offspring, and she determined to end this happiness. So she afflicted Hercules with a sudden madness; and in his delirium he killed his wife, and threw his children into the fire. When at last he recovered his senses, he suffered terribly over the thought of the crimes that he had unwittingly committed, and would have gone off to the mountains to spend his days in sorrow and remorse, had not Juno demanded that he should expiate his deeds of bloodshed. Accordingly she sent Mercury to lead him from his solitude among the hills and to take him to his cousin Eurystheus, king of Argos, whom he was compelled to serve for a whole year. During this time he performed the twelve great labors that have made his name famous as the doer of mighty deeds.

The first task that Eurystheus gave the hero was to procure the skin of a monstrous lion that inhabited the Nemean forest. This creature's frequent attacks had brought terror to all the countryside, for it was not content with carrying off cattle and sheep, but had killed the children at play, and mangled shepherds who were watching with their flocks. When the people heard that Hercules was setting out to fight the lion, they tried to persuade him to give up the adventure; but he, who had strangled two huge serpents in his infancy, was not afraid of a lion, however fierce and strong it might be. So he boldly entered the forest, and having tracked the great brute to its den, he attacked it fearlessly and killed it with his bare hands. Then, throwing the body of the lion over his shoulder, he started back to the palace of Eurystheus; but when the king saw Hercules approaching, he begged him to leave his burden outside the city gates. So the hero skinned the lion, and took the shaggy pelt to be henceforth his favorite covering.

Hercules's second labor was to kill the Hydra, a nine-headed monster that infested the marshes of Lerna. With the blows of his great oak club the hero was able to strike off eight of the heads, but the central one was immortal and could not be destroyed. Further to complicate the difficulty, Hercules found that as soon as he struck off one head, two others sprang up in its place. To prevent this discouraging miracle from continuing, the hero bade his friend Iolaus, who had accompanied him, take a lighted brand and sear the wounds as soon as they were made. Through this wise precaution the Hydra was finally killed, and its one immortal head was buried under a huge rock. While this difficult struggle was going on, Juno, always eager to thwart the hero, sent a large crab to pinch Hercules's feet as he wrestled with the Hydra. He succeeded in crushing it with his club; but Juno did not leave its body on the trampled and blood-stained ground. In recognition of its services to her, she placed it in the sky as the constellation of Cancer (the Crab). Before Hercules left the dead Hydra he dipped some arrows in its venomous blood, knowing that any wound received from their poisoned tips would surely be fatal. These arrows were later of great service to Hercules, and only once did he regret their deadly quality.

The next task that Eurystheus set was the capture of the golden-horned and brazen-hoofed stag of Cerynea, which ran so swiftly that it did not seem to touch the ground. Hercules pursued the stag for many miles, but was unable to overtake it until he drove it into the cold regions of the north, where its fleetness was hindered by the great drifts and the ice-covered ground. Finally the stag ran into a deep snow bank, and so Hercules captured it and took it home in triumph.

The fourth labor to which Hercules lent his great strength was the killing of a wild boar that haunted Mount Erymanthus in Arcadia. While on this expedition, the hero was attacked by the centaurs, and when he shot at them with his poisoned arrows, one of the deadly missiles flew far and struck his loved tutor Chiron, who was galloping toward the combatants, hoping to settle the quarrel peaceably. When Hercules saw Chiron fall, he rushed to his side and tried to stanch the fatal wound; but the dying centaur knew that his end had come, and sorrowfully bade the hero farewell. To reward Chiron for his long service, the gods transferred him to the heavens as the constellation Sagittarius.

Hercules was next sent to kill the flock of fierce birds whose cruel beaks and sharp talons made havoc in the country around Lake Stymphalus. The foul mist that rose from the stagnant water over which the birds hovered was so deadly to breathe that Hercules could hardly approach the lake; but with the help of his poisoned arrows he was able to wound the birds at a distance. After hours spent in this pestilent atmosphere he killed the entire flock and returned to the court of Eurystheus to report his success.

The most unpleasant of all Hercules's labors was the cleaning of the stables where Augeas, king of Elis, kept his herd of a thousand oxen. These stables had not been cleaned for thirty years; and when Hercules caught one glimpse of the filth within them, he felt that this was too degrading a task for him to undertake. But the work had to be done; and since he could not put his hand to anything so foul, he looked about for some other means to accomplish the labor. Not far from the stables flowed two rivers, the Peneus and Alpheus, and these Hercules turned out of their courses and made them rush through the filthy building until every part of the stables of Augeas was washed perfectly clean. Then he restored the rivers to their former beds, and returned home to report this task fulfilled.

The next labor that was assigned to the hero was the capture of a mad bull given by Neptune to King Minos. In the early days of his power, Minos had boasted that he could obtain anything that he wished from the gods; and had accordingly begged of Neptune a bull for the sacrifices. The kindly sea-god sent a splendid offering, but when Minos saw the bull's size and beauty, he resolved to keep it. So he substituted another animal for the sacrifices. This angered Neptune so much that he made the bull go mad; and it rushed here and there over the island, causing great terror among the people. The creature was finally caught and overcome by Hercules, who rode it through the waves to Greece. The offspring of this bull was the famous Minotaur which the hero Theseus pursued through its labyrinth, and slew.

The eighth labor of Hercules was to bring from Thrace the horses of Diomedes. These splendid creatures the king fed on human flesh; and in order to get a sufficient supply of fresh meat, he decreed that all strangers who came into his kingdom should be imprisoned, fattened up, and then served as food to the horses. To punish Diomedes for his years of cruelty, Hercules fed him to his own steeds, and then led them back to Eurystheus, who was proud to be the possessor of such a prize.

At the court of Eurystheus was the king's beautiful daughter, Admete, who loved purple and fine linen, and decked herself with all the jewels that her father's wealth could command. One day Admete heard a traveler telling wonderful tales of the girdle that was worn by Hippolyte, queen of the Amazons; and at once the spoiled princess demanded of her father that he send Hercules to procure for her the coveted girdle. So the hero set out again, accompanied by his friend Iolaus; and after a hard and perilous journey came to the country of the Amazons. These were a fierce, warlike nation of women who kept in their tribe only the girls who were born among them and disposed of the boys by killing them, or by giving them to the neighboring peoples. The girls were trained in severe military discipline, and became a race of very redoubtable warriors whom no king cared to treat with contempt. When Hercules came before the queen Hippolyte, she received him kindly, listened to the explanation of his visit, and even promised to give him the girdle that the selfish Admete coveted. Before the hero and his friend set out on their journey homeward, the queen entertained them royally with feasting and games that lasted several days. Meantime Juno saw an opportunity for indulging her hatred of Hercules; and taking the form of an Amazon, she mingled freely with the women. By pretending to have received a heaven-sent message, she persuaded them that the stranger had used the girdle as a mere pretext for his visit, and that his real intention was to carry off the queen. The Amazons believed this artfully-contrived report, and rushed in a body to protect Hippolyte. They attacked Hercules fiercely, but he beat them off and finally escaped with his friend, but not before he had killed several of the Amazons, including the queen who had befriended him.75 With the dearly-bought girdle he returned homeward, and on the way he heard the proclamation of Laomedon that whoever would save his daughter Hesione from the sea-monster should receive a large reward. Hercules killed the beast and freed the maiden, but was obliged to leave Troy without the promised gold, because of Laomedon's perfidy and greed.76

When the ancients looked each evening at the glowing west, they pictured it as a far-distant country, more wonderful than any ever seen by mortal eyes. Here in this land of heart's desire lay the Garden of the Hesperides, where a dragon guarded the golden apples that grew on a wonderful tree which had sprung up miraculously to grace the wedding of Jupiter and Juno. In this far-off sunset land were also the Isles of the Blest,77 where mortals who had led virtuous lives were transported without ever tasting of death. Here the blessed of the gods enjoyed an eternity of bliss; and wandered happily over the Isles, which had a sun and moon and stars of their own, and never felt the touch of wintry winds. In this mysterious region of the west was the island of Erythea, called "the red" because it glowed in the light of the setting sun. To this spot Hercules was sent to take possession of the oxen of Geryon—a monster with three bodies. On his journey to the island, Hercules's way was blocked by a huge mountain; and with one blow of his strong oak club he cleft the opposing rock, and allowed the waters of the sea to flow through. This is now the strait of Gibraltar, and the cliffs on either side are called the Pillars of Hercules.

When the hero reached the island of Erythea, he found the oxen guarded by the giant Eurytion and his three-headed dog; but even this did not daunt the slayer of the Hydra. He boldly attacked the giant; and after a fierce battle, in which his oak club stood him in good stead, killed both Eurytion and the monstrous dog. Then he went in search of the oxen, and, after herding them closely, drove them toward his own country. On the journey homeward he passed Mount Aventine, where the giant Cacus lived in a rocky cave. One night, as Hercules was asleep near the mountain, the giant stole part of the cattle; and, to deceive the hero, he dragged them backwards by their tails into his cave. Hercules might have been tricked by this stratagem if the stolen oxen had not lowed loudly as the rest of the herd passed the cave, and so betrayed their hiding place. Hercules rushed into the giant's dark, ill-smelling dwelling, slew him, and recovered all the stolen cattle.

Hercules and the Centaur

CHAPTER XXIV
HERCULES

Part II

ONE of the most difficult of Hercules's labors was to procure the golden apples that the Hesperides, daughters of Hesperus, god of the west, guarded very jealously. At the foot of the tree coiled a fierce dragon whose nostrils poured out fire, and whose deadly breath would have slain any venturesome robber, even if he had escaped the dragon's claws. As Hercules did not know in what part of the great glowing west the Garden of the Hesperides lay, he wandered many miles before he met with any one who could direct him where to go. The first help he received was from the nymphs of the Eridanus River, who were sporting on the river bank and called to Hercules to come and join in their games. Much as he would have liked to rest, the hero dared not tarry; but he begged the friendly nymphs to tell him the way to the Garden of the Hesperides. They could not help him, but they advised him to go to old Proteus, "the Ancient of the Deep," who could tell him whatever he wished to know better than any one else. So Hercules went down to the seashore, and found the hoary god asleep in his cool green cave. Knowing the old man's wiles, the hero grasped him firmly and held him fast through all the bewildering changes by which he sought to frighten away the stranger. At last, finding himself securely caught, the Wizard assumed his own form, and asked Hercules what it was that he wished to know. The hero stated his errand, and Proteus told him, "in words that ne'er deceive," that he must find the giant Atlas who alone knew where the Garden of the Hesperides lay.

Hercules then started again on his search, and in the course of his journey came to the Caucasus Mountains, where he found Prometheus, the stealer of the sacred fire, bound with adamantine chains to the rock, while a vulture daily feasted on his liver.78 Hercules killed the foul bird, broke the chains, and set Prometheus free; and in return for his deliverance the grateful Titan directed his rescuer where to find the giant Atlas. Following Prometheus's advice, Hercules traveled straightway to Africa; and on the way he passed through the land of the Pygmies, a tiny race of warriors who waged continual warfare with neighboring tribes, and especially with their deadly enemies, the cranes. Hercules was not aware that he had reached the country of the Pygmies;79 but one day, when he had fallen asleep from weariness, he was wakened by sharp prickings over his body; and looking around he saw a host of diminutive men, attacking him with their tiny weapons. The hero laughed at these brave efforts, caught up a few of the doughty little warriors, and, wrapping them in his lion skin, carried them back with him to the court of Eurystheus.

As he journeyed through Africa in search of Atlas, Hercules came to the country of Anteus—a mighty giant and wrestler, and the son of Terra, the Earth. All strangers who came into the land were obliged to wrestle with him, and if they were defeated, they were immediately killed. As no one had ever overcome Anteus, he had brought an untimely death on many a brave hero; so Hercules was eager to defeat him and avenge the unknown dead. As soon as they had grappled for the first struggle, the slayer of the Hydra knew that he had met more than his equal in strength. For a long time they wrestled, Anteus growing stronger after each fall, and Hercules growing fainter from every additional blow of the giant's hand. Again and again the undaunted hero threw his adversary to the ground, but Anteus rose with redoubled vigor and continued the unequal contest. Then, all at once, Hercules remembered the tale he had once heard told of a giant who drew strength from his mother Earth; and believing that this was the case with Anteus, he made a mighty effort and lifted the giant from the ground. Anteus struggled to get his feet again on the earth; but Hercules kept him in the air, and held him there until he felt the powerful body beginning to weaken. Little by little the miraculous strength oozed away, and soon Anteus grew so weak that Hercules easily crushed the limp form with his hands.

The hero then traveled on in search of Atlas, whom he finally found standing on the coast of Africa, with the great weight of the heavens resting on his broad shoulders. As Hercules looked up at the enormous figure, which reached so far into the clouds that nothing could be seen above his waist, he noticed that the forests had grown up so thick and tall all around that only a glimpse of the giant's huge legs could be seen through the heavy foliage. As the hero stood watching this figure that for centuries had stood here in obedience to the divine command of Jupiter, he saw dark clouds beginning to gather about the giant's head, and soon a storm broke over the sea and land. Amid the beating of the rain and the crash of the thunder, Hercules thought he heard the voice of Atlas speaking to him; but it might have been only a peal of thunder. When the storm was over and the mists rolled away from the earth, Hercules saw the head of Atlas through rifts in the scurrying clouds. The snow-white hair gave the giant's face a benign look as it fell thick and white over the stooping shoulders that bore so terrible a weight. In a voice that he strove hard to make gentle, Atlas asked the hero what he was seeking, and Hercules told him that he had come to get some of the golden apples from the Garden of the Hesperides.80 Atlas laughed at these words, and his great shoulders shook so with merriment that a few of the stars fell out of their places. Then he told Hercules that such a feat was impossible even to so great a hero; but that if some one would take the heavens from his shoulders for a few hours, he himself would get the apples.81

Hercules was delighted with this offer of assistance, and agreed to take the giant's burden while the latter went on his friendly errand. Very carefully Atlas transferred the heavens to the shoulders of Hercules, and then sped westward to the Garden of the Hesperides. The hero was a bit troubled when he saw Atlas shake his huge shoulders and stretch himself in delight at his freedom, for it would be strange, indeed, if the giant were ready to resume his burden after having tasted the joy of liberty. With some anxiety Hercules watched him step into the sea that came only to his knees though he had waded out a mile from the shore. As Atlas went deeper and deeper into the waves, at first his huge bulk loomed like a cliff against the horizon; but soon it dwindled into a mere speck, and was presently lost to view. How long he stood holding the heavens Hercules never knew; but he found himself growing very weary of his burden, and anxious over Atlas's long absence. Suddenly he saw a dark spot on the horizon, and he knew that it was the giant returning.

It had not been a difficult task for Atlas to reach the Garden, or to pluck the golden apples from the carefully-guarded tree; and Hercules, delighted with the giant's success, thanked him for his trouble and asked him politely to take the sky again on his shoulders, for the journey back to the court of Eurystheus was a long one. Now Atlas had no desire to stand for another dozen centuries with his old burden; and seeing a good opportunity of getting rid of it forever, he told Hercules that he would carry the apples to Eurystheus himself; and meanwhile the hero could keep the heavens supported until Atlas returned. Pretending that he was quite satisfied with this arrangement, Hercules bade the giant good-by; then hastily asked him to wait a moment while he made a pad for his shoulders to ease the weight of the unaccustomed burden. The unsuspicious giant good-naturedly agreed to this, and took the heavens from Hercules; but instead of making a cushion, the hero picked up the golden apples, which Atlas had dropped on resuming his burden, and started back to his own country, leaving the giant to stand on the seashore forever, or until the pitying gods should release him.

The twelfth and last labor of Hercules was to bring from Hades the three-headed dog, Cerberus. With the help of Mercury and Minerva, he descended into the dread realm of Pluto, and begged that grim monarch to let him take Cerberus into the upper world. Pluto was not willing at first to lose the guardian of his gates even for a short time; but at length he consented to let Hercules do as he desired on condition that Cerberus should not be bound or any weapons used upon him. So the fierce three-headed creature was carried, snarling and struggling, in the hero's strong arms; and when the pair approached the throne of Eurystheus, the horror-struck monarch implored Hercules to take the monster back as quickly as possible, for the sight of its dripping jaws, from which oozed the deadly nightshade, so terrified Eurystheus that he sought refuge in a huge jar, and would not come out until his courtiers assured him that Cerberus was safely out of the country.

When the twelve labors were ended, Hercules's term of service at the court of Eurystheus was over, and he was free to wander where he willed. He spent many years roaming through various lands and assisting other heroes who, like himself, were in search of adventures. He took part in the battle between the Centaurs and Lapithæ;82 joined in the Argonautic expedition; organized the first siege of Troy, and braved the terrors of Hades to bring Alcestis back to her repentant husband.83 The expedition against Troy was one of revenge, for the false Laomedon had never paid the gold that he had promised for the release of his daughter Hesione from the sea-monster; and Hercules now set out to punish the treacherous king.84 So he sailed for Troy with eighteen ships, and the city fell into his hands with but little resistance. Laomedon was killed, his son Priam placed on the throne of Troy, and Hesione given in marriage to Telamon, one of the Greeks who accompanied Hercules.

Hercules serving Omphale

The hero's splendid career received a check, however, for in a quarrel he killed his friend Iphitus, and the gods, angry at this unnecessary bloodshed, compelled him to go once more into bondage. So for three years Hercules served Omphale, queen of Lydia; and during this time he lived very effeminately, wearing sometimes the dress of a woman and spinning wool with the handmaidens of Omphale, while the queen wore his lion's skin and wielded his renowned club. When his years of servitude were over, he set out again on his wanderings; and during one of his journeys he met the beautiful Deïaneira, daughter of Œneus of Calydon and sister of Meleager, famous in the Calydonian hunt. Hercules immediately sought the maiden's hand in marriage; but she had another suitor, the river god Achelous, who had already obtained her father's consent. Deïaneira, however, much preferred her new lover, and begged him to free her from the betrothal with Achelous. So Hercules challenged the river-god to a wrestling match, the conditions of the contest being that he who won should have the maiden in marriage. Achelous readily agreed to this way of settling their rival pretensions, for he had no doubt as to the result of the wrestling.

The opponents were well matched as to strength, but the river-god had one great advantage, for he could assume any form he pleased, and thus bewilder any one who tried to grapple with him. Among his many changes, he took the form of a serpent; but when Hercules grasped it by the neck and was about to strangle it, Achelous became a bull and rushed at the hero with lowered horns. Skillfully eluding this unexpected attack, Hercules seized the bull by one horn and held on so firmly that when the creature tried to wrench himself free the horn broke. This decided the victory in favor of Hercules, and Achelous departed sullenly to his bed in the river. The broken horn was appropriated by Fortuna, the goddess of plenty, who filled it with her treasures, and adopted it thenceforth as her symbol, calling it Cornucopia.

Fortuna

There was nothing now to hinder the marriage of Hercules with Deïaneira, and the wedding took place with much mirth and feasting. After several days of festivity Hercules departed with his wife; and in the course of their journey homeward, they came to the river Evenus, which had grown so swollen and turbid from the heavy rains that it was impossible to ford it. As the travelers stood helpless on the bank, the centaur Nessus came galloping up to them, and offered to carry Deïaneira across the river in safety. Grateful for this timely assistance, Hercules placed his wife on the back of the centaur, who swam with her through the swift-flowing stream. When they reached the opposite bank, Deïaneira expected the centaur to stop, that she might dismount; but Nessus set off at a brisk trot, hoping to kidnap his fair rider before her husband could overtake them. Hercules heard the cries of his terrified bride, and as soon as he swam the river he sent a swift arrow after the treacherous Nessus. The poisoned tip sank deep into the centaur's side, and he knew at once that he had received his death-wound. With a pretense at repentance, he asked Deïaneira to forgive his rash deed; and then, as if granting her a favor, he told her to take his robe which was stained with blood, and keep it carefully, for it had wonderful properties. He assured her that if the time ever came that Hercules's love grew cold, she had only to persuade him to put on this magic robe, and his devotion to her would become more ardent than ever before. Deïaneira took the robe, but said nothing to her husband of the centaur's gift, hoping that she would never have to make use of it.

For many years Hercules and his wife lived happily together; for, although the hero went on other adventures, he was always eager to return to Deïaneira, and she had no need to be reminded of the centaur's gift. On one of his expeditions, however, he brought back with him a fair maiden named Iole, of whom his wife soon grew to be extremely jealous. Not long after the arrival of Iole, Hercules wished to offer sacrifices to the gods in honor of his safe return; so he sent to Deïaneira for a suitable robe. His wife, trembling for the success of her venture, bade the messenger Lichas carry to Hercules the magic robe of Nessus, which she had carefully guarded all these years. The hero, not knowing the history of the fatal garment, threw it over his shoulders, and as soon as it touched his flesh, the poisoned blood began its deadly work. The body of Hercules burned suddenly as if on fire, and agonizing pains convulsed his frame. He tried to unloose the fatal robe, but it clung to his skin, and he tore off part of his flesh in trying to set himself free. In his rage and pain he turned upon Lichas, the unhappy bearer of the poisoned robe, and seizing him in his still powerful arms flung him into the sea from the top of Mount Œta, where they had assembled for the sacrifices. Then the hero tore up huge oak trees by their roots and built a lofty funeral pyre on which he stretched his pain-wracked limbs. Calmly he bade his servants apply the torch, but no one was willing to do this, even to ease his sufferings; so Hercules turned to his friend Philoctetes, and after giving him the poisoned arrows, begged him in pity to light the funeral pyre. The youth placed beside Hercules the hero's famous oak club, and covered his body with the lion's skin. Then he applied a torch to the wood, and the flames rose with a roar and cracking to the skies. But only the mortal part of the hero perished, for Jupiter would not allow the divinity that he had bestowed upon Hercules to suffer extinction. Purged of his mortality, the hero took his place in high Olympus, and even revengeful Juno was so reconciled to his presence, that she gave him her daughter Hebe in marriage.

CHAPTER XXV
PERSEUS

WHEN the wicked King Danaüs persuaded his daughters to kill their husbands on their wedding night, there was one, Hypermnestra, who refused to slay her lover, and by saving him brought upon the head of cruel Danaüs the doom that he had striven to escape.85 The grandson of Hypermnestra and Lynceus was Acrisius, king of Argo, a kindly ruler who dearly loved his only daughter Danaë, and kept her always near him to delight his eyes with her great beauty. Unfortunately the king chanced to learn from an oracle that he would one day be killed by his grandson; and hoping to prevent this, he shut Danaë in a high brazen tower which no one was allowed to enter on pain of death. He placed around the tower a strong guard, so that no one could get even a glimpse of the imprisoned princess; but though no mortal wooer could approach her, Danaë's loveliness was not hidden from Jupiter's eyes, and as he looked down from high Olympus he pitied the maiden's loneliness and loved her for her great beauty. Fearing to frighten her if he assumed any mortal disguise, and not daring to appear before her in his divine splendor, he took the form of a golden shower, which fell softly on the sill of the tower window and charmed the lonely captive with its brightness. Each day this strange visitor came to glorify her darkened room, and Danaë looked forward eagerly to its appearance. Thus by means of the golden shower Jupiter won the maiden's confidence and love, and spent many hours with her in the high tower room. Danaë was not lonely any more, but people who passed beneath her window could hear her singing to herself all day long.

One morning the astonished attendants rushed to King Acrisius and told him that in the brazen tower was a mother and child—his daughter Danaë had given birth to a son who was so beautiful that they called him Perseus. The king was enraged at this news, and threatened to put the boy to death; but as he was unwilling to stain his hands with the blood of his grandson—even though this grandson might cause his own death—he put Danaë and her infant in a cask, and set them adrift on the sea. For days the strange boat tossed about on the ever-rocking waves, and the poor frightened mother prayed to the gods to save her and her hapless child. Jupiter heard her cries, and no storms came to beat the frail boat upon the rocks, nor did any rough seas imperil the voyager's safety. At last the cask was washed gently up on the shores of the island of Seriphus, where a friendly fisherman rescued Danaë and her child and took them to the king, Polydectes. This ruler received them kindly, and allowed them to live at his court; and here the young Perseus grew up into manhood, learning all the games and sports that belonged to the training of a Grecian youth.

Meanwhile Polydectes had become so enamored of Danaë that he wished to marry her, and grew very angry at her continued refusals. His wrath was increased when Perseus forbade him to distress Danaë any longer with his unwelcome attentions. As Polydectes did not dare to kill Perseus or banish him from the kingdom—for he knew that his suit would then be hopeless—he began to taunt the youth with his inexperience, and asked him why he did not set out on some adventure to prove his mettle like other heroes. Perseus did not consider himself a hero, but he hoped some day to do great things; and the sneers of the king worked on his proud heart, as that wily old monarch had expected. The youth then demanded to have his courage and endurance put to the test, and Polydectes promptly told him to go and slay the Gorgon Medusa, and bring her head back as the proof of his valor. Perseus needed no urging to set out at once, though he well knew the danger of the undertaking. His mother implored him to remain with her, but the youth was determined not to endure Polydectes's taunts any longer, and he was eager to prove his bravery, even at the risk of his life.

There were three of the Gorgons, all of them hideous to behold; but Medusa was by far the most terrible,86 for besides her frightful appearance she had the power to turn those who looked at her into stone. She was once a beautiful maiden, who had had the misfortune to offend Minerva, and that goddess, to punish her, changed her into a dragonlike creature with long tusks, a scaly hide, brazen claws, and instead of hair a writhing mass of snakes. To this monster Polydectes sent the young Perseus, feeling sure that he would never return home alive.

The young hero had not journeyed far before he noticed that some one was walking beside him, and, turning to look more closely at the stranger, he was at once surprised and frightened at recognizing Mercury. But the messenger of the gods bade him have no fear, for he himself had come to help in the perilous quest for the Gorgon's head. Then Mercury lent Perseus his own winged sandals, and told the youth that he would have to do some swift moving in the course of his adventures. The god also lent him a magic helmet that rendered the wearer invisible, and bade him offer thanks to Pluto as the sender of this invaluable gift. Not to be outdone by the other gods in kindness, the august Minerva lent Perseus her shield—the terrible Ægis of Jupiter—which the warrior-goddess carried with her to battle. Thus equipped for the combat Perseus had no fear of encountering the dread Medusa of the snaky locks, and pressed forward eagerly on his journey. He had already inquired of Mercury the way to the

Gorgon's cave, but the god could not direct him, and told him that he must find the Grææ and learn the way from them.

The Grææ were three hideous old women who had been gray-haired from birth,—and so received their name,—and they lived in a far-off land, where eternal darkness reigned. They had only one tooth and one huge eye among them, and passed these around to each other in turn. As they alone could tell him where Medusa dwelt, Perseus started northward on Mercury's winged sandals, and after flying for many days in search of the Three Sisters, he came at last to their cheerless land. He found the Gray Old Women seated under a drooping willow-tree that fell so far over them that it almost hid their shrunken forms.

"There sat the crones that had the single eye,
Clad in blue sweeping cloak and snow-white gown;
While o'er their backs their straight white hair hung down
In long thin locks, dreadful their faces were,
Carved all about with wrinkles of despair;
And as they sat they crooned a dreary song,
Complaining that their lives should last so long,
In that sad place that no one came anear,
In that wan place desert of hope and fear;
And singing, still they rocked their bodies bent,
And ever each to each the eye they sent."

—WILLIAM MORRIS, *The Doom of King Acrisius.*

As Perseus approached the spot where the Gray Old Women sat crooning to themselves, he took good care to keep on his magic helmet, and he watched closely to see when the eye was being transferred from one old head to the other. Just as the eldest sister was taking out the great eye, and the one who was next in turn was holding out her shriveled hand to receive it, Perseus stepped quickly between them and snatched it away. The old woman began to grope for it in her pitiable blindness, and then arose a fierce dispute among the sisters as to who really had the eye. To end the quarreling Perseus spoke gently to them, telling them that he had taken their treasured eye, and would return it to them as soon as they had informed him where to find Medusa of the snaky locks. For a while the Gray Old Women pretended that they had never heard of Medusa, but finding that the unseen speaker was determined to keep their precious eye until he had received the desired information, they told him the way to the Gorgon's Cave. Perseus then returned to them the huge eye, which seemed to stare at him with a very knowing look, and sped off on his winged sandals to the country where Medusa dwelt.

As he flew along the seacoast he saw in the distance a dark cavern among the rocks, and in front of it, on the glaring white sand, lay a monster which, even from his great height above the water, Perseus could not glance at without shuddering. Remembering Minerva's caution when she gave him her shield, he used its bright surface as a mirror in which were reflected all the objects below; and never once was he tempted to turn his eyes toward the dreadful figure on the beach. Its scaly hide glistened in the sunlight, its brazen claws shone like live coals, and the snakes that lay coiled around its head shot out their tongues and hissed whenever the Gorgon stirred in its sleep. As Perseus drew nearer he saw, reflected in his polished shield, the forms of men and animals that had been turned to stone by one glance at Medusa's face. These were very numerous around the mouth of the cave, and Perseus silently prayed to the gods that his figure might not be added to the number. Some distance away lay the other two Gorgons, Medusa's sisters, but the young hero had no thought for them. His whole attention was centered on the blow that he must deal the sleeping Medusa before the snakes hissed so loudly that she would awaken. Even in his shield the sight of that twisting, wriggling mass of reptiles was so repulsive that Perseus shuddered and was tempted to turn away; but just then he heard a whisper. "Be quick. Strike swift and sure;" and as he recognized the voice of Mercury, all his courage returned.

Grasping his sword more firmly and holding his bright shield above the sleeping monster, he swooped suddenly down upon it, and with one swift stroke cut off the great head with all its coils of serpents. It was only a moment's work to sheathe his sword and grasp the hideous trophy in his hands; but even then the danger was not over, for the snakes on Medusa's head began to hiss so loudly that their noise awoke the other two sleeping Gorgons, and they looked around to find why their sister had disturbed their rest. Seeing Medusa's headless body on the sand, they set up such terrible cries that the noise re-echoed like thunder through the cavern, and as far away as Perseus had already flown, he could hear the awful sounds that made the seashore seem like some vision in a dreadful nightmare.

Perseus

As he hurried over the sea with Medusa's head held firmly in his hand, some of the blood dripped down into the white-capped waves and was cherished by Neptune, who had once loved Medusa when she was a beautiful maiden. From these drops of blood the sea-king created the wonderful winged horse, Pegasus, who was to share in the adventures of another famous hero, Bellerophon. Some of the Gorgon's blood had also dropped on the hot African sand, as Perseus was flying upward from the Gorgon's cave, and from this sprang a brood of poisonous reptiles that ever afterward infested that region and brought death to many an unwary explorer.

The journey homeward was long and wearisome, and Perseus was often obliged to seek the seashore to rest. Once as he was flying along the coast of Africa, borne aloft on the winged sandals, he saw old Atlas standing where he had stood for many centuries with the weight of the heavens on his bent shoulders. The clouds wrapped his head so completely that Perseus could see only his immense body. Forests had grown up so high all around him that his huge legs were scarcely visible among the heavy foliage, and his broad shoulders looked like mighty bowlders rising up above the tree-tops. But though his head *was* so far in the clouds, Atlas knew that Perseus was approaching,—for giants have certain senses unpossessed by mortal men,—and he shook the clouds from about his face, and blew away the mists with his breath. Then, when the air was clear, and Perseus could see the white hair that was previously hidden above the clouds, he pitied poor Atlas for his heavy punishment and stopped to speak with him. The giant looked down from his great height and begged the hero to uncover Medusa's head,—which Perseus had kept wrapped in his cloak,—for he was anxious to gaze upon it and become himself an image of stone. He told how weary he was of standing for all these ages without ever being able to rest, and he could not endure the thought of keeping up this torture for eternity. So Perseus lifted up the Gorgon's head, being careful to keep his own averted, and Atlas gazed long and eagerly at the dead face, with its wreath of lifeless serpents. Then slowly the giant's great bulk began to harden, and the stooping shoulders became firm, unfeeling stone. As Perseus stood there watching the strange transformation, he seemed to see no longer the floating white hair of Atlas, but a pile of snow on a mountain top; and he looked no more on the huge limbs surrounded by forests, but he saw rents and clefts on a mountain side that just showed themselves through the thick trees. Thus was the burden of Atlas forever removed from his aching shoulders, and the heavens now rested securely on a mountain.

When Perseus resumed his journey along the coast, he soon came to a place where the cliffs rose abruptly from the sea; and as he looked down at the rocks below him, he saw, outlined against their dark surface, a figure that made him pause in his swift flight, and wonder if a sudden madness had taken hold on his fancy; for chained to the rock was a maiden so beautiful that even her constant weeping had not marred the perfect loveliness of her face. Keeping the Gorgon's head carefully concealed under his cloak, so that the captive maiden could get no glimpse of the snaky locks, Perseus flew to the girl's side, and, taking off his magic helmet, spoke to her gently. At any other time she would have been startled at this sudden appearance of a stranger; but the thought of her dreadful fate, so near at hand, drove all other fears from her mind. The spray from the sea dashed over her, and the cold winds blew on her shivering form; but of this she seemed to be hardly aware. Her eyes were fixed in wild terror upon a cavern in the rocks, where Perseus could see a huge dragon lying stretched out on the cool, slimy seaweed.

When the young hero spoke to the maiden, she did not seem to hear him, but, at his gentle persistence, she at last turned her eyes away from the dreaded cavern and told him her story. She said that her name was Andromeda, and that her mother, Cassiopeia,87 had angered the sea-nymphs by presuming to rival them in beauty. To punish the queen for her vanity, the nymphs sent a fierce sea-monster to devastate the homes along the coast; and when the terrified people consulted an oracle to know how they might save themselves from further disaster, they were told that the monster would not depart until the Princess Andromeda was sacrificed to its fury. So the king, her father, and her wretched, remorseful mother, and a procession of weeping attendants had led her, that very day, to the rocks, and had chained her fast to await the monster's pleasure.

Just as Andromeda was speaking, there was a rustling sound in the cave, as if the dragon were stretching its huge wings. Then came a sudden whir and rush, as the monster glided out of the dim interior of its cave, and came speeding through the water toward its victim. The scaly hide glittered in the sunlight, and the great coils of its snaky body beat up the waves as it came with incredible swiftness toward the captive maiden, whose terrified shrieks almost unnerved the young hero who had come to rescue her. Quickly he donned his magic helmet and grasped the keen-edged sword that had already stood him in good stead. As the monster's head emerged from the waves, Perseus rushed upon it unseen, and with a quick thrust pierced the creature in its one vital spot. The dragon sank back into the blood-stained water, and then made a few ineffective plunges toward its victim; but Perseus's blow had been sure, and the creature's great body finally disappeared beneath the waves. While Andromeda was thanking her deliverer with grateful tears, he struck off the chains that bound her to the rock, and led her to where her parents and an astonished group of watchers had been looking on at the strange combat. The great joy of Andromeda's father was equaled only by the mother's happiness over her rescued child; and they both welcomed the young hero who had saved her from so terrible a fate.88

When Perseus had been entertained royally for several days, the king bade him demand any reward that he wished for his heroic services; and the youth boldly asked Andromeda's hand in marriage. To this the parents gladly consented, although she was already betrothed to her uncle Phineus, and the preparations were begun at once for the wedding. While the marriage celebrations were in progress, the jilted suitor, who had been too timid to attempt any rescue of Andromeda, now came forward to claim his wife. His pretensions were laughed at, however, and he left the court angry and plotting revenge. The following day he appeared with a band of followers and suddenly attacked Perseus, who had barely time to defend himself. The friends of the young hero rallied to his support, but they were outnumbered by the attacking party, and a disastrous battle might have ensued, had not Perseus bethought himself of a sure means of defense. Catching up the cloak in which he had wrapped the Gorgon's head, he cried: "Whoever is my friend, let him turn away his eyes." The courtiers of King Cepheus, and the men fighting around Perseus obeyed him; but Phineus and his followers believed this to be a mere trick to gain time, and looked on while Perseus unveiled Medusa's snaky head. Some of the gazers had their spears in uplifted hands; some were fitting arrows to their bows as they turned their eyes a moment toward Perseus; but in whatever position they stood, just so they were suddenly turned into stone. By some chance Phineus had been watching his men instead of looking at the Gorgon's head; and when he saw their dreadful transformation, he fell on his knees before Perseus, and with outstretched hands implored the hero to spare his life. But Perseus forced him to look upon the hideous face of Medusa, and he became a stone image with averted head and supplicating arms.

Having thus disposed effectively of his enemies, Perseus covered up his death-dealing trophy, and the wedding ceremonies were resumed. Later he departed with his bride to the country of Polydectes, where that king had been keeping his mother a prisoner until she would consent to marry him. He had long ago believed Perseus dead, and was therefore much astonished to see him appear unharmed and victorious. Hearing of the cruel treatment his mother had received from Polydectes, the young hero determined on a swift revenge. In the presence of the king and his court, he suddenly displayed the head of Medusa; and the whole company, just as they stood, were turned into stone. Then Perseus set sail with his wife and mother for his own country; but before he left he returned to Pluto the magic helmet, to Mercury the winged sandals, and to Minerva the wonderful Ægis. The august goddess of wisdom seemed to have taken a strange fancy to the Gorgon's head, so Perseus gave her this trophy of his victory, and she fixed it in the middle of her shield.

When Perseus, with Andromeda and Danaë, arrived in Argo, they found that old Acrisius had been driven from his throne, and that a usurper was enjoying the kingdom. It did not take long for the hero who had slain Medusa to kill the unlawful claimant, and reinstate his grandfather. The old man had been languishing for years in prison, and was hardly able to endure the great joy of his release at the hands of one whom he had long since believed to be dead. Things seemed to be settled very happily in spite of the oracle; but the decrees of the gods are sure to be fulfilled, and one day when Perseus was playing quoits, he accidentally threw one wide of the mark. It struck Acrisius, who was looking on at the game, and killed him instantly. This unfortunate mishap so preyed upon Perseus's mind that he could not remain in Argo, but exchanged his kingdom for that of Mycenæ, over which he ruled for many years very wisely and well. When at last Perseus died, the gods placed him among the stars with his wife Andromeda, and with Cassiopeia, who had long since been cured of her vanity.

CHAPTER XXVI
BELLEROPHON

AT the court of Prœtus, king of Argos, there dwelt as guest of honor a young prince named Bellerophon. He was a kinsman of Prœtus and a grandson of Sisyphus, king of Corinth, so much honor was shown him. As he was strong, brave, and fearless, he was a leader in all the games; and his beauty won such favor at the court that Prœtus's wife, Queen Anteia, sought his love. Since the youth could not in loyalty return her affection, he found it difficult to remain in Argos; for the queen was not content to receive only the courtesy due her, but importuned Bellerophon for his love. He tried many times to find some pretext for leaving his kinsman; so when Prœtus proposed that he should make a journey to Lycia to deliver some important messages to its ruler, the youth was eager to go. Meanwhile the queen, angered at his indifference, had told her husband that Bellerophon delighted in treating her with contempt in return for all her kindness, and that she could not endure his presence in Argos any longer. She demanded further that Prœtus should put the young man at once to death, but that he should not let Bellerophon suspect that she had been the instigator of the deed. The king readily believed his wife's artfully contrived story, and declared that the insolent youth should be made to pay dearly for his ingratitude. As Bellerophon was already a hero at the court, Prœtus dared not condemn him openly to death; so when the prince departed on his journey to Lycia, he carried with him some letters89 whose purport he was far from suspecting; for the sealed message that he bore so light-heartedly was a request to King Iobates to put the bearer at once to death.

King Iobates was the father-in-law of Prœtus; and the ruler of Lycia had often relied on his powerful relative as an ally in time of war; so the king of Argos was confident that his instructions would be carried out. The expedition to Lycia might, therefore, have had a different ending had not Bellerophon forgotten to deliver his letters for several days. Meanwhile King Iobates, supposing him to be on a friendly visit, received him very hospitably and made him a member of the royal household. After much feasting and entertainment, the young prince suddenly remembered the sealed message intrusted to his care, and hastened to deliver it to Iobates with many apologies for his forgetfulness. When the king read the letter, he was surprised and horrified at its contents, for he could not, in cold blood, kill the guest who had sat at his table; and yet he did not wish to refuse any demand made by Prœtus. When the courtiers saw his white face and troubled looks, they wondered what the message contained; but no one suspected its real import.

At last a solution of the difficulty came to the king's mind, and he began to praise Bellerophon for the bravery and courage that had made the young prince famous throughout Greece. He lamented that no such fearlessness dwelt among the men of Lycia, for otherwise the Chimæra would not be living in security and laying waste the king's lands. When Bellerophon heard what terror was inspired by the mere mention of the Chimæra's name, he wondered whether he would be afraid to face this fearful creature with its lion's head, goat's body, and dragon's tail. When he expressed surprise that no hero had slain it, the wily Iobates at once implored him to help the stricken country and to go himself to fight the Chimæra. Bellerophon might have been eager for this adventure, had he not learned to love the king's daughter Philonoë, who had found the handsome stranger more to her liking than all the youths of Lycia. He was, therefore, loath to leave the princess and depart on so perilous a venture; but at the repeated urging of Iobates, he began to make preparations for the journey.

Before setting out he first consulted the soothsayer Polyidus,90 who advised him to procure the winged horse Pegasus91 if he hoped to succeed in slaying the Chimæra. This advice was probably well-meant, but it was very discouraging; for how could Bellerophon expect to bridle the famous immortal steed that had never known the touch of any man's hand? He knew too well that Pegasus was rarely seen by mortal eyes, for he dwelt on the calm heights of Mount Helicon, a spot sacred to the Muses, and seldom came to earth except to visit the fountain of Pirene, near Corinth, whose clear waters sometimes tempted him to leave his lofty home. Very few people had ever seen the snow-white horse, with his wonderful silvery wings that carried him through the air as buoyantly as an eagle in its flight. Whenever Pegasus deigned to come to earth to taste the sweet waters of Pirene he sped over the grassy meadows so swiftly that even the fleetest runner could not hope to catch him. He had never been bridled in all his wild, free life, and for beauty and strength and sheer joy of living there was nothing like him in the whole wide world. "Sleeping at night as he did, on a lofty mountain top, and passing the greater part of the day in the air, Pegasus seemed hardly to be a creature of the earth. Whenever he was seen, up very high above people's heads, with the sunshine on his silvery wings, one would have thought that he belonged to the sky, and that, skimming a little too low, he had got astray among our mists and vapors, and was seeking his way back again.... In the summer time, and in the beautifullest of weather, Pegasus often alighted on the solid earth, and, closing his silvery wings, would gallop over hill and dale for pastime as fleetly as the wind."92

When Bellerophon was advised to catch this glorious winged steed, it was no wonder that he felt discouraged, for nowhere could he find an old man, a maiden, or a child who had ever had so much as a glimpse of the snow-white Pegasus. Some one told him, however, that the immortal steed had once been tamed by Minerva, and owed obedience to her; so he went immediately to the temple of the warrior-goddess, and begged her to help him. For many hours he prayed before Minerva's shrine, but there came no answer to his petition; and, at last, worn out with fatigue and discouragement, he fell asleep on the steps of the temple. When the first rays from Apollo's golden sun-car fell on the white marble pillars of the temple, Bellerophon awoke, and to his great astonishment he found in his hand a golden bridle. Believing this to be the answer to his prayers, he set out hopefully on his search for the winged horse; and before journeying very far, he came to the fountain of Pirene, where the beautiful, clear stream bubbled up beside a grassy meadow so redolent of ripening clover that it might tempt a far more fastidious horse than the immortal Pegasus. Bellerophon spent many days beside the fountain, but he never caught a glimpse of the white-winged steed, nor saw any mark of his hoofs upon the sod. Once an old man stopped to ask him why he was lingering so long beside the fountain, and then shook his white head incredulously when Bellerophon spoke of Pegasus and his silvery wings.

At last the young hero grew so discouraged that he decided to return to the court of Iobates; but on the very morning that he was intending to leave Pirene, he chanced to wake just at dawn, and, leaning over the fountain to bathe his flushed face he saw reflected in the water an image that made his heart beat fast with hope and joy. It seemed like a great white bird, flying high up among the clouds, where the sunlight shone on its silvery wings. Nearer and nearer it came, sweeping the air in great wide circles, and at last it alighted beside the fountain. Bellerophon meantime had hidden himself in the bushes, and now he watched the beautiful creature as it folded its gorgeous wings and bent its arching neck to drink the clear water. Then Pegasus daintily cropped a few clover blossoms, shook his long white mane, and began to run up and down over the meadows, capering madly like a colt just set free in the pasture. After rolling luxuriously in the thick grass, and racing like the wind across the meadow, Pegasus grew tired of his play, and folding his snow-white wings, trotted quietly up to the fountain to take one more drink before flying back to his home on Mount Helicon.

Then Bellerophon crept noiselessly out of his hiding place, and while the unsuspicious Pegasus was drinking the cool water and his eyes were no longer watchful, the youth boldly sprang upon his back and took firm hold of the thick mane, being careful meantime not to let Minerva's golden bridle slip from his fingers. Bellerophon had ridden many a horse, but never one as wild and spirited as this; for the glorious Pegasus had not known, until now, the ignominy of bearing a mortal rider on his back, and he did not intend to submit to the disgrace. When he felt the touch of Bellerophon's knees on his broad flanks, he made a tremendous bound into the air, and before the youthful rider could realize what had happened, he found himself hundreds of feet above the earth. The winged horse snorted, and shook with anger, and tried to unseat his rider by every trick known to equine ingenuity. He bounded forward with a sudden jerk, reared, turned over and over in the air, until half the time Bellerophon was riding with his head downward; but in spite of all his efforts, he could not throw off the strange thing that clung to his back. All at once Bellerophon saw his chance to slip the golden bridle between the maddened horse's teeth, and suddenly Pegasus became as gentle and tractable as if he had always obeyed the will of a master.

Happy to find the conflict over, the young hero turned the head of his white-winged steed toward the mountain-region where the dread Chimæra dwelt. It was a wild and rocky part of the country that Bellerophon looked down upon, and he saw all around him the evidence of ruin wrought by the fire-breathing monster. The dwellings of the peasants were in smoking ashes; carcasses of half-eaten cattle were strewn about the barren pastures; and human bodies were also to be seen, torn and mangled by the Chimæra's ruthless claws. On the mountain side was a deep hole in the rocks, and from it issued clouds of black smoke that had a horrid stifling smell as it rose up from the cavern's mouth. As Bellerophon descended nearer to the earth, the delicate nostrils of his horse dilated at the first contact with the foul smoke, and he found it hard to persuade Pegasus to fly closer to the Chimæra's den. When they did approach through the thick clouds of smoke, Bellerophon saw the monster's great body stretched out at full length in the cave, while all the three heads lay on half-eaten carcasses that were strewn about the floor. The lion and the goat part of the Chimæra were asleep, but the snake was wide awake; and when it saw Bellerophon approaching on his winged horse, it raised its head and began to hiss so loudly that it roused up the other creatures until they too were intent and watchful.

Then the smoke poured out of the cave more thickly than before; and if Pegasus had not carried him quickly away from the poisonous fumes, Bellerophon would have been suffocated long before he was able to get near enough to deal the Chimæra a mortal blow. But the brave horse bore him out of danger, and kept him far above the thick smoke until the monster crawled out of its lair. Then like the swift rush of air, Bellerophon swooped down upon the Chimæra and cut off its three horrid heads with his sword; but even then the danger was not over, for the headless creature sprang into the air, and clutched wildly for its enemy with its long claws. So sure an instinct for destruction did the Chimæra have that, mangled and dying as it was, it struck directly at Bellerophon and would have torn him into pieces had not the faithful Pegasus borne him swiftly out of reach of the deadly claws. After a few vain attempts to grasp its destroyer, the Chimæra's great body gave a convulsive shudder, and fell back stone-dead upon the blood-soaked ground.

Then Bellerophon sped back to the court of Iobates and announced that the Chimæra was dead. The king was glad to hear that the monster could no longer devastate his land, but he was sorry to see Bellerophon returning unhurt and victorious, and with such a wonderful prize as the winged horse, Pegasus. Most people had never believed that this immortal steed really existed, and had thought that the stories about it were merely old wives' tales. Iobates did not dare to kill so popular a hero as the young prince became after this adventure, but he sent him off on other perilous journeys, hoping that on one of them he might meet his death. Bellerophon, however, never came to any harm, for he had always the sure help of Pegasus, and he returned safe from each expedition with trophies to lay at the feet of his beloved princess, Philonoë. At length the king was convinced that Bellerophon was under the special protection of the gods, and, hoping to win their favor, he gave the young hero his daughter in marriage, and appointed him his successor to the throne.

For several years Bellerophon lived happily in Lycia; but his many victories with Pegasus had made him presumptuous, and he felt that his true place was with the immortals. So one day he mounted his winged steed and flew far above the earth into the white clouds that wrap the top of Mount Olympus. Angered at this insolence and daring, Jupiter sent an enormous gadfly which stung Pegasus so cruelly that he gave a sudden leap forward, and this unexpected movement threw his too-confident rider from his back. The luckless Bellerophon felt the reins slip through his fingers, and he plunged downward through mist and clouds many, many miles to the earth. This terrible fall would have killed any one but a mythological hero, but Bellerophon, though bruised and shaken, only lost his eyesight. Ever afterwards he wandered through the fair places of the earth, lame and blind and lonely, lamenting the foolish pride that had led him to risk the anger of the gods. What his end was no one ever knew, but he probably died in some distant land, alone and forgotten, while Pegasus went back to the sunny slopes of Mount Helicon and never visited the earth again, even to drink the sweet waters of Pirene.

CHAPTER XXVII
THE STORY OF JASON

Part I

IN Thessaly there once ruled a wise and good king named Æson, who dwelt happily with his wife Alcimede, and his little son Jason. The king's reign did not last long, however, for his wicked brother Pelias collected a band of armed warriors and made war upon Æson, who, after a feeble resistance, surrendered his throne to the invader and escaped secretly from the kingdom with his wife and child. The dethroned monarch took refuge in a distant country, and lived in concealment until Jason was old enough to be sent to some place of greater safety, for they knew that the cruel Pelias would try to seek him out and kill him. So they intrusted the boy to the care of the centaur Chiron, after telling that wise teacher who the lad really was, and begging him to bring Jason up with the desire some day to avenge their wrongs.

Chiron instructed the youth in all the arts of which he himself was master, and when the young prince reached manhood, he was one of the bravest and most skillful of the centaur's pupils. Jason had been told many times of his uncle's tyranny, and he burned to avenge the wrongs of his parents; but his wise teacher cautioned him to wait until he had strength and power enough to face the wicked usurper. When he deemed the youth sufficiently trained to leave his care, Chiron sent Jason forth, bidding him satisfy now his desire for revenge. He advised his pupil, however, to be careful and to do no harm to any one except the man who had wronged him. Jason promised to obey his tutor's instructions, and, girding on his sword, set out on the journey to his native city.

It was springtime when Jason turned his steps toward his father's kingdom, and the rains had swollen all the streams, making them difficult to ford. One day as he stood on the bank of a river, wondering where he had best attempt to swim across, he saw an old woman looking despairingly at the rushing, foaming water. Jason spoke gently to her, and offered to carry her across the river. This unexpected assistance was gratefully accepted, and Jason bravely waded into the shallowest part of the stream. The swift current and his unwieldy burden made the crossing very difficult, so that when Jason at last reached the opposite bank, he was glad to rest. He did not mind the wetting, but he was sorry to find that he had lost one of his sandals in the river. As it was useless to try to find it, he set off with only the remaining one, but first he stopped to say good-by to the old woman. To his surprise he no longer saw a bent and trembling figure beside him, but he stood in the presence of a beautiful, imperious woman, whose royal bearing would have proclaimed her a goddess even if the startled youth had not seen beside her the peacock that ever attends the stately Juno. Jason trembled at this transformation of his aged passenger, but Juno smiled graciously upon him and bade him have no fear, for she had come to promise him her aid and protection.

Before he could render suitable thanks, the goddess had disappeared, and Jason continued his journey, full of courage and confident of success. Soon he came to his native city, where he found a great crowd of people assembled at the temple, for Pelias, the king, was offering on that day special sacrifices, and a public festival had been proclaimed throughout the city. Jason joined in the crowds that were hurrying to the temple, and stood quite near his uncle, while the king, unconscious of his presence, was performing the sacrifices. When the ceremony was over, Pelias glanced around at the assembled company, and started back pale with terror when he saw Jason; for although he did not recognize his nephew, he had been warned by an oracle to beware of a youth who would appear before him wearing only one sandal. Trembling, but striving to hide his fear, Pelias spoke to the stranger and asked him his name. Then Jason confronted his uncle boldly, declared his own parentage, and demanded that the usurper should at once resign his throne and restore old Æson to his rightful place in the kingdom.

Pelias did not dare openly to defy this fearless youth, but neither did he intend to give up his power and wealth; so being a crafty man he sought to beguile Jason with soft words, and promised to send at once for the absent king and queen. He urged his nephew to remain meanwhile at the court, and invited him to join the royal household that evening in a splendid banquet. Jason needed no persuasion to eat, drink, and be merry; and as the wily Pelias plied him with rich viands and the choicest wine, his heart warmed toward his uncle, and he felt less eager to carry out his long-cherished vengeance. During the feast the bards sang of brave deeds done by heroes, and one old musician told of the famous golden fleece that many had sought to take by stealth; but of those who went on the quest, no one ever came back to tell why he had failed.

Jason listened eagerly while the old singer told how the famous fleece once belonged to a ram that the friendly Neptune sent to Phryxus and Helle to enable them to escape from the persecutions of their stepmother Ino. This was the same Ino who cared so tenderly for the infant Bacchus; but to her stepchildren she was very cruel. Their own mother Nephele had been sent away by King Athamas because he had wearied of her, and wished to marry Ino; and when the banished mother learned how neglected and ill-treated her children were, she begged Neptune to help them. So the sea-god sent a golden-fleeced ram, which Phryxus and Helle mounted and thus escaped from their cruel stepmother. Only Phryxus reached the land of Colchis, however; for when the ram flew over the sea, Helle grew frightened at the sight of the waves tossing so far beneath her, and suddenly lost her hold on the golden fleece. Her brother reached out to clutch her as she slid from the ram's back, but it was too late, and the unfortunate maiden fell into that part of the sea that is since known as the Hellespont. Phryxus reached Colchis safely, and here he sacrificed the ram to Neptune, and hung its golden fleece on a tree under which he placed a dragon to guard it night and day.

As Jason listened to this story he felt as though here was a task worth his mettle; and it needed no urging from Pelias to make him declare himself ready to set forth on the adventure without further delay. The wily king praised Jason's courage, and prophesied that he would be called the greatest among heroes, while in his heart he felt assured that the troublesome nephew would never return alive. He promised to render Jason every assistance in his power, and offered to fit him out with a well-manned ship; but the young adventurer had been thinking over the matter more calmly, and had begun to distrust his uncle's apparent kindness. So he went for counsel to the shrine of Jupiter at Dodona, where there was an oracle called the Speaking Oak; and, on consulting this, he learned, to his great satisfaction, that Juno was still watching over his welfare, and would aid him in the quest of the golden fleece. The Speaking Oak then bade him cut off one of its great limbs, and carve from it a figurehead for his ship. It told him also that the ship in which he was to sail should not be made of timber cut from any ordinary trees, but should be built of the wood taken from pine-trees that grew on Mount Pelion.

When Jason had carved his figurehead, he found that it had the gift of speech and could counsel him wisely in all his affairs, so as soon as the ship was ready, the figurehead was fastened to its prow, and Jason set out on his memorable voyage. He called his ship the Argo,93 and himself and his fellow adventurers the Argonauts. Among his companions were many men famous for their brave deeds: Hercules, Admetus, Castor and Pollux, Meleager, Orpheus, and Theseus. All these were eager for new adventures, and no one doubted that with so many heroes to aid him, Jason would succeed in winning the golden fleece. Even Pelias, as he watched the voyagers sail away, wished that he had sent the daring youth on a still more perilous journey.

The voyage to Colchis was full of strange happenings, both on land and sea. The first disaster that overtook the Argonauts occurred when Hercules went ashore to get some fresh water, with a youth of the party named Hylas. There had been several occasions on which it was necessary for some of the heroes to land in order to get food or water, but the delay had been brief and the voyage quickly resumed. This time they were in need of new oars, so Hercules offered to procure them, and took with him his favorite companion Hylas. While he himself was felling trees, he sent Hylas in search of fresh water; and the youth, after wandering about for some time, came at last to a fountain whose waters were so pure and cool that he lingered long beside it. The nymphs who lived in the fountain were charmed with the beauty of Hylas, and determined to keep him with them; so when he bent over the water, they drew him gently down into its clear depths. Hercules, after waiting long for the lad's return, went in search of him; but no trace of Hylas could be found anywhere in the lonely forest. Though he called again and again, no voice answered him; for Hylas lay in the green bed of the fountain, and his ears were deaf to the cries of his friend. Hercules's grief was so great over the loss of Hylas that he refused to accompany the expedition any further, and made his way home alone and on foot.[94]

On another occasion Jason landed in Thrace; and here he learned that the blind King Phineus was tormented by some Harpies—creatures half women and half bird—that ate or befouled all the food placed before the wretched king. The only meals Phineus could take were by stealth, and the poor king's life was rendered miserable by the constant presence of these foul monsters. When the two sons of Boreas, who were happily gifted with wings, heard Jason relate the story of the Harpies to his companions, they promptly offered to help the blind Phineus; and, flying at the loathsome birds with drawn swords, the brothers drove them out of Thrace into an island so far away that they never came back to trouble the king.

CHAPTER XXVIII
THE STORY OF JASON

Part II

ONCE, in the course of the voyage, Jason was attacked by a flock of brazen-feathered birds that showered their sharp metal plumage down on the Argonauts, and wounded some of them sorely. Jason soon found that weapons were of no avail against these formidable enemies, so he consulted the figurehead that had always counseled him wisely. In obedience to its advice the heroes clashed their swords and spears furiously against their shields until the birds, terrified by the noise, flew away and never returned.

When the Argo approached the Symplegades,—or Clashing Islands,— Jason remembered the words of Phineus, who had advised him to let free a dove, whose speed was less than that of his swift vessel, before he attempted a passage. If it flew easily between the rocks, then the ship could safely follow it with no chance of being ground to pieces as the islands clashed together. When the Argonauts reached this dangerous spot, Jason sent a dove out before him. He watched its flight anxiously, and when it glided between the rocks with only a tail feather caught, he guided the ship so close behind it that, as he slid through the opening made by the rebound of the islands, the deadly rocks merely grazed his rudder. Since their destructive power depended on allowing no vessel to pass them unharmed, the evil force that the islands possessed was now broken, and they were henceforth chained fast to the bottom of the sea.

At last the Argo reached the shores of Colchis, and Jason made known to King Æetes his desire to possess the golden fleece. The owner of that wonderful pelt was very naturally not ready to give it to even the boldest stranger; but he treated the Argonauts kindly, and even promised to bestow upon Jason the coveted fleece if he could catch and harness to a plow two brazen-hoofed, fire-breathing bulls. Then, having done this, he must plow up a certain piece of ground sacred to Mars, and sow the field with dragon's teeth just as Cadmus had done.95 Last of all he must conquer the armed giants that would spring up in the field after the sowing, and then slay the dragon that guarded the golden fleece. This was certainly enough to daunt any hero, but Jason, relying on the help of Juno, agreed to the king's terms and went down to the seashore, where his ship lay, to consult the figurehead who had never yet failed him. On the way he met Medea, the king's daughter, who was much taken with the young stranger's beauty, and hoped to induce him to marry her. Medea herself was very beautiful, and being also a sorceress she was an invaluable ally in the adventure that had brought Jason and his friends from a far-distant land. So before many days had passed Medea plighted her troth to the young hero who needed help sorely and the king's daughter promised to give him the aid of her magic arts.

On the day appointed for the great task, Jason boldly approached the fire-breathing bulls, for Medea had given him a charm by which the fierce brutes were rendered harmless, and were easily yoked and harnessed to the plow. Then, in the presence of the astonished spectators, who expected to see him crushed beneath the brazen hoofs, Jason plowed the field; and having sown it with dragon's teeth, stood ready, sword in hand, to meet the attack of the giants who sprang up out of the ground clad in full armor. When he saw the glittering spears turned toward him, Jason's heart began to quail lest, after all, Medea's help should prove ineffective; and even the sorceress herself felt a momentary doubt of her own power to save her lover from his foes. As the armed men were about to rush upon him, Jason threw a stone in their midst, according to Medea's instructions, and the giants turned against each other and began a furious battle that ended in the destruction of the whole armed host.

Then the hero, accompanied by Medea, hastened to the tree where the golden fleece hung, and here a charm was needed to lull to sleep the dragon that guarded the treasure. As soon as the great eyes that had never been known to close began to shut one by one, Jason stepped softly up behind the monster and cut off its head. It was but a moment's work to tear the fleece from the tree where it had hung for so many years, and to bear it in triumph to the Argo, where Jason's friends stood anxiously awaiting his coming. The men were already at the oars, for he had told them to be ready to sail at a moment's notice when he should appear bearing the golden fleece. In spite of Æetes's promise the hero did not trust him, and so made his preparations for departure very secretly. When he and Medea boarded the Argo with their prize, the rowers bent with all their strength to the oars, and the ship slid silently and swiftly out of the harbor.

Æetes soon learned that the Grecian vessel had left his shores, carrying on board the golden fleece, his daughter, and—worst of all—his only son and heir Absyrtus; so he hurriedly manned his royal barge with rowers, and set out after the Argonauts. Although the fugitive vessel made good speed, the king's ship began to gain on it; and as Jason watched the distance between the vessels growing less and less, he was filled with despair and begged the sorceress to aid them with her magic. Medea did not care what fate befell the Argonauts, but she had no desire to leave Jason and return to her father's court; so she did not hesitate to resort to any means of preventing the king from overtaking her. She therefore killed her brother Absyrtus, and, cutting his body into pieces, dropped them one by one over the side of the vessel. Æetes, seeing the remains of his only son floating on the water, stopped to collect them so that the body might have suitable burial; and by this delay the Argonauts were allowed to escape. The wretched king then returned to Colchis, where he buried Absyrtus with prayers to the gods to bring vengeance upon his inhuman daughter.

When the Argo with its triumphant crew reached Thessaly, they found that their arrival caused great surprise as well as joy, for King Pelias had never supposed they would return, and felt himself secure against any further trouble from the youth with only one sandal. He was therefore much dismayed at seeing Jason return, especially as he came unharmed and bearing so rich a trophy as the golden fleece. The usurper knew that his days of power were over, and when Jason again demanded the kingdom in his father's name, Pelias was forced to resign his throne to the lawful king. Old Æson was then summoned from his place of banishment, and restored to his rightful place; but he was so weak and decrepit that power had no charm for him, and he accepted his throne very reluctantly.

So Jason begged his wife to use her magic in behalf of the old king; and Medea, anxious to please her lover, willingly promised to restore Æson to all the vigor of manhood. To prepare the magic potion that was to bring youth and health, the sorceress went out into the meadows on nine successive nights beginning with the new moon, and gathered herbs whose magic properties she alone could tell. Then she set a caldron in the deepest part of the woods, and built under it a slow fire that burned always night and day. In the caldron she threw the magic herbs, flowers with acrid juice, stones from the far east and sand from the all-surrounding ocean, hoar frost gathered by moonlight, a screech-owl's head and wings, and the entrails of a wolf. Then she added some bits of tortoise shell and the liver of a stag—for these animals are tenacious of life—and the head and beak of a crow that outlives nine generations of men. All these she boiled together,96 stirring them with an olive branch; and when she lifted out the branch, it was full of new leaves and heavy with young olives. These preparations being finished, and the time being full moon, Medea went forth alone into the forest with old Æson, just at midnight when all creatures slept, and no breath of wind stirred the trees. She laid the old man on a bed of herbs, and after putting him into a deep sleep, cut his throat and let out the sluggish blood of age. Then she poured into the wound the juices from her caldron; and when these began to flow through the king's weak frame, he underwent a wonderful change, for his hair and beard lost their whiteness and took on the glossy hue of youth. His paleness changed to the ruddiness of manhood; and his feeble limbs felt all the vigor of a hero in his prime.

Medea

When the daughters of Pelias saw this miracle of old Æson transformed into a stalwart man, they begged Medea to use her magic in restoring their father to his former youthfulness; and the sorceress promised to help Pelias just as she had the father of Jason. So she prepared a caldron full of boiling water, and pretended to put into it the necessary ingredients for the magic potion; but when the devoted, though too-credulous daughters of Pelias killed their father, and put his body into the caldron, as Medea had directed, they did not restore him to youth, but merely ended very effectively the life that they so ardently wished to prolong.

Though Medea's great beauty and her power as a sorceress kept Jason faithful to her for many years, he at last grew weary of her and prepared to wed a maiden named Creusa.97 Pretending to approve of his choice, and concealing her rage at Jason's heartlessness, Medea sent the bride a beautiful, though poisoned, robe. The unsuspicious Creusa was delighted with this rich gift; but as soon as it rested on her shoulders the hapless maiden was seized with terrible convulsions, from which she shortly died. Then Medea killed with her own hands the children that she had borne to Jason—so that she might have no reminder of his falseness—and fled in her dragon-car to Athens, where she sought the protection of King Ægeus, the father of Theseus. Here she lived many years, for the king, not knowing her history, and being enamored of her beauty, married her and made her his queen.

Jason, filled with remorse and despair, now led a most unhappy life, and spent most of his time on the seashore beside the great hulk of the Argo, which was slowly rotting away on the beach. One day a sudden gale detached a loose beam from the vessel, and it fell on Jason's head, killing him instantly. Thus ended forever the voyages of the Argonauts.

CHAPTER XXIX
THE CALYDONIAN HUNT

ONE of the heroes of the Argonautic expedition was Meleager, son of Œneus and Althæa, king and queen of Calydon. When Meleager was born, his mother saw in a vision the three Fates spinning the thread of her child's life; and she heard them foretell that he would live until the brand then burning on the hearth should be consumed. Althæa, terrified by the vision, awoke; and snatching the brand from the fire she plunged it into an earthen jar full of water. When she saw that the last spark was extinguished, she carefully hid the brand on whose existence depended the life of her son. Meleager, thus saved from death, grew up into splendid and vigorous manhood, and was welcomed by Jason as a fitting companion for the famous voyage to Colchis.

While his son was absent on this expedition, Œneus offended Diana by omitting to offer to her the customary yearly sacrifice; so the angry goddess sent a fierce boar to devastate the country. This creature was of such enormous size and strength that no hunters dared attack it, and it laid waste the fields of Calydon by trampling on the young corn, rooting up vines and olive trees, and devouring flocks and herds, thus creating wild confusion among the panic-stricken people. When Meleager returned from his voyage, and learned of the disaster that had overtaken the land, he summoned a band of heroes and set out to slaughter the wild boar. Jason, Nestor, Telamon the father of Ajax, Theseus and his friend Pirithous, Peleus (afterwards the father of Achilles), the twin brothers Castor and Pollux on their snow-white horses—all these and many others came at Meleager's call to join in the hunt.

With the youths came also Atalanta, daughter of Jasius, king of Arcadia. This princess had been left when an infant on Mount Parthenium, and exposed to the hunger of wild beasts, for her father was angry at finding that the gods had sent him a daughter instead of the longed-for son. Atalanta was not devoured, however, nor did she perish from cold, for a kindly she-bear nursed the deserted infant, and she grew up strong and fearless. Later on some shepherds found the sturdy little maiden in the woods; and taking her to their rude home, they cared for her, and taught her to follow the chase. Thus she had grown up like a boy, fearless, bold, and skilled beyond most youths in the use of the bow and spear.

When the company of heroes saw Atalanta ready to join them in the chase for the wild boar, they were disposed to scoff at the idea of a maiden taking part in an adventure whose dangers might make a brave man fearful; but Meleager, won by Atalanta's beauty, welcomed her eagerly, and begged her to share in the hunt. Then the company set forth into the forest, and they did not have to wait long for their quarry, for, as soon as the wild boar heard the barking of the dogs and the sound of snorting steeds, he rushed out of his lair and savagely attacked the hunters. One after another of the heroes was gored by the boar's long tusks, or thrown down and trampled on by the cruel hoofs, or put to flight. Jason threw his spear, but it only grazed the boar's side. Telamon rushed forward, but stumbled over a projecting root and fell to the ground. Nestor, thrown headlong by a furious attack from the boar, sought safety in the branches of a tree. Theseus hurled his lance, but it was caught by a bough and turned aside. Then an arrow from Atalanta's bow pierced the brute's side, and blood flowed from the wound. The infuriated boar turned savagely upon her, but Meleager, who was ever near the maiden, hurled his spear with so true an aim that the boar fell dead upon the bloody and trampled ground.

Then the heroes crowded around Meleager, congratulating him on his victory; but he refused to accept the honor of having slain the boar, and gave to Atalanta its head and rough hide as trophies belonging to the victor. His companions were angered that such honor should be given a mere girl, and they feared the scorn and ridicule that would be heaped upon them when they returned to report the success of the hunt. Meleager, however, did not heed their murmured threats, nor did he listen to the reproaches of his two uncles, Plexippus and Toxeus, who had accompanied him. To see themselves thus rivaled by a boyish girl was too humiliating for the pride of these two princes; and they began to insult Atalanta by chiding her for joining in the sports of men, and showing such unmaidenly boldness. Then they attempted to snatch from her the trophies of the hunt; and at this Meleager, who had been incensed at their taunts to Atalanta, turned upon them in a blaze of fury, and killed them both with his sword.

Meanwhile Althæa had heard that the boar was slain, and was on her way to the temple with a thank-offering when news was brought her that her two brothers had been killed—and by the hand of her son. Then the sister's desire for vengeance crowded out of her heart the mother's love for her son; and she brought out of its place of concealment the brand on whose existence depended Meleager's life. She lit a fire, and then hesitated for a moment whether to commit this dreadful deed or not; but the thought of her murdered brothers hardened her heart, and she threw the brand into the fire. As the flames wrapped around it, Althæa fancied that she heard it give a groan and, seized with remorse, she was about to snatch it from the fire, but the memory of her dead brothers stayed her hand, and she sat by the fire watching the flames consume the brand. While this was going on, Meleager suddenly felt his body seized with deadly pangs; and, though not knowing the cause, he was certain that his death was at hand. Then, like a brave man and a warrior, he lamented that he must die in this mysterious way and not meet his death fighting like the heroes of old. He called upon his mother and father, upon his sisters, and upon his loved Atalanta, but no one could save him from his fate. When the last bit of the brand fell into the ashes, Meleager died; and his mother, now filled with horror and remorse at her deed, committed suicide.

Atalanta, having won fame and the spoils of a celebrated hunt, was now welcomed at her father's court and returned there to live. But though she spent much time at the palace, she could not be induced to give up the chase, and roamed the forests as before, glorying in her freedom. Her father could not persuade her to marry, although many noble suitors sought her hand; for an oracle had once warned her that marriage would be her ruin. To her father's continued insistence she at last returned this answer—that she would wed the suitor who could beat her in a foot-race; but the conditions of the race were to be that the runner, if defeated, should lose his life. Rather than accept these terms, many of the suitors withdrew; but some remained to run the race, for the maiden's beauty was worth a great venture. None of them, however, succeeded in beating the fleet-footed Atalanta; and each man paid the price of defeat with his life. In vain the old king implored his daughter to alter the hard conditions, but Atalanta was determined never to wed.

At one of the races a youth named Hippomenes98 was made the judge; and when he learned the terms of the contest, he turned to the competitors and asked them why they were so foolish as to risk their lives for the sake of a maiden's beauty. As he was speaking, Atalanta appeared dressed for the race, and when he looked at her, Hippomenes said: "Pardon me, youths, I knew not the prize you were contending for." When the race was over, and the defeated runners put to death, Hippomenes, undaunted by this result, boldly asked that he might try his fate. Atalanta looked at him pityingly, for he was a youth of noble bearing, and she felt a strange reluctance to see him go so blithely to his death. She would not admit to herself that she could fall in love so quickly with a stranger; and yet she half hoped that in this race she would not come first to the goal. As Hippomenes prepared himself for the running, she thought: "What unkind god wishes to bring disaster upon this youth, and commands him, at the risk of a life so dear, to seek this marriage. In my own opinion I am not of such great value. It is not his beauty that moves me, though he is good to look upon, but I pity him because he is still a boy. He himself cannot affect my sympathies, but his youth moves me."99 Then she tried to persuade Hippomenes to give up the race; but the more he looked at Atalanta, the more determined he was to win her, and he demanded the right to compete alone with the fleet-footed maiden.

Reluctantly Atalanta prepared for the race, and as Hippomenes waited eagerly for the sound of the trumpet he breathed an ardent prayer to Venus to help him win the peerless maiden. Venus, the patroness of lovers, heard his prayer, and, unseen by any watchers, slipped into his hand three golden apples gathered from a wonderful tree on her own island of Cyprus. When the signal was given for the start, each runner shot forward like an arrow from the bow; but Atalanta soon outdistanced her lover, and his fate seemed assured; but just as she passed him he threw in front of her a golden apple, and the maiden, surprised at this unexpected interruption, stopped to pick it up. Hippomenes pressed eagerly forward, but Atalanta soon overtook him and as she sped by him he tossed another golden apple in her path. Caught by its glitter the maiden stooped again, and while she paused to recover the apple, Hippomenes shot ahead. This advantage was soon lost, however, for again Atalanta outran him and was speeding past him toward the goal. Then the lover, with another prayer to Venus, threw the third golden apple; but by this time the maiden had begun to fear that she might be beaten by the handsome stranger, and so hesitated to stop for the tempting golden fruit. Venus impelled her, however, to pause long enough to snatch the apple quickly from the ground, and in that moment's delay Hippomenes passed her and reached the goal.100

Cybele

Thus for the first time the race was won by another than Atalanta, and Hippomenes claimed the maiden as his rightful reward. Triumphantly he carried off his prize, and for a long time he and Atalanta were so happy that the words of the oracle seemed unlikely to be fulfilled; but unfortunately the lovers forgot to do honor to Venus, and the goddess was so angered at their ingratitude that she caused them to give offense to Cybele (Rhea) by desecrating her sacred grove. To punish them for this impiety, Cybele changed them into a lion and lioness, and yoked them to her car, which they were ever afterward compelled to draw.

CHAPTER XXX
THESEUS

Part I

THESEUS was among the heroes who joined Jason in the famous Argonautic expedition; and he also accompanied Meleager on the Calydonian hunt. Thus it seems that he was well-known throughout Greece for a brave and daring youth who was ready to follow his friends into any adventure, no matter how dangerous. When Theseus was a mere child, his father Ægeus, king of Athens, went on a journey to some distant country, taking with him his wife Æthra and his little son. He returned alone to Athens, leaving Theseus and his mother in the stranger's land; but before he departed he hid his sword and sandals under a large rock, and bade Æthra leave them there until she deemed her son strong enough to raise the stone. If Theseus proved equal to the test, he was to take the sword and sandals and go straightway to his father's court at Athens, where he would be acknowledged as the king's son and heir.

Æthra carefully obeyed these instructions, and when the time came that she considered Theseus strong enough to meet his father's test, she led him to the rock and bade him raise it. With a mighty effort the youth lifted the huge stone, and to his surprise he found beneath it a pair of sandals and a fine sword—both so perfectly preserved that they might have been placed there only the day before. Then Æthra explained the presence of these gifts, and told her son how the king, his father, had placed them there beneath the rock, so that he might know whether Theseus was to be a future hero or a weakling. While his mother was speaking, the youth eagerly girded on the bright sword and put the sandals on his feet, and he needed no urging when Æthra bade him set out at once for his father's kingdom. She warned him of the perils that beset the road to Athens, for giants and robbers would bar his way, and many other dangers lay in wait for the traveler; but Theseus was young and fearless, and he would have faced greater dangers than these to reach King Ægeus and the wonderful city of Athens.

He had gone but a few miles on his journey, when he was accosted by the giant Periphetes, son of Vulcan, who stood in the road, with his huge club in his hand and refused to let Theseus pass. When the young hero pushed boldly forward, Periphetes raised his club to strike the youth to the ground, as he had done many another wayfarer; but as he lifted his arm for the blow, Theseus plunged his sword quickly into the giant's side, and

Periphetes fell dead upon the very roadway where he had been for so long a terror to all travelers.

Elated with his victory, Theseus took the stout club of his fallen enemy and continued his journey to the Isthmus of Corinth, where he found that the road soon grew very narrow and led along the edge of a rocky precipice. Here he encountered a famous robber named Sciron, who compelled all those who passed his way to wash his feet. When the terrified traveler, unable to refuse, was thus occupied, the robber would suddenly raise his foot and kick the man over the side of the cliff into the sea below, where a hungry tortoise lay waiting with ever-open jaws. When Theseus was told the condition on which he would be allowed to pass, he drew his sword and set upon his enemy so fiercely that Sciron quickly withdrew his demand, and offered to let the hero go on his way undisturbed. Then Theseus, as he held his sword point at the robber's throat, commanded Sciron to perform the same menial task that he had set so many others; and when the robber, not daring to refuse, was kneeling before him, Theseus hurled him over the precipice and gave one more meal to the hungry tortoise, who never again was able to feast on the bodies of luckless travelers.

 The next adventure that befell the hero was with a cruel giant called Sinis, or the Pine-Bender, because he delighted in bending over some tall pine-tree until its top reached the ground; and having done this, he would call to some unsuspicious passer-by to help him hold it down. The stranger usually complied with this request, and then the giant would take his great hand from the tree, which would at once spring back to its upright position, hurling the unfortunate helper into the air, and often dashing him to pieces against the rocks. When Theseus encountered the giant and was asked for his help, he remembered that his mother had told him long ago of this brutal giant's jest, and he determined that travelers should no more be killed or even terrorized by this curse of the highway. So when Sinis bent down a particularly large and strong pine-tree and begged Theseus to help him hold it, the hero deftly fastened the giant himself to the tree which sprang upward as soon as it was released and dashed the huge body against the mountain side, crushing it to pieces.

After disposing of the giant, Theseus continued his journey and next encountered Procrustes (called the Stretcher), a fearful giant who, under the pretense of hospitality, lured travelers into his house. Though an offer of food and entertainment was so unusual that it might have aroused suspicion, most of those who passed Procrustes's house accepted his invitation and entered. In the house was an iron bedstead on which the giant forced all his guests to lie. If they were too short, he stretched their limbs to suit the size of the bed; and if they were too long, he cut off their legs to make them fit its dimensions. Theseus entered Procrustes's home, and partook freely of the food set before him. Then he suddenly fell upon the giant, who was unprepared for such an attack, bound him to his own bedstead, and by making his huge body fit into it, inflicted on Procrustes the same cruel death that he had delighted to visit on others.

When Theseus finally reached Athens, he went straightway to the palace, and on his way he learned that his father had married the sorceress Medea. When he arrived at the royal apartments and came before Ægeus, his cloak so completely hid his sword that the king could not possibly recognize it as the one he had left for his son. Nevertheless he welcomed the stranger, who seemed a brave and handsome youth, and bade him take a place at the banquet-table. But though the king did not know whom he was entertaining, Medea, the sorceress, was perfectly well aware of the stranger's identity, and mixed a deadly poison in the wine-cup that was intended for the guest. Handing this to Ægeus, she bade him honor the youth with a cup of their choicest wine; and the king, suspecting nothing, was about to offer the poisoned drink to Theseus when he suddenly saw the sword beneath the stranger's cloak. Looking down at the youth's sandals, he recognized them as the ones that he had buried under a rock long ago, and he knew then that the sword was also his own. With a cry of joy he started forward to embrace his son, and as he did so the cup of wine that he held in his hand was overturned and its contents poured on the table. Some of the drops of poisoned wine fell on a dog that was lying at the king's feet, and immediately it gave one convulsive shudder and died. Realizing that the deadly draught had been meant for him, and knowing that only the jealous Medea could have dared to commit such a crime, Theseus sprang toward her with drawn sword, intending to put an end to her wickedness; but the sorceress fled from the banquet-hall, mounted her dragon-car, and escaped to a distant country, which was afterwards called by her name Media.

King Ægeus was delighted to find that his son had grown to be such a brave and handsome youth, and he listened with pride while Theseus related all the adventures that had befallen him on the way to Athens. Then the king made a great feast in honor of his son, and publicly proclaimed him his heir. The time passed very happily to Theseus until the day when he saw a sad procession of weeping people wending its way through the streets, and observed in the midst of them seven youths and seven maidens dressed in funeral garments. He inquired where this solemn cortège was going, and was told that the casting of lots had just been concluded and the victims had been chosen for the Minotaur. Then the young prince learned for the first time that since Minos, king of Crete, had conquered the Athenians in a recent war, he had exacted of them a terrible tribute. Each year seven youths and seven maidens were offered to the Minotaur,101 an insatiable monster that dwelt in an intricate labyrinth built for its special use by King Minos, and designed by the celebrated architect Dædalus.

The labyrinth was so intricate that no one who entered it could ever hope to find his way out; and the victims which Athens supplied each year were probably killed by terror and suspense as they threaded their way through the labyrinth's tortuous windings, long before the fearful Minotaur came upon them. The architect who designed this wonderful cave should have earned the lasting gratitude of Minos; but Dædalus unfortunately lost the king's favor, and for some slight offense was shut up in a tower with his son Icarus. The boy gave himself up for lost, but the father began at once to contrive some means of escape, and ingeniously fashioned two pairs of wings, which were to gain freedom for himself and his son. When the last feather was adjusted, Dædalus fastened one pair of wings securely on Icarus, and cautioned him not to fly too high lest the heat of the sun should melt the wax with which the feathers were held together. The youth, impatient to be free, paid slight attention to these warnings; and as soon as his wings were fastened, he sprang boldly from the tower window and flew straight toward the clouds. Higher and higher he rose, exulting in this glorious motion, and soon the heat of the sun's rays began to soften the wax on his wings. When it was too late, Icarus realized his danger and came nearer to the earth; but the wax was melting fast, and in a moment the feathers separated and the adventurous boy was plunged headlong into the sea. His body was never recovered, but that part of the sea was afterwards called the Icarian Sea. Dædalus enjoyed a happier fate than that of his son, for he reached Sicily in safety and built a temple there to Apollo. In the temple he hung up his wings as an offering to the god.102

CHAPTER XXXI
THESEUS

Part II

WHEN Theseus heard the story of the Minotaur and its wonderful labyrinth, he determined that it should no longer exact its yearly tribute of human lives, for he would offer himself as one of the victims and end the terrible sacrifice by slaying the monster. When he announced this intention to his father, the king sought to persuade him to remain at home; but Theseus joined the youths and maidens who had been chosen by lot to go to Crete, and they set sail for the country of the Minotaur. According to the custom, the ship hoisted only black sails, which Theseus promised to change for white ones when he returned unharmed, having slain the monster.

Nothing befell the voyagers until they reached the coast of Crete, but here the ship was stopped by the giant Talus, whose body was made of brass and was always so red hot that if he held any one in his embrace, the victim was burnt to cinders. This giant was a very effective guardian of the island, and kept off all strangers who had no business along that coast. As he knew that the black-sailed ship brought to his master, King Minos, the yearly tribute from the Athenians, he let the vessel pass; and the voyagers, having landed, were led before the king. The cruel mouth of Minos relaxed into a smile when he saw the youths and maidens, for they were all young and beautiful,—the very flower of the Athenians,—and it gave him special satisfaction to consign such a chosen company to death. Beside Minos stood his daughter Ariadne, who looked compassionately at those who were destined for the sacrifice, and when she saw Theseus, she pitied him above all the rest, and wished she might save him from his loathsome fate.

When the young hero asked that he might go first into the labyrinth, and alone, King Minos smiled at what he considered a child's boast—for he had heard that Theseus hoped to slay the Minotaur; but when he learned that the bold youth was his enemy's only son, he gladly allowed him to do as he wished, although it was contrary to all custom. Theseus was therefore placed alone in a cell of the prison, and here he did not feel quite so bold or so eager to face the Minotaur as he had when he talked over the adventure at his father's court. His sword had been taken away, and he had no other weapon with which to fight the monster, so his confidence was somewhat shaken; and as he watched the night deepening the gloom of his prison, he felt disheartened and almost unnerved for his coming battle. Just then the door of the prison opened softly, and Ariadne, the king's daughter, entered. To Theseus's great surprise she gave him a sharp sword and a ball of thread—two things that she assured him were necessary for him to have if he hoped to come alive out of the labyrinth. She bade him fasten one end of the thread to the entrance of the cave, and keep the ball tight in his hand, so that it might lead him back through the intricate windings after he had slain the Minotaur.

Theseus was very grateful to Ariadne for her assistance, without which he would never have been able to encounter the monster or to escape from its wonderful labyrinth. He assured the maiden that his father would send her a generous reward of gold and jewels; but she refused to accept any return for her kindness until Theseus ventured to suggest that if she would become his wife, he would be proud to take her back with him to Athens. To this Ariadne gladly agreed, and they plighted their troth in the murky darkness of the prison. When at dawn of the following day the hero, now full of courage and sure of success, was led to the labyrinth, he fastened one end of the thread to the entrance. Then, with his hand on his sword, which was hidden under his long cloak, he stepped boldly into the cave from which no human being had ever come out alive. The passage was narrow and dark, and strewn everywhere with whitening bones, so Theseus stepped very cautiously, with his ball of thread held fast and his hand ever ready on his sword. Suddenly the Minotaur rushed upon him at an unlooked-for turn in the road, and though the hero had no warning of its presence he met it boldly. A terrible battle ensued, in which Theseus struck fiercely at the Minotaur, wounding it mortally, while the pain-maddened brute tore gashes in his flesh and almost suffocated him with its deadly breath. At last the hero gave a swift thrust with his sword that cut through the monster's great head, and in a moment the Minotaur lay dead among the bones of its former victims.

With the help of the thread, which he had never lost, even in the thick of the fight, Theseus was able to retrace his steps and to reach the entrance to the labyrinth, where he found Ariadne anxiously awaiting him. At the sight of the blood-stained sword she knew that her lover had slain the Minotaur, and together they hurried to the black-sailed ship, to which Ariadne had already conveyed the youths and maidens who had been Theseus's companions on the voyage. As quickly as possible the ship sped out of the harbor; but before they could quite clear the Cretan shores, the giant Talus came upon them, and, seeing that some of his master's prisoners were escaping, he tried to catch hold of the vessel by its rigging. As he leaned forward to do this, Theseus dealt him such a mighty blow that he toppled over into the sea and was drowned. At this spot there were later discovered some thermal springs, which gave evidence of the terrible heat in the giant's brazen body.

Only once did the vessel stop on its swift voyage homeward, and this was at the island of Naxos. Here the whole company landed to explore the beauties of the island, and to find some spring from which to get a supply of fresh water. Ariadne wandered apart from the gay company, and being weary, threw herself down on the bank of a stream to rest. Here she fell fast asleep, and when Theseus later found her there, he at once conceived the treacherous idea of deserting her. So he summoned all his companions, and went stealthily down to the ship, where he embarked, leaving Ariadne alone on the island. For some days the deserted maiden sat on the seashore watching in vain for the Athenian ship to return; but she did not mourn her faithless lover long, for the gods sent her a greater happiness than she could ever have had with the fickle Theseus. The island of Naxos was the favorite spot of Bacchus, god of wine, who landed one day with a merry company of followers, and found the weeping Ariadne. In a short time he won her love and confidence, and persuaded her to be his wife. The wedding celebrations so occupied Ariadne's mind that the treacherous Theseus was soon forgotten.103

The Athenians had been so eager to return to their native city that they had no thought but to reach home as quickly as the vessel could bear them; and Theseus forgot his promise to his father that, in case of success, white sails should replace the black ones that were hoisted on the outgoing voyage. Old Ægeus went each day to the seashore, and stood on a high rock, watching the sea for some sign of the returning ship. When, at last, he saw it loom up on the horizon, with its black sails showing ominously against the sky, he at once concluded that his son was dead; and in his grief over this great loss he threw himself into the water, which has since been known as the Ægean Sea.

When Theseus entered Athens in triumph, the first news he heard was the tidings of his father's death; and realizing that it had occurred through his forgetfulness, he was filled with remorse. Though this misfortune made him king of Athens, he allowed the city no rejoicings on his accession to the throne; and the power and wealth at his command gave him no happiness, for his conscience still accused him of causing his father's death. He tried to divert his mind by absorbing himself in state duties, but soon found that nothing would bring forgetfulness as long as he stayed in Athens; so he set out again in search of adventures, and led an expedition against the Amazons, who had been harassing his land. After a long and fierce battle he defeated them and took their queen, Antiope, prisoner. The Amazons then attacked Athens, and penetrated into the heart of the city, but were finally driven out. Shortly after this Theseus married the queen, Antiope,104 and a son was born to them whom the delighted father named Hippolytus. When, later on, the Amazons again made an invasion into the country under the pretext of rescuing their queen, Antiope was killed by an arrow sent at random into the court of the palace.

The next adventure in which Theseus engaged was to lead the Athenian army against Pirithous, king of the Lapithæ, who had been secretly carrying off some of his herds. Full of anger at these continued plunderings, Theseus came suddenly upon the marauders as they were boldly making off with their booty; but as soon as he and Pirithous were brought face to face, they were seized with such an admiration for each other that they had no longer any feelings of enmity. They threw down their weapons, clasped each other's hands, and swore eternal friendship. To prove his devotion to his new friend, Theseus agreed to accompany him to the court of Adrastus, king of Argos, and to be present at the marriage of Pirithous to Hippodamia, the daughter of the king. Many guests came to the wedding, and among them were Hercules and a number of the centaurs. The beauty of the bride so won the admiration of the centaurs that they determined to kidnap her, and a terrible battle ensued between them and the Lapithæ, who were aided by Theseus and Hercules. Finally the centaurs were driven away, but not before many of them had been killed or wounded. The bride who had been the cause of this strenuous fighting did not live long, however, and Pirithous soon found himself like Theseus, a disconsolate widower.

Theseus

Having been so unfortunate in their wives, the two heroes determined not to seek again any king's daughters in marriage, but to choose some one of divine parentage. So Theseus decided upon Helen, the child of Jupiter and Leda105 whom the ruler of the gods wooed in the form of a snow-white swan. Pirithous's choice fell upon Proserpina, the wife of Pluto. Theseus succeeded in carrying off Helen; but as she was at that time a mere child, he left her in the care of his mother Æthra until she should be old enough for marriage. Meanwhile Helen's twin brothers, Castor and Pollux, having discovered who her abductor was, waited until he was absent on the venture with his friend Pirithous, and then went to the rescue of their sister, whom they took forcibly from Æthra, and carried triumphantly home to Sparta.

Of these twin brothers, Castor was mortal, and some time later was slain in battle. Pollux, who was immortal, then begged Jupiter to let him die also, that he might not be separated from his brother. The ruler of Olympus, touched by this evidence of devotion, allowed Castor to return to life on condition that Pollux would spend half of his time in Hades. Later on both brothers were translated to the heavens, where they form a bright constellation, one of the signs of the Zodiac.106

Although Theseus's attempt to win an immortal bride was unsuccessful, the two friends were not discouraged; and the hero accompanied Pirithous to Hades when he made the bold attempt to carry off Proserpina. Pluto, having discovered their intention, was so enraged at the insult that he fastened Theseus to an enchanted rock, and bound Pirithous to the ever-revolving wheel of his father Ixion. When Hercules went down to Hades to ask Pluto's permission to carry the three-headed dog Cerberus to the court of Eurystheus,107 he freed Theseus from the enchanted rock and thus enabled him to return to Athens.

Though somewhat advanced in years Theseus decided to marry again, and chose as his bride the beautiful Phædra,108 a younger sister of Ariadne. An embassy was accordingly sent to ask for the maiden's hand in marriage, and later she was brought to Athens; but she was not at all pleased with her elderly husband, and much preferred his handsome young son Hippolytus, whose years were better suited to her own. She tried to persuade Hippolytus to elope with her, and when he indignantly refused to be so disloyal to his father, Phædra's affection for him turned to hate, and she determined to make him pay dearly for thus scorning her love. So she went to the king and told him that Hippolytus was trying to persuade her to desert the husband she adored; and the infatuated Theseus, believing her story, vowed to punish the youth for his treachery. Learning that his son was then driving his chariot along the seashore, the king implored Neptune to avenge his wrongs; and the obliging sea-god sent a huge wave over the chariot, which dashed it against the rocks and threw the lifeless body of Hippolytus on the beach. When Phædra saw what had happened as the result of her false accusations, she was filled with remorse and despair; and after confessing her wickedness to the king, she hung herself. One story relates that Diana, pitying the innocent Hippolytus, restored him to life with the aid of Æsculapius; and, to remove him from the power of his irresponsible father, placed him in the care of the nymph Egeria.

Theseus, having grown bitter from his many misfortunes, now became so stern and tyrannical that his people began to hate him and to wish for another ruler. At last, driven to desperation by his harsh measures, they banished him to the island of Scyros, where the king Lycomedes treated him at first with great kindness; but he soon grew tired of the old man's presence and decided to get rid of him. So one day when Theseus was walking along the cliff's edge, a servant stole up behind him and threw him into the sea. When the Athenians heard of the fate that had befallen their king, they repented of having sent him into banishment; and now, in a sudden revulsion of feeling, they made him a national hero. Later on he was deified as a sort of demigod; his bones were brought piously back to Athens; and a magnificent temple was erected in his honor on the Acropolis.

CHAPTER XXXII
ŒDIPUS

LAIUS and Jocasta, king and queen of Thebes, were very happy when the gods gave them a little son, and they sent to the oracle at Delphi to learn what auspicious omens attended the child's birth. To their horror they were informed that the boy would kill his father, marry his mother, and bring great misfortune upon his native city.

Hoping to avert this dreadful calamity, Laius commanded a servant to take the child away and kill him; but the man, not wishing to commit so heartless a crime, hung the infant by his ankles to a tree, and left him there to perish of hunger or from the teeth of wild beasts. The king, believing that his command had been carried out and that the boy no longer lived, was happy in the conviction that the oracle would never be fulfilled. Meanwhile the helpless child was left hanging to the tree until a shepherd, chancing to pass by, heard his pitiful cries and went to his rescue. The kindly peasant then carried the infant to his master Polybus, king of Corinth, who befriended the little stranger and later adopted him as his son and heir, for he had no children of his own. He called the boy Œdipus, which means swollen-foot.

The young prince grew up in entire ignorance of his real parentage, and never suspected that he was not king Polybus's son until one day, at the royal banquet, a guest, drunk with wine, was heartless enough to tell him that he was only an adopted child. At first Œdipus believed this statement to be just a malicious invention; but as he saw the glances that the other guests exchanged, he was filled with dread lest the words might be really true. So he went in haste to the woman he had always called his mother, and demanded the truth about his birth. The queen, fearing that Œdipus might kill himself if he knew that he had been deceived about his parentage, assured him that he was indeed her son. The youth believed her repeated assertions, and yet he was not wholly satisfied; so he went to consult the oracle at Delphi. From this he could learn nothing but the terrible prophecy that he would kill his father, marry his mother, and bring misfortune upon his native city.

Determined not to be forced into committing any of these crimes, Œdipus fled from Corinth and became a wanderer. Once, while he was walking on the high-road, bewailing the cruel fat that drove him away from the people he loved, he was met by a chariot in which sat an old man and his servant. This was Laius, king of Thebes, who was journeying thus far from his native city to consult the oracle of Delphi. The servant who drove the king's chariot commanded Œdipus to move out of the road, and flourished his whip to enforce his demand. The young prince was not accustomed to be thus ordered about, and refused to move so that the king's chariot might pass. The driver then struck Œdipus with his whip, at which the youth grew so enraged that he avenged the insult by killing the servant with his sword. The king hurled his spear at Œdipus and called loudly to his other servants, who were some distance behind; but before they could come to their master's rescue, Laius was stretched dead in the road. Thus the first part of the prophecy was fulfilled.

When the attendants came hurrying to the king's assistance, they were horrified at finding both him and his charioteer dead; but although they searched everywhere, no trace of the murderer could be found. Œdipus meanwhile had escaped and was on his way to Thebes, whither the servants were now preparing to carry their dead master. Though strangers were usually noticed as they came through the city gates, Œdipus was scarcely observed during the many days that Thebes was in mourning for the dead king. When the funeral ceremonies were over, the young stranger heard one day a herald proclaiming in the streets that the throne of Thebes should belong to him who could kill the Sphinx and thus free the country from its baneful presence. The hand of the queen Jocasta was also promised as a further reward.

When Œdipus asked one of the natives what this creature called the Sphinx might be, the old man to whom he spoke turned on him a look of surprise, and remarked that he must indeed be a stranger to Thebes if he did not know that the city was suffering from the presence of the Sphinx. This monster, he said, was half woman and half lion, with the claws and wings of a huge bird; and it had stationed itself just outside the city gates, where it crouched upon a rock so close to the high-road that no traveler could pass it unseen, especially as it kept watch both night and day. To each passer-by the Sphinx propounded a riddle, and those who solved it could pass undisturbed, but those who failed were at once torn to pieces by the monster's claws. Thus far no one had been able to solve the riddle, and many travelers had already been destroyed.

When Œdipus heard this story, he determined to seek the Sphinx and try his fate. Even if he himself were slain, he would not regret having given his life to the nation that had befriended him, especially since the oracle had prophesied for him such a series of crimes that he had no love for life. So, sword in hand, he went out of the city gates, and walked boldly along the road to the rock where the crouching Sphinx lay in wait for its prey. As soon as it saw Œdipus, it stopped him, and demanded that he should answer the riddle or else lose his life.

"Tell me your riddle then," cried the hero, boldly; and the Sphinx replied:—

"What is it that in the morning goes on four feet, at noon on two feet, and in the evening upon three?"

For some minutes Œdipus did not answer, but he crept nearer to the Sphinx, with his sword gripped firmly in his hand. The monster began to lick its cruel lips, and stretch out one long claw toward its victim, when Œdipus answered:—

"It is man, who in childhood creeps on hands and knees, in manhood walks erect, and in old age moves with the help of a staff." The Sphinx, with a cry of rage and disappointment, spread its wings, preparing to fly away to some other place where it could find new victims; but Œdipus suddenly rushed upon it with his drawn sword, and drove it over the edge of a precipice which was so steep that the monster was instantly killed by its fall.

When Œdipus returned to the city and announced that he had slain the Sphinx, the people greeted him as their deliverer. They placed him in the royal chariot, proclaimed him their king, and carried him in triumph to the palace, where the queen Jocasta welcomed him. Shortly after this she married Œdipus, thus fulfilling the second part of the prophecy.

In spite of the crimes that he had unknowingly committed, Œdipus reigned many years in Thebes, and proved himself so wise and just a ruler that the people never regretted having chosen him for their king. Two sons were born to him and Jocasta, and two beautiful daughters. The former were named Eteocles and Polynices, and the latter Ismene and Antigone. Œdipus himself was so content that he almost disbelieved the fatal prophecy at Delphi; but his happiness was destined to be short lived, for the city was suddenly afflicted with a pestilence and famine which caused such distress throughout the land that the stricken people came flocking to Œdipus, praying him to deliver them from the scourge. The king sent at once to consult the oracle at Delphi, and his messengers returned with this answer from Apollo:—

"The plague, he said, should cease,
When those who murdered Laius were discovered,
And paid the forfeit of their crime by death
Or banishment."109

Every effort was then made to discover who had slain the former king Laius, and it was not long before the crime of Œdipus was revealed. At the same time the old servant who had been commanded to kill the infant son of Laius and Jocasta was found, and made to confess his part in the tragedy. Œdipus was now convinced of his real parentage, and discovered to his horror that he had already been guilty of the three crimes that the oracle had foretold. In vain he had fled from Corinth to escape being near his supposed parents; and in vain, too, had he sought refuge in another city, believing that the one he had left was his birthplace. When the queen Jocasta realized the full horror of her relationship to Œdipus, she committed suicide; and the king, rushing into her apartment at the sound of her cries, saw her lifeless body on the ground. In despair at this sight Œdipus, the unwilling cause of the tragedy, was seized with a sudden madness and put out both his own eyes, declaring that the sunlight would be forever hateful to him.

Œdipus and Antigone

Blind, penniless, and on foot, he left the palace and the city on which he had brought such disaster, and wandered over the land accompanied by his devoted daughter Antigone, who clung to the fallen king the more lovingly because of his misery and disgrace. After many days of wandering in the rain and cold, begging their scanty food and resting in any wayside spot that offered them shelter, Œdipus and his daughter came to Colonus, a village near Athens. Here was a deep and almost impenetrable forest, which the Greeks believed to be sacred to the Furies. In this grewsome spot Œdipus declared that he would stay the rest of his days; and bidding his daughter farewell, he entered the dark forest alone. Antigone, weeping and clinging to her father's arm, besought him to let her stay beside him, for what could he—old and blind and helpless—do in that fearful spot but perish? Œdipus gently released her clinging hands, and refused to allow her to go any farther with him, assuring her that to him who lived ever in the eternal night of blindness, there were no terrors in the darkness of the forest.So Antigone sadly returned to Athens, and the blind king groped his way among the thick underbrush and fallen trees. At nightfall a terrible storm came up, and its forerunner, the wind, shook the forest as if it were some child's toy; but still the old king felt his way among the trees, and the lightning, as it flashed into the dark places of the forest, illumined a figure bent and shaking, but grim, determined, and unafraid. The next day when the storm was over, a party of men sent by Theseus, king of Athens, went in search of Œdipus, but no trace of him was ever found; and the ancients believed that the Furies dragged him down into Hades, where he received a fitting punishment for his crimes.110 The plague having been removed from Thebes by the death of Œdipus—according to the words of Apollo—the city returned to its former prosperity; and then began a fierce dispute between the king's two sons as to which of them should succeed to the throne. A compromise was finally agreed upon whereby the eldest son, Eteocles, was to reign for one year, and at the end of the year the second son, Polynices, was to accede to the throne and rule for the same length of time. The dispute being settled amicably, Polynices set out for adventures in foreign lands during his brother's reign; and at the end of the year he returned to claim his right to wield the scepter of power. Eteocles refused, however, to relinquish the throne; and with the help of the soldiers, drove Polynices out of the city.

Antigone and Ismene

Furious at this treachery, but unable to retaliate single-handed, Polynices fled to the court of Adrastus, king of Argos, where he was hospitably received. On relating the story of his wrongs, he so won the sympathy of the king that the kindly monarch promised to help him regain his kingdom. Later on the banished prince married Adrastus's daughter, and the king equipped a large army to go with Polynices to Thebes. At the head of the troops he placed seven valiant chiefs who were determined to win the city from the usurper, or perish in the attempt. These leaders gave this celebrated expedition the name of "The Seven against Thebes." If courage and boldness were enough to overthrow a city, the besiegers would have won an easy victory; but their bravery was of no avail against a place so well fortified and defended as Thebes. After a seven years' siege the leaders of the attacking forces grew weary of espousing a hopeless cause, and decided that the quarrel between the two brothers must be settled by a duel. Accordingly Polynices and Eteocles met face to face, and fought so fiercely that both of them were killed. The only one left in the city who could rightfully assume the reins of authority was Creon, the father of Jocasta, who was now proclaimed king of Thebes.111 By Creon's order the body of Eteocles was given all the honors of a royal burial; but the corpse of Polynices was left on the battle-field a prey to dogs and vultures. Then the king issued a proclamation that if any one dared to touch the body of the dead prince, he would be buried alive. The friends of Polynices did not venture to defy this edict; but his sister Antigone, horrified at the thought of leaving her brother's body to suffer such disgrace, determined to ignore the king's barbarous decree. As she was unable to procure any assistance, she dug a grave with her own hands and buried Polynices, performing such funeral rites for the repose of the dead as she could accomplish alone. While she was engaged in this act of devotion she was seen by the soldiers of Creon, who dragged her at once into the presence of the king. Although Antigone was one of his own family, and was also the promised wife of his son Hæmon, the relentless monarch condemned her to death. Hæmon pleaded with his father to spare the life of his betrothed, since her deed, though in defiance of the king's order, had been one of praiseworthy devotion; but Creon would not revoke his decision, and condemned Antigone to the most horrible of deaths—that of being buried alive. While this inhuman sentence was being carried out, Hæmon leaped into the grave where Antigone was kneeling, and declared that he would die by her side. As the terrible process of walling-in the lovers was slowly completed, Antigone died in Hæmon's arms; and when he felt her lifeless body lying limp in his embrace, he ended his own life with his dagger.

CHAPTER XXXIII
THE APPLE OF DISCORD

JUPITER, father of the gods, once fell in love with the beautiful sea-nymph "Thetis of the silver feet," the daughter of Nereus and Doris. Before he arranged for the marriage, the ruler of Olympus first consulted the Fates to see whether any misfortune was likely to attend his nuptials; and the three sisters who spin the thread of life night and day declared that Thetis was destined to be the mother of a son who would be far greater than his father.

Although Jupiter could not imagine how any god could supplant him in Olympus, he was nevertheless unwilling to act in defiance of what the Fates decreed; so he gave Thetis in marriage to Peleus, king of Phthia, who had long loved her and had sought her hand in vain. The sea-nymph was not very well pleased at having to accept a mere mortal as a husband, even though he was a king, after having been wooed by the greatest of the gods. To induce her to consent to the marriage, Jupiter promised that he and the other gods would come down from high Olympus to attend the wedding; and the prospect of this great honor soothed the pride of Thetis so that she consented to marry Peleus.

The preparations for the wedding were begun in the coral caves of her father Nereus, and all the ocean-deities and sea-nymphs helped to beautify the palace under the sea. When the wedding day arrived, Jupiter, with all the attending gods, came to grace the marriage feast. The guests took their seats at the well-filled table, and pledged the bride in brimming cups of wine. There was nothing to mar the joy of the occasion until suddenly an uninvited guest appeared in the banquet-hall, and the laughter died away into an ominous silence. This unexpected visitor was Eris (or Discordia), the goddess of discord, who had not been asked to the wedding because her hideous face, snaky hair, and vicious temper made Thetis fear that her presence would anger the other guests. The strife-breeding goddess regarded this omission as an insult, so she went unbidden to the marriage feast, determined to vent her wrath and spite on those who had received the coveted honor. For a moment she stood looking at the assembled company with glances full of hatred, and she laughed mockingly when she saw them shrink away as she breathed over them her poisonous breath. Then she threw on the table a golden apple, and immediately vanished.

The guests were eager to see the beautiful fruit, and as they passed it about among themselves they were surprised to find engraved on its smooth surface the words "For the Fairest." Immediately there arose a lively discussion as to whom the apple should rightfully belong; and each of the goddesses present was inclined to believe that the fruit was intended for her. At last all the contestants for the golden apple withdrew their claims except Juno, Minerva, and Venus,—each of whom disputed hotly for its possession. Juno contended that her power and majesty gave her the best right to the prize; Minerva claimed that the beauty of wisdom surpassed all other charms; while laughter-loving Venus asked who could rightfully be called "the fairest" if not the goddess of beauty.

As the dispute grew more and more bitter, the goddesses called upon the other guests to decide their respective claims; but no one was willing to assume this responsibility. Since the apple could be given to but one of the three, the other two would be sure to vent their anger and disappointment on those who made the decision, each believing that the judges willfully refused to admit her superior charms. So, at the suggestion of one of the company, the entire wedding party adjourned to Mount Ida, where the beautiful shepherd Paris was tending his flocks. Jupiter appointed him to be the judge of the contest. The bewildered shepherd took some moments to recover from the surprise of having this brilliant company break in upon his solitude; and he stood watching them in awe and reverence, not daring to speak in the presence of the immortals.

Paris was not, however, an uncouth peasant lad, for although occupying the lowly position of shepherd, he was really the son of Priam and Hecuba, king and queen of Troy. When he was a mere infant, he was left on the mountain to perish, because an oracle had foretold that he would cause the death of his family and the destruction of his native city. But though so inhumanly exposed to cold and the hunger of wild beasts, the child did not die, for he was found by a shepherd, who adopted him and brought him up to follow his own calling.

When Paris grew to manhood he was so handsome that the wood-nymphs, who were his companions, all sighed for love of him. Among them was the fair and gentle Œnone, whom Paris secretly married, and with whom he lived happily on Mount Ida. Though his foster-father had told him the story of his birth, Paris had no longing for the glitter and grandeur of palaces, for he felt sure that king Priam would wish to kill him if he learned that the son he feared and hated was alive.

Paris

Paris had grown so accustomed to the solitude of the mountain that when the wedding party suddenly came upon him, he stood fearful and silent while Jupiter, showing him the golden apple with its inscription, bade him judge which of the three goddesses should receive it. Before he could make any answer, Juno told him if he gave the apple to her he would thereby win great wealth and honor. Minerva promised him the gift of wisdom far exceeding that of mortal men; but laughter-loving Venus whispered in his ear that if he awarded her the apple, he should have the most beautiful woman in the world for his wife. Whether it was the alluring beauty of Venus that blinded his judgment, or the reward which she offered that tempted him, it is impossible to tell. Perhaps it was for both of these reasons that Paris turned quickly and placed the coveted apple in Venus's hand. This decision brought upon him the wrath of both the discredited goddesses, who began from that moment to cherish a hatred for the house of Troy, and to plot its destruction.

Venus told Paris that in order for her to fulfill her promise, he must now go down to the city of Troy and make himself known to his parents. She assured him that he need have no fear of his father, for she herself would so order his affairs that the king would welcome him and acknowledge him as his son. Later on she would arrange that he should be furnished with ships in which to sail to Greece, for to this country he must inevitably go, since Helen, wife of Menelaus, king of Sparta, was the most beautiful woman in the world. Obeying carefully all the instructions of the goddess, who had now become his protectress, Paris left his shepherding and went down to the court of his father, King Priam. He was so blinded by the vision of his glorious future that he did not think how heartless he was to desert the loving and faithful Œnone, who mourned for him until the hills echoed with the sound of her cries.

To tell the story of Paris's return to his native city, of his voyage to Sparta, and of his abduction of Helen, would be to tell the story of the Trojan war and of how dearly Paris and his household paid for the most beautiful woman in the world. When the sons of Priam were falling, one by one, beneath the fierce blows of the Greeks, Paris was wounded by a poisoned arrow shot by Philoctetes, who had received these famous weapons from Hercules when he lit that hero's funeral pyre.112 As the poison entered Paris's veins, and he knew that he had received a mortal wound, he sent at once for Œnone, who had always loved him so dearly that he believed she must have forgiven his treachery and desertion. He knew how skilled the nymph was in the use of healing herbs, and she had once told him, in the happy days of their love on Mount Ida, that if he ever were wounded, he should send for her and she would heal him. Paris therefore dispatched a messenger in all haste to bring his wife from her home among the hills; but Œnone refused to accompany the messenger, for she knew that it was not for love of her that her husband desired her presence. So Paris died of his poisoned wound, and when Œnone heard of his death, she went down to the city and saw the funeral pyre with its flames leaping toward the sky. Filled with remorse at her refusal to come to his aid, Œnone could not look on at the sight of Paris's burning body and live; so she sprang upon the blazing pyre and perished beside her lover.

APPENDIX

I

The only powers that dared oppose the will of Jupiter were the Fates and Destiny, who issued their irrevocable decrees without regard to the wishes of the ruler of Olympus. Jupiter's sovereignty is thus described by Homer:—

"He whose all-conscious eyes the world behold,
The eternal Thunderer sat, enthroned in gold,
High heaven the footstool of his feet he makes,
And wide beneath him all Olympus shakes.

* * * * *

He spoke, and awful bends his sable brows,
Shakes his ambrosial curls, and gives the nod,
The stamp of fate and sanction of the god;
High heaven with trembling the dread signal took,
And all Olympus to the center shook."

—POPE'S TRANSLATION.

The principal temples of Jupiter were the Capitol at Rome, and the Temple of Jupiter Ammon in Libya. At Dodona was the oracle of Jupiter, called the "Speaking Oak," where the responses were given by the trees whose rustling branches made sounds that were interpreted by the priests. The oracle was said to have been established at Dodona in the following manner: two black doves took their flight from Thebes in Egypt. One flew to Dodona in Epirus; and alighting in a grove of oaks, it proclaimed, in human language, to the people of that region, that they must establish there an oracle of Jupiter. The other dove flew to the temple of Jupiter Ammon, and delivered a similar command there. Another account says that two priestesses were carried off from Thebes in Egypt by the Phœnicians, and set up oracles at Dodona and the Libyan Oasis.

A magnificent temple at Olympia was dedicated to Jupiter, and here, every fifth year, the Greeks assembled to celebrate games. These festivals lasted five days, and were known as the Olympic Games. Vast numbers of spectators flocked to them from every part of Greece and from Asia, Africa, and Sicily. The Greeks usually reckoned time by Olympiads or five-year periods,—the space of time between the celebrations. The first Olympiad was about 776 B.C.

Inside the temple at Olympia stood a wonderful statue of Jupiter made of ivory and gold. The parts representing flesh were of ivory laid on a framework of wood, while the drapery and ornaments were of gold. It was the work of Phidias, and was considered the highest achievement of Grecian sculpture. The height of the figure was forty feet, and the pedestal was twelve feet. The god was represented as seated on his throne, with his brows crowned with a wreath of olive and in his hand a scepter. The statue was considered one of the Seven Wonders of the world, but our knowledge of it is confined to literary descriptions and to copies on coins.

II

Poems:—

ometheus Bound SCHYLUS

ometheus Unbour:RCY B. SHELLEY

ometheus   ENRY W. LONGFE

ometheus   MES R LOWELL

The following are Byron's lines:—

"Titan! to whose immortal eyes
The sufferings of mortality,
Seen in their sad reality,
Were not as things that gods despise;
What was thy pity's recompense?
A silent suffering, and intense;
The rock, the vulture, and the chain;
All that the proud can feel of pain;
The agony they do not show;
The suffocating sense of woe."

III

There is a full account of the story of Pandora in Hawthorne's "Wonder Book."

Poems:—

ındora   ANTE G. ROSSETI

asque of Pandora ENRY W. LONGFE

IV

Other mythologists than Ovid, in treating the story of the flood, state that Deucalion and Pyrrha took refuge in an ark, which, after sailing about for many days, was stranded on the top of Mount Parnassus. This version was far less popular with the Greeks, though it shows more plainly the common source from which all these myths are derived.

"Who does not see in drowned Deucalion's name,
When Earth her men, and Sea had lost her shore,
Old Noah!"

—FLETCHER.

V

The city of Delphi, containing the famous oracle of Apollo, was built on the slopes of Mount Parnassus in Phocis. It had been observed at a very early period that the goats feeding on Parnassus were thrown into convulsions when they approached a certain deep cleft in the side of the mountain. When a goatherd ventured near the spot, he found a peculiar vapor arising from the cavern, and as he inhaled it, he was affected in the same way as the animals had been. The inhabitants of the country, unable to explain the goatherd's convulsive ravings, imputed his utterings to divine inspiration. A temple was therefore erected on the spot, and the prophetic influence was attributed to various gods, but was finally assigned only to Apollo. A priestess was appointed who was named the Pythia, and her office was to sit upon a tripod placed over the chasm from which the divine afflatus proceeded. The priestess and the tripod were both adorned with laurel; and as she inhaled the hallowed air, her words— believed to be inspired by Apollo—were interpreted by the priests.

The Pythian Games were celebrated at Delphi every three years, and were instituted by Apollo in commemoration of his conquest of the Python. At these games were chariot racing, running, leaping, wrestling, throwing quoits, hurling javelins, and boxing. Besides the exercises in bodily strength, there were contests in music, poetry, and oratory. These occasions gave the poets and musicians an opportunity to show their productions to the public.

VI

There was in Troy a celebrated statue of Minerva called the Palladium. It was said to have fallen from heaven, and the Trojans believed that the city could not be taken so long as this statue remained within it. Ulysses and Diomede entered the city in disguise, and succeeded in obtaining the Palladium, which they carried off to the Grecian camp.

The finest and most celebrated of the statues of Minerva was the one by Phidias in the Parthenon at Athens. This was forty feet in height, and was covered with ivory and gold. It represented the goddess as standing with a spear in one hand, and in the other a statue of victory. Her helmet, highly decorated, was surmounted by a sphinx. The Parthenon itself was constructed under the supervision of the famous sculptor; and many of the reliefs which enriched the exterior were by the hand of Phidias himself. The statue of Minerva is not in existence, but parts of the frieze of the Parthenon are in the British Museum and are known as the Elgin Marbles.

The hero Theseus instituted at Athens the festival of Panathenæa in honor of Minerva. The chief feature of the festival was a solemn procession in which the Peplus, or sacred robe of Minerva, was carried to the Parthenon, and left on or before the statue of the goddess. The Peplus was covered with embroidery worked by virgins of the noblest families in Athens. The festival was peculiar to the Athenians, but among them persons of all ages and both sexes took part in the celebrations. In the procession the old men carried olive branches and the young men bore arms. The women carried baskets on their heads containing the sacred utensils and cakes necessary for the sacrifices.

VII

The most famous representations of Juno are the torso in Vienna from Ephesus, the Barberini in the Vatican at Rome, the bronze statuette in the Cabinet of Coins and Antiquities in Vienna, and the Farnese bust in the National Museum at Naples.

Juno's festivals, the Matronalia, in Rome, were always celebrated with great pomp. Less important feasts were held in each city where a temple was dedicated to her. On one of these occasions, an old priestess was very anxious to go to Juno's temple at Argos, in which she had served the goddess many years in her maiden days, and which she had left only to be married. The way was long and difficult, and the old priestess could not attempt to walk such a distance; so she bade her sons Cleobis and Biton harness her white heifers to her car. The youths were anxious to do her bidding; but they could not find the heifers, however diligently they searched. As they did not wish to disappoint their mother who had set her heart on attending the services, they harnessed themselves to the car, and thus conveyed her to the temple. The mother, touched by their filial devotion, then prayed to Juno to bestow on her sons the greatest gift in her power; and when the old priestess went in search of the youths, after the services were over, she found them dead in the portico of the temple where they had lain down to rest. Juno had taken them, while they slept, to the Elysian Fields to enjoy an eternity of bliss as a reward for their devotion.

VIII

There is another version of the story of how Hercules brought Alcestis back from Hades. This is in the Alcestis of Euripides, and Browning has related it in his "Balaustion's Adventure." In this account the wife of Admetus is not surrendered willingly by Pluto, but the great hero Hercules wrestles with Death for the body and life of Alcestis, and by winning the victory over this dread adversary, restores Admetus's wife to his arms.

Other poems:—

IX

The combat between a hero and a dragon is a favorite theme in mythology and folklore. Besides the myth of Apollo's slaying of the Python are the well-known stories of Siegfried's killing of Fafnir, St. George and the Dragon, Perseus and the Sea Serpent, Cadmus and the Serpent, and Hercules and the Hydra.

The principal temples dedicated to the worship of Apollo were at Delos, his birthplace, and at Delphi.

One of the Seven Wonders of the ancient world, the famous Colossus of Rhodes, was a statue of Apollo. His head was encircled with a halo of bright sunbeams, and his legs were set wide apart to allow vessels to pass in and out of the harbor with all their sails spread.

Among the many remains of ancient sculpture, none is better known— unless it be the Venus of Milo—than the statue of Apollo called the Belvedere, from the name of the apartment of the pope's palace at Rome in which it is placed. The artist is unknown, but the work is supposed to be of the first century of our era, and is modeled on the type of Greek sculpture of the Hellenistic period. It is restored to represent the god at the moment when he has shot the arrow that slays the Python.

Poems:—

X

The story of Clytie is frequently alluded to in poetry, and the sunflower is often used as an emblem of constancy. Moore's lines are well known:—

"The heart that has truly loved never forgets,
But as truly loves on to the close;
As the sunflower turns on her god when he sets
The same look that she turned when he rose."

XI

The sisters of Phaëton, the Heliades, spent their days by the Eridanus River shedding tears, wringing their white hands, and wailing over the loss of their brother, until the gods, in pity for their grief, turned them into poplar trees. Their tears, which continued to flow, became amber as they dropped into the stream.

XII

The Diana of the Ephesians, referred to by St. Paul in Acts xix: 28, was not the chaste moon-goddess of the Greeks, though a world-renowned sanctuary was dedicated to Diana at Ephesus.

Poems:—

·aise of Artemis	ƆMUND GOSSE
ymn to Diana	ƐN JONSON
rtemis in "Epic of	ᴤWIS MORRIS
iobe	΄ALTER S. LANDOR

The most beautiful statue of Diana is the Diana of Versailles, in the Louvre, Paris (also called the Diana of the Hind).

XIII

Before Orion was slain by an arrow from Diana's bow he loved Merope, daughter of Œnopion, king of Chios, who consented to the union on condition that the lover should win his bride by some heroic deed. But instead of meeting this requirement, Orion attempted to elope with Merope. The plan was frustrated, however, by the king; and the bold youth was punished by the loss of his bride and also of his eyesight. Then Orion wandered about, blind and helpless, and finally reached the Cyclops' cave, where one of them took pity on him and led him to the sun, from whose radiance his sight was restored.

XIV

The story of Endymion is a favorite theme in poetry. The best-known poem on this subject is the Endymion of Keats. Other poems are by James R. Lowell, Henry W. Longfellow, Arthur H. Clough, Elizabeth L. Landon, and Lewis Morris.

XV

In the story of Hyacinthus, as told by the poet Ovid in the "Metamorphoses" (Book 10, line 16, etc.) the account says: "Behold the blood that had flowed on the ground and stained the herbage ceased to be blood; but a flower of hue more beautiful than the Tyrian sprang up resembling the lily, except that this is purple and that silvery white." It is evident that the flower here described is not our modern hyacinth, but some species of iris or larkspur.

XVI

Another unfortunate ending to one of the friendships of Apollo was the death of Cyparissus, a clever young hunter, whose companionship the sun-god often sought. Cyparissus accidentally killed Apollo's pet stag, and he grieved so sorely over this mischance that he pined away and died. Apollo then changed his body into a Cyprus tree, which the god declared should henceforth be used to shade the graves of those who, when living, were greatly beloved.

XVII

There were many oracles of Æsculapius, but the most celebrated one was at Epidaurus. Here the sick consulted the oracle and sought the recovery of their health by sleeping in the temple. The treatment of the sick was probably nothing like that of modern therapeutics, but resembled what is now called animal magnetism or mesmerism.

Serpents were sacred to Æsculapius, probably because of the superstition that those animals have a faculty of renewing their youth by a change of skin. The worship of Æsculapius was introduced into Rome in a time of great sickness, and an embassy was sent to the temple at Epidaurus to implore the help of the god. Æsculapius was so favorably inclined to the petitioners that he accompanied the returning ship in the form of a serpent. When they reached the river Tiber, the serpent glided from the vessel, and took possession of an island in the river. Here a temple was later erected in honor of Æsculapius.

XVIII

According to the more ancient Greek conception, Venus was the daughter of Jupiter and Dione, goddess of moisture; but Hesiod says that she came from the foam of the sea, and was therefore called by the Greeks

Aphrodite—the foam-born. She was generally represented as a beautiful nude figure, or wearing her wonderful girdle, the Cestus—in which lay "love and desire and loving converse that steals the wits even of the wise." The most famous statue of Venus is the one that was found on the island of Melos (Milo), and is now in the Louvre, in Paris. It is probably the work of some sculptor of about the third century B.C. He followed an original of the age of Praxiteles, probably in bronze, which represented the goddess, partly draped, gazing at her reflection in an uplifted shield. A masterpiece of Praxiteles was the Venus of Cnidos, based upon which are the Venus of the Capitoline in Rome, the Venus de Medici in Florence, and the Venus of the Vatican, which is much superior to the other two.

Poems:—

ɔorus to Aphrodite in "Atalanta in Ca	LGERNON C. SWINBURNE
ɔhrodite in "Epic of Hades"	EWIS MORRIS
ɛnus of Milo	DWARD R. SILL
ɛnus and Adonis	ILLIAM SHAKESPEARE
donis in "Epic of Hades"	EWIS MORRIS
eath of Adonis trans. by	HEOCRITUS, ANDREW LANG
ɪus Veneris	LGERNON C. SWINBURNE

The "Lament for Adonis" by Bion has been translated by Andrew Lang, Edwin Arnold, and Mrs. Browning.

The following stanza is from Tennyson:—

"Idalian Aphrodite beautiful,
Fresh as the foam, new-bathed in Paphian wells,
With rosy slender fingers backward drew
From her warm brows and bosom her deep hair
Ambrosial, golden round her lucid throat
And shoulder; from the violets her light foot
Shone rosy-white, and o'er her rounded form
Between the shadows of the vine bunches
Floated the glowing sunlights, as she moved."

XIX

The worship of Aphrodite was probably of Semitic origin, but was early introduced into Greece. The Aphrodite of Homer and Hesiod displays both Oriental and Grecian characteristics. Among the Phœnicians Venus is known as Astarte, among the Assyrians as Istar. There were temples and groves dedicated to Venus in many places, and in some of them—Paphos for instance—gorgeous annual festivals were held. The festival of Venus that was celebrated in Rome in April was called the Veneralia.

Sapho calls Aphrodite the "star-throned, incorruptible, wile-weaving child of Zeus."

XX

One of the many myths connected with Venus was that of Berenice who, fearing for her husband's life, prayed to the goddess to protect him as he set out to battle. She vowed to give her beautiful hair as a sacrifice to Venus if he returned home in safety. The prayer was granted, and Berenice's luxuriant tresses were laid on the goddess's shrine, whence they soon mysteriously disappeared. When an astrologer was consulted in regard to the supposed theft, he pointed to a comet in the sky, and declared that the gods had placed Berenice's hair among the stars to shine forever in memory of her wifely sacrifice.

XXI

References and allusions to Cupid abound in poetry. A few of the best-known poems are:—

ros	DMUND GOSSE
de to Psyche	)HN KEATS
ie Lost Eros	TOMAS ASHE
ie Unknown Eros	OVENTRY PATMOI
ory of Cupid and	TILLIAM MORRIS
ue and Cry After	EN JONSON

The following is a charming little poem by John Lyly:—

"Cupid and my Campaspe play'd
At cards for kisses, Cupid pay'd.
He stakes his quiver, bow and arrows,
His mother's doves, and teeme of sparrows,
Looses them too; then downe he throwes
The coerall of his lippe, the rose
Growing on's cheek (but none knows how),
With these, the crystal of his brow,
And then the dimple of his chin;

All these did my Campaspe winne;
At last hee set her both his eyes;
She won, and Cupid blind did rise.
O love! has she done this to thee?
What shall (alas) become of mee?"

XXII

There is a very old story of a woman's love for her husband and her efforts to win him back from Death which is known in every part of India. On a certain night in the year millions of Hindu women celebrate a rite in honor of Savitri. The story is told in the Mahabharata, an ancient epic of India.

Walter Pater, in "Marius the Epicurean," gives the story of Cupid and Psyche as contained in Apuleius. Many of the incidents of the story will be found in modern fairy tales and romances such as "Beauty and the Beast"; Grimm's "Twelve Brothers"; the Gaelic stories: "The Three Daughters of King O'Hara," "Fair, Brown and Trembling," "The Daughter of the Skies"; and the Norse tale, "East of the Sun and West of the Moon."

XXIII

The most amusing use made of the story of Pyramus and Thisbe is in Shakespeare's "Midsummer-Night's Dream," Act III, Sc. 2, and Act V, Sc. 1, which is a burlesque of what was, in the original story in Ovid, a tragedy.

XXIV

Poems on "Hero and Leander" have been written by Chistopher Marlowe, Leigh Hunt, Thomas Hood, and Thomas Moore. Keats wrote a sonnet, "On a Picture of Leander."

Byron attempted Leander's feat of swimming across the Hellespont, a thing that was considered impossible until the English poet proved its feasibility by performing it himself. The distance in the narrowest part is almost a mile, and there is a constant current setting out from the Sea of Marmora. Since Byron's time the swimming of the Hellespont has been achieved by others; but it still remains a test of strength and skill.

XXV

Various modern stories have been based upon the myth of Pygmalion. One of the best known is "The Venus of Ille," by Prosper Mérimée.

Poems:—

XXVI

Amphion had a twin brother named Zethus who, however, had none of the musician's artistic ability. The brothers heard that their mother Antiope had been put aside by her second husband Lycus, in order that he might marry another wife; so Amphion and Zethus hastened to Thebes, where they found things worse than they had imagined, for Antiope was thrust into prison and subjected to very cruel treatment. The brothers besieged the city; and, after taking possession of it, put Lycus to death. Then they tied Dirce, who had been the cause of their mother's suffering, to the tail of a wild bull, and let it drag her over the stones until she was dead. This punishment of Dirce is the subject of a famous piece of sculpture called the "Farnese Bull" (as it once belonged to the Farnese family), now in the National Museum at Naples.

Poem:—

XXVII

Orpheus's lute was placed in the heavens as the bright constellation Lyra.

The story of Orpheus and Eurydice is often alluded to in poetry. Pope has used it to illustrate the power of music in his "Ode for St. Cecilia's Day," and the wonderful beauty of the nightingale's song over the grave of Orpheus is alluded to by Southey in his "Thalaba."

The song of the nightingale seemed to the ancients so plaintive that, wishing to account for its sadness, they invented the story of Philomela. King Tereus, having wearied of his wife Procne, tore out her tongue by the roots and then married her sister Philomela, pretending that his wife was dead. Procne informed her sister of the horrible truth by means of a web into which she wove her story. To revenge themselves upon the king, the sisters killed the boy Itylus (son of Tereus and Procne) and served him up as food to his father. To punish them for this wickedness the gods changed Procne into a swallow, and Philomela into a nightingale, which forever bemoans the murdered Itylus. The king, Tereus, they transformed into a hawk.

Poems:—

XXVIII

The Muses were the daughters of Jupiter and Mnemosyne, goddess of memory. Although they sometimes united in one grand song, they had separate duties and powers. Apollo as leader of the choir of Muses was called Musagetes.

Clio, the Muse of history, recorded the great deeds of heroes, and was usually represented with a laurel wreath, and a book and stylus.

Euterpe, the Muse of lyric poetry, was represented with a flute and garlands of flowers.

Thalia, the Muse of comedy, was also the patroness of pastoral poetry, and so was often represented with a shepherd's crook as well as a mask.

Melpomene, the Muse of tragedy, wore a crown of gold, and wielded a dagger and a scepter.

Terpsichore, the Muse of choral dance and song, was usually portrayed in the act of dancing.

Erato, the Muse of love poetry, held a lyre.

Polyhymnia, the Muse of sacred poetry, also presided over rhetoric.

Calliope, the Muse of epic and heroic poetry, wore a laurel crown.

Urania, the Muse of astronomy, held mathematical instruments.

XXIX

Mars's attendants, or some say his children, were Eris (Discord), Phobos (Alarm), Metus (Fear), Demios (Dread), and Pallor (Terror).

As founder of Rome, Romulus was its first king, and ruled over the people so tyrannically that the senators determined to get rid of him. So one day when an eclipse plunged the city into sudden darkness, the senators killed Romulus, cut his body into pieces, and hid them under their wide togas. When daylight returned, and the people looked about for their king,—for all the citizens had assembled on the Forum,—the senators informed them that Romulus had been carried off by the immortal gods and would never return. After this Romulus was worshiped as a god under the name of Quirinus, and a temple was built on one of the seven hills of Rome, which has since been known as Mount Quirinal. Yearly festivals in honor of Romulus were held in Rome under the name of Quirinalia.

XXX

Homer gives two versions of the story of Vulcan's lameness,—one, that Jupiter threw him out of heaven for helping his mother against Jupiter's will; and the other, that he was born deformed, and that Juno, ashamed of his ugliness, cast him out of heaven.

(1) "Yea once ere this, when I was fain to save thee (Juno), he caught me by my foot and hurled me from the heavenly threshold. All day I flew, and at the set of sun I fell in Lemnos, and little life was in me."

(2) "She (Thetis) delivered me when pain came upon me from my great fall through the ill-will of my shameless mother who would fain have hid me away for that I was lame."

He spake and from the anvil rose limping, a huge bulk, but under him his slender legs moved nimbly. The bellows he set away from the fire, and gathered all his gear wherewith he worked into a silver chest; and with a sponge he wiped his face and hands and sturdy neck and shaggy breast, and did on his doublet and took a stout staff and went forth limping.— *Iliad*, Book I and Book XVIII.

Vulcan's children were mostly monsters; but he is also the reputed father of Servius Tullius, sixth king of Rome, by a slave Ocrisia whom he visited in the form of a bright flame, which played harmlessly about her.

Vulcan was worshiped by all blacksmiths and artisans; and great festivals, called the Vulcanalia and the Hephæstia, were celebrated in his honor.

XXXI

There were many versions of the creation of the world among the Greeks and Romans, but the most popular was the following: At first there was nothing but a confused mass in which land, sea, and air were all merged in one substance. Over this shapeless mass reigned a careless deity named Chaos who shared his throne with his wife Nyx (or Nox) the goddess of Night. They were dethroned by their son Erebus (Darkness) who ruled over the universe with his children Æther (Light) and Hemera (Day). These two then succeeded to the throne, and by their combined efforts, together with the help of their own child Eros (Amor or Love) created Pontus (the Sea) and Gæa (the Earth), also called Ge, Tellus, Terra. The earth was divided into two equal parts by Pontus, and around it flowed the great river Oceanus. Soon Gæa created Uranus (Heaven), and these two powerful deities took possession of all the universe, and became the parents of twelve gigantic children, the Titans, whose strength was so great that their father Uranus grew much afraid of them. To prevent their ever uniting against him he hurled them, soon after their birth, into the dark abyss called Tartarus, which was situated far under the earth. Here he chained his six sons, Oceanus, Cœus, Crius, Hyperion, Iapetus, and Saturn (Cronos or Time) and his six daughters (also called the Titanides), Ilia, Rhea, Themis, Thetis, Mnemosyne, and Phœbe. Later on, Uranus thrust into Tartarus his other children, the Cyclops, who made the darkness hideous with their incessant clamor.

Gæa was not pleased at this treatment of her children, so she descended into Tartarus to urge the Titans to conspire against their father. But they were all too fearful of the great Uranus and none dared defy him except Saturn, who, having been released from his chains by his mother, went out of Tartarus armed with a scythe that Gæa had given him. He came upon Uranus unawares, bound him fast, and took possession of the throne. Then he released his sisters and brothers, and the Titans, glad to escape from their dreadful bondage, agreed to accept Saturn as their ruler. He chose his sister Rhea (Cybele) for his wife, and gave his brothers and sisters different parts of the universe to govern.

Meanwhile old Uranus had told Saturn, when the latter wrested from him his throne, that he himself would one day be dethroned by his children. So when Rhea bore her first son, Saturn determined to defy the prophecy and promptly swallowed him. One child after another was thus disposed of; and at last Rhea resolved to save her youngest son by stratagem. As soon as Jupiter was born, his mother concealed him, and was able to persuade Saturn into swallowing a large stone which she had wrapped in swaddling clothes. Then Rhea intrusted her child to the care of the Melian nymphs, who bore him off to a cave on Mount Ida. Here a goat (Amalthea) was procured as nurse, and it fulfilled its duties so well that it was later placed in the heavens as a constellation.

When Rhea considered her son strong enough to cope with his powerful father, she urged him to attack Saturn, who, surprised at the sudden appearance of a son of whose existence he was unaware, was defeated and forced to resign his power to Jupiter. Then by means of a nauseous drink prepared by Metis, a daughter of Oceanus, Saturn was made to disgorge the unfortunate children he had swallowed: Neptune, Pluto, Vesta, Ceres, and Juno.

XXXII

Poems:—

The following stanza is from Shelley's "Arethusa:"—

"Arethusa arose
From her couch of snows
In the Acroceraunian mountains,—
From cloud and from crag,
With many a jag,
Shepherding her bright fountains.
She leapt down the rocks,
With her rainbow locks
Streaming among the streams;—
Her steps paved with green
The downward ravine
Which slopes to the western gleams:
And gliding and springing
She went ever singing,
In murmurs as soft as sleep;
The earth seemed to love her,
And Heaven smiled above her,
As she lingered toward the deep."

The river Alpheus does, in fact, disappear underground in part of its course, finding its way through subterranean channels until it again appears on the surface. It was said that the Sicilian fountain Arethusa was the same stream that, after passing under the sea, came up again in Sicily. Hence the story arose that a cup thrown into the Alpheus appeared again in Arethusa.

It is this fable of the underground course of the Alpheus that Coleridge alludes to in his poem of Kubla Khan:—

"In Xanadu did Kubla Khan
A stately pleasure dome decree,
Where Alph, the sacred river, ran
Through caverns measureless to man,
Down to a sunless sea."

XXXIII

Many beautiful temples were dedicated to Ceres and Proserpina, both in Greece and Italy; and their yearly festivals, the Cerealia and Thesmophoria, were celebrated with great pomp.

To commemorate her long search for her daughter, Ceres instituted at Eleusis the Eleusinian Festivals and Mysteries. The Festivals were held in February and September. The lesser festival, in February, represented the restoration of Proserpina to her mother; the greater, held in September, lasted nine days and represented the abduction of Proserpina. All classes might participate in these festivals. The Mysteries of Eleusis were witnessed only by the initiated, and were surrounded with a veil of secrecy that has never been fully withdrawn. The initiates passed through certain symbolic ceremonies from one degree of mystic enlightenment to another till the highest was attained. The Mysteries apparently resembled the ceremonies of the modern masonic orders.

XXXIV

The following stanzas are from Swinburne's "Garden of Proserpine":—

"We are not sure of sorrow,
And joy was never sure;
To-day will die to-morrow;
Time stoops to no man's lure;
And love, grown faint and fretful,
With lips but half regretful,
Sighs, and with eyes forgetful
Weeps that no loves endure.

"From too much love of living,
From hope and fear set free,
We thank with brief thanksgiving
Whatever gods may be,
That no life lives forever;
That dead men rise up never;

That even the weariest river
Winds somewhere safe to sea."

XXXV

Besides Pluto, god of the Infernal Regions, the Greeks also worshiped
Plutus, a son of Ceres and Jason, who was known exclusively as a god of
wealth. Abandoned in infancy, he was reared by Pax, goddess of peace,
who is often represented as holding him in her lap. Because Plutus would
bestow his favors only upon good and worthy mortals, Jupiter deprived
him of his sight; and he then distributed his wealth indiscriminately.

Virgil thus describes the crowd of spirits that wait to be ferried by Charon
across the river:—

"The shivering army stands,
And press for passage with extended hands,
Now these, now those, the surly boatman bore;
The rest he drove to distance from the shore."

XXXVI

The Furies visited the earth to punish filial disobedience, irreverence to
old age, perjury, murder, treachery to guests, and even unkindness toward
beggars. They avenged the ghosts of those who died by a violent death
and had no one to avenge them. Therefore they persecuted Orestes, who
killed his mother, and brought to punishment the murderers of Ibycus.
This poet, beloved by Apollo, was journeying to the musical contest at
Corinth, and was attacked by two robbers. As he lay dying he called upon
a flock of cranes, that were passing overhead, to take up his cause and
avenge his death. When his body was found, there was great lamentation
among the Greeks, and every effort was made to discover the murderers,
but without success. Later on, when a vast assemblage was witnessing a
play in which the Chorus personated the Furies, the people sat terrified
and still as death when the Choristers, clad in black, appeared bearing in
their fleshless hands torches blazing with a pitchy flame. As they advanced
with measured step, the company could see their bloodless cheeks and the
writhing serpents that curled—in place of hair—around their brows. Then
they began to sing: "Woe, woe to him who has done the deed of secret
murder. We, the fearful brood of night, fasten ourselves upon him, flesh
and soul. Unwearied we pursue him; no pity checks our course; still on to
the end of life, we give no peace, no rest." As the Furies finished their
weird chant a number of dark objects came sailing across the sky, and in
the solemn stillness that had fallen over the assembly a terrified cry arose

from one of the benches, "Look, comrade, the cranes of Ibycus!" Having informed thus far against themselves, it was not long before the murderers were seized, and, having confessed their crime, were put to death.

The effect upon the audience of this appearance of the Furies (as related in the story of Ibycus) is not exaggerated, for it is recorded that Æschylus, the tragic poet, having on one occasion represented the Furies in a chorus of fifty performers, the terror of the spectators was such that many fainted and were thrown into convulsions, and the magistrates forbade a like representation for the future.

Poem:—

:anes of [HILLER

XXXVII

The story of the true and false Dreams and the horn and ivory gates rests on a double play of words: ἐλέφας (elephas), ivory, and ἐλεφαιρομαι (elephairomai), to cheat with false hope; κερας (keras), horn, and κραίνειν (krainein), to fulfill.

Poem:—

ιe Ivory GateORTIMER CC

Dreams were sometimes sent through the gates of horn to prepare mortals for misfortunes, as was the case of Halcyone. Ceÿx, king of Thessaly, once left his beloved wife, Halcyone, to go on a journey to the oracle of Delphi. On the outgoing voyage, a tempest struck the ship on which the king was sailing, and he with all his crew perished in the waves. Every day the queen went down to the seashore to watch for the returning vessel, and every night she prayed to the gods to bring her husband safely back to her. Juno, knowing that these prayers were in vain, pitied the faithful Halcyone, and wished to prepare her for the great sorrow that must soon come with the news of Ceÿx's death. So she sent Iris to the cave of sleep, and the rainbow goddess bade one of the Dreams go forth from the gate of horn to visit the sleeping queen. The Dream glided to Halcyone's bedside, and, assuming the form of Ceÿx, appeared before her pale, like a dead man, and dripping with the salt sea. He told his wife that the storm had sunk his ship, and that he himself was dead. Terrified at this vision, Halcyone sprang from her couch and hastened to the beach, where she found the body of her husband washed up by the waves. In pity for her grief, the gods changed both Halcyone and Ceÿx into birds that ever afterward lived on the waters, and were known as the Halcyon birds. These birds uttered shrill cries of warning to all seamen whenever a storm threatened, but were themselves so fearless of the sea that they built their nests and hatched their young on the ever-tossing waves.

XXXVIII

The Nereides trained Arion, the wonderful winged steed that had the power of speech, to draw his father's chariot over the waves. He was said to be the first and the fleetest of horses, and passed successively into the hands of Cepreus (Pelops' son), Hercules, and Adrastus—the last of whom won all the chariot races, thanks to the fleetness of Arion.

Neptune was a patron of horse trainers, and was himself especially devoted to horses.

The Cyclops are described differently by different authors. Homer speaks of them as a gigantic and lawless race of shepherds who dwelt in Sicily. Each of them had a single eye in the center of his forehead. The chief of the Cyclops was Polyphemus who fell in love with the Nereid Galatea. He took great care of his appearance, harrowed his coarse hair with a currycomb and mowed his beard with a sickle. When he looked into the sea, he smiled complacently and said: "Beautiful seems my beard, beautiful also my one eye—as I count beauty—and the sea reflects the gleam of my teeth whiter than Parian Stone" (Theocritus, Idyll VI.) Galatea did not return the Cyclops's affection, however, for she loved the river god Acis. Polyphemus came upon the lovers one day in the woods, and was so enraged at the sight of them that he killed his rival with a rock. As the blood of Acis crept in a stream from under the rock it grew paler and paler until it turned into water. Soon it became a river which still bears the name of the unfortunate Acis.

XXXIX

Milton alludes to the ocean deities in the song at the conclusion of "Comus."

"Sabrina fair ...
Listen and appear to us,
In name of great Oceanus,
By the earth-shaking Neptune's mace,
And Tethy's grave majestic pace;
By hoary Nereus' wrinkled look,
And the Carpathian wizard's hook,
By scaly Triton's winding shell,
And old soothsaying Glaucus' spell,
By Leucothea's lovely hands,
And her son that rules the strands;

By Thetis' tinsel-slippered feet,
And the song of Sirens sweet;" etc.

Proteus is called the Carpathian wizard because his cave was on the island
of Pharos, or Carpathos.

XL

Wordsworth's sympathy with the classical conception of nature is shown
in the following sonnet:—

"The world is too much with us; late and soon,
Getting and spending, we lay waste our powers;
Little we see in Nature that is ours;
We have given our hearts away, a sordid boon!
This sea that bares her bosom to the moon;
The winds that will be howling at all hours,
And are upgathered now like sleeping flowers;
For this, for everything, we are out of tune;
It moves us not. Great God! I'd rather be
A Pagan suckled in a creed outworn;
So might I, standing on this pleasant lea,
Have glimpses that would make me less forlorn,
Have sight of Proteus rising from the sea;
Or hear old Triton blow his wreathed horn."

XLI

Palæmon was usually represented riding on a dolphin. He was called
Portumnus by the Romans, and was believed to have jurisdiction over the
ports and shores. Some authorities state that the Isthmian Games held on
the isthmus of Corinth were in honor of Neptune instead of Palæmon.

The divinities of the lakes, rivers, fountains, etc., were hoary river gods,
slender youths, beautiful maidens, and sometimes children. The famous
statue called "Father Nile" is in the Vatican at Rome.

XLII

Bacchus was worshiped very widely throughout the ancient world, and
many festivals were held in his honor. The most noted were the Greater
and Lesser Dionysia, the Liberalia, and the Bacchanalia. Bacchus is
generally represented as crowned with ivy or grape leaves and bearing an
ivy-circled wand (the thyrsus). He rides in a chariot drawn by panthers or
leopards.

Poems:—

XLIII

As the ass was reverenced in Phrygia, the acquisition of ass's ears may not have been such a disgrace as we imagine.

Ovid thus describes Midas' golden touch:—

"Whose powerful hands the bread no sooner hold,
Than all its substance is transformed to gold;
Up to his mouth he lifts the savory meat,
Which turns to gold as he attempts to eat:
His patron's noble juice of purple hue,
Touch'd by his lips, a gilded cordial grew,
Unfit for drink; and, wonderous to behold,
It trickles from his jaws a fluid gold.
The rich poor fool, confounded with surprise,
Starving in all his various plenty lies."

(Croxall's trans.)

XLIV

Fauns and satyrs have been favorite subjects in art and especially in sculpture. The most famous are the Faun of Praxiteles (Vatican, copy); the Dancing Faun (Lateran, Rome); Dancing Faun, Sleeping Faun, Drunken Faun, and Faun and Bacchus (National Museum, Naples); Sleeping Satyr, or the Barberini Faun (Glyptotek, Munich).

The use of the Faun in literature is best known in Hawthorne's "The Marble Faun."

Reference is made to fauns and naiads in Milton's "Lycidas." Robert Buchanan has two poems entitled "The Satyr" and "The Naiad."

XLV

Poems:—

XLVI

Keats in "Endymion" alludes to Dryope thus:—

"She took a lute from which there pulsing came
A lively prelude, fashioning the way
In which her voice should wander. 'Twas a lay
More subtle-cadenced, more forest-wild
Than Dryope's lone lulling of her child."

Poem:—

XLVII

James R. Lowell has taken the story of Rhœcus as the subject of one of his finest poems.

"Hear now this fairy legend of old Greece,
As full of freedom, youth and beauty still,
As the immortal freshness of that grace
Carved for all ages on some Attic frieze."

Poem:—

XLVIII

Janus is not the only one among the Greek and Latin deities whose name has been given to a part of the week or year. In Latin, the names of the days are—dies Solis (Sunday); dies Lunæ (Moon day); dies Martis (Mars' day); dies Mercurii (Mercury's day); dies Jovis (Jove's day); dies Veneris (Venus's day); dies Saturni (Saturn's day).

XLIX

Austin Dobson has a poem "The Death of Procris."

Moore, in his Legendary Ballads, devotes one ballad to "Cephalus and Procris."

L

The finest poetic treatment of the sadness of Tithonus over his immortal old age is in Tennyson's "Tithonus." The following are a few lines from this poem, which should be read in its entirety:—

"Let me go; take back thy gift;
Why should a man desire in any way
To vary from the kindly race of men,
Or pass beyond the goal of ordinance
Where all should pause, as is most meet for all?

* * * * *

"Coldly thy rosy shadows bathe me, cold
Are all thy lights, and cold my wrinkled feet
Upon thy glimmering thresholds, when the steam
Floats up from those dim fields about the homes
Of happy men that have the power to die."

LI

The story of Hercules's accepting Arete (Virtue) as his guide—the "Choice of Hercules"—may be found in The Tatler, No. 97.

The Nemean games instituted by Hercules in honor of Jupiter were celebrated at Nemea, a city of Argolis.

The most famous statue of Hercules is the Farnese Hercules in the National Museum at Naples. Another well-known piece of sculpture is The Infant Hercules Strangling a Serpent, in the Uffizi at Florence.

Quite worth the student's consideration are the poems "Deïaneira" and "Herakles" in the classical but too-little-read "Epic of Hades" by Lewis Morris. The following is an extract from the description of the Centaur Nessus:—

"Take
This white robe. It is costly. See, my blood
Has stained it but a little. I did wrong;
I know it, and repent me. If there come
A time when he grows cold—for all the race
Of heroes wander, nor can any love

Fix theirs for long—take it and wrap him in it,
And he shall love again."

LII

Poem:—

ᴉe FortunatNDREW LAᴉ

The following is from Pindar:—

"The Isles of the Blest, they say,
The Isles of the Blest,
Are peaceful and happy, by night and by day,
Far away in the glorious west.

They need not the moon in that land of delight
They need not the pale, pale star;
The sun is bright, by day and night,
Where the souls of the blessed are.

They till not the ground, they plow not the wave,
They labor not, never! oh, never!
Not a tear do they shed, not a sigh do they heave,
They are happy forever and ever!"

LIII

The chosen device of Charles V. of Germany represented the Pillars of
Hercules entwined by a scroll that bore his motto "Plus Ultra." This
device, represented on the German dollar, has been adopted as the sign of
the American dollar ($).

LIV

The Pygmies were a nation of dwarfs, so called from a Greek word
meaning the cubit or measure of about thirteen inches, which was said to
be the height of these people. They lived near the sources of the Nile, or,
according to others, in India. Homer tells us that the cranes used to
migrate every winter to the Pygmies' country, where they occasioned a
fierce warfare. H. M. Stanley, in his last African expedition, discovered a
race of diminutive men that correspond very well in appearance to those
mentioned by Homer.

Terra is the same goddess as Gæa (the Earth).

Poem:—

ttle of Pygmies and (MES BEATTIE

LV

The Apples of the Hesperides may have been suggested by the oranges of Spain.

See the poem "The Golden Apples," in William Morris's "Earthly Paradise."

LVI

Two poems on the Medusa which are well worth reading are "The Doom of King Acrisius" in William Morris's "Earthly Paradise," and Shelley's lines "On the Medusa of Leonardo Da Vinci in the Florentine Gallery."

LVII

There are translations of Simonides's "Lament of Danaë" by William C. Bryant and John H. Frere.

Tennyson has a singular use of the proper noun in the "Princess" when he says:—

"Now lies the Earth all Danaë to the stars,
And all thy heart lies open unto me."

LVIII

Cassiopeia was said to have been an Ethiopian; and was, therefore, in spite of her boasted beauty black. Milton alludes to her in "Il Penseroso" as:

"that starred Ethiop queen that strove
To set her beauty's praise above
The Sea-Nymphs, and their powers offended."

Though Cassiopeia attained the honor of being set among the stars, she was placed—through the efforts of the sea-nymphs—in a part of the heavens near the pole, where she is half the time held with her head downward, to teach her humility.

LIX

For a Gaelic Andromeda and Perseus, see "The Thirteenth Son of the King of Erin" in Curtin's "Myths of Ireland."

Poem:—

ndromeda   HARLES KIN(

LX

From the incident of Bellerophon's bearing to Iobates the letters that contained his own death-warrant, came the expression "Bellerophontic letters." This is used to describe any written message that a person may deliver, unknowingly, and that is prejudicial to himself.

On Mount Helicon, the home of the Muses and Pegasus, was the fountain Hippocrene, which was opened by a kick from the hoof of Pegasus.

Poems:—

gasus in Pound   ENRY W. LONGFELLOW

llerophon in Argos and iñILLIAM MORRIS

gasus in Harness   HILLER

LXI

The most famous soothsayer was Melampus, who was also the first mortal endowed with prophetic powers. The story is told that before his house stood an oak tree containing a nest of serpents. The old serpents were killed by some servants, but Melampus took care of the young ones, and fed them carefully. One day when he was sleeping under the oak tree, the serpents licked his ears with their tongues; and when he awoke he was surprised to find that he now understood the languages of birds and creeping things. In this way he was able to foretell future events, and he became a celebrated soothsayer. Once Melampus was taken captive and put into prison; but he overheard the woodworms saying that the timbers of the prison were so nearly eaten through that the roof would soon fall in. He told this to his captors, who immediately took advantage of the warning and left the building; but not before they rewarded Melampus by setting him free.

LXII

The best description of Hercules's lament for Hylas is in Lang's translation of the thirteenth Idyl of Theocritus.

Poem:—

ylas   \YARD T\

The naming of Jason's ship may have been after its builder, or from the city of Argos, or from the word "Argo," meaning swift or white.

The story of the Symplegades may be a reference to the rolling and clashing of icebergs. The dove incident occurs in many ancient stories, from that of Noah down.

Poems:—

ılking Oak   LFRED TENNYSO

fe and Death of JILLIAM MORRIS

son and King AtҎEDERICK TENN

LXIII

Medea's preparations for her magic potion are like the incantations of the witches in Macbeth, Act IV, Sc. I.

"Round about the caldron go;
In the poison'd entrails throw.

* * * * *

Fillet of a fenny snake,
In the caldron boil and bake;
Eye of newt and toe of frog,
Wool of bat and tongue of dog,
Adder's fork and blind-worm's sting,
Lizard's leg and howlet's wing:

* * * * *

Witches' mummy; maw and gulf
Of the ravin'd salt-sea shark,
Root of hemlock digg'd i' the dark," etc.

LXIV

Medea's sorceries were assisted by the prayers that she addressed to Hecate, a mysterious divinity who embodied the terrors of the darkness. She haunted cross roads and graveyards; and, being goddess of sorcery and witchcraft, wandered only by night and was seen only by dogs, whose barking told of her approach.

Translations of the Medea of Euripides are by Augusta Webster, William C. Lawton, and Wodhull.

LXV

Poems on Atalanta:—

talanta's Race in "The Earthly Par ILLIAM MORRIS

talanta in Calydon ⎵GERNON C. SWINBURNE

ippomenes and Atalanta ⎵ALTER S. LANDOR

LXVI

Dædalus shared with Æolus the honor of inventing sails for the ships hitherto propelled by oars.

Dædalus could never bear the idea of a rival; and when his nephew Perdix was apprenticed to him, the lad gave such promise of excelling his teacher in mechanical arts that Dædalus grew to hate him. One day when Perdix was walking on the seashore he picked up the spine of a fish, and later on he imitated it in iron, thus inventing the saw. He also invented a pair of compasses. Then Dædalus, envious of his nephew's skill, pushed him off a tower and killed him; but Minerva, pitying the boy, changed him into a partridge, which bears his name.

LXVII

Castor and Pollux were deities of boxing, wrestling, and all equestrian exercises. They were generally seen mounted on snow-white horses, and their appearance on the battle-field was a good omen for the army among whom they came. The Romans believed that they fought at the head of their legions at the famous battle of Lake Regillus.

LXIX

Poems:—

ıeseus and Hippolyta ⎵ALTER S. LANDOR

riadne   REDERICK TENNYSON

ippolytus of Euripides

1ædra   LGERNON C. SWINBURI

1ædra in "The Epic of EWIS MORRIS

LXX

The story of Œdipus is taken from the "Œdipus Rex," "Œdipus Coloneus," and "Antigone" of Sophocles (trans. of Plumptre or of Lewis Campbell).

Other poems:—

vell-foot the Tyrant   ERCY B. SHELLEY

1e Downfall and Death of King ŒDWARD FITZGERALD

ntigone   UBREY DE VERE

1e Sphinx   \LPH W. EMERSON

:agment of an Antigone   ATTHEW ARNOLD

LXXI

In her "Characteristics of Women," Mrs. Jameson has compared the character of Antigone with that of Cordelia in Shakespeare's "King Lear." The scene of Œdipus going alone into the forest at Colonus is similar in pathos and tragedy to Lear's defiance of the midnight tempest on the lonely heath.

LXXII

For references in poetry to the judgment of Paris:

dgment of Paris MES BEATTIE

dgment of Paris HN STUART BL.

:none   LFRED TENNYS(

LXXIII

Other minor deities not mentioned in the text are:

Victoria (Nike), goddess of victory.

Phosphor, the morning star.

Hesperus, the evening star, god of the west.

Hygeia, a daughter of Æsculapius, watched over the health of man.

The Graces, daughters of Jove, presided over banquets, dances, and also social pleasures and polite accomplishments. They were three in number—Euphrosyne, Aglaia, and Thalia. They are also called Gratiæ.

Momus was the god of laughter.

The Seasons were the four daughters of Jupiter and Themis. Their collective name was Horæ (the Hours). As the Hours they attended the sun-car of Apollo.

Fama, goddess of Fame.

Faunus, god of fields and shepherds. He was also gifted with prophetic powers.

Fauna, the sister wife or daughter of Faunus. She was also called the Bona Dea.

Pales, a deity who presided over cattle and pastures.

Manes, the souls of the departed who had become deified.

FOOTNOTES

1 See Appendix, page 325.

2 See Appendix, page 327.

3 See Appendix, page 327.

4 See Appendix, page 328.

5 See Appendix, page 328.

6 See Appendix, page 329.

7 From the Greek word "parthenos," which means "maiden."

8 See Appendix, page 331.

9 See Appendix, page 332.

10 See Appendix, page 332.

11 See Appendix, page 334.

12 See Appendix, page 333.

13 See Appendix, page 334.

14 See Appendix, page 334.

15 See Appendix, page 335.

16 See Appendix, page 335.

17 Mercury's wand was called the Caduceus.

18 See Appendix, page 335.

19 Cf. "Story of Cyparissus," Appendix, page 336.

20 See Appendix, page 336.

21 See Appendix, page 337.

22 See Appendix, page 338.

23 See Appendix, page 340.

24 See Appendix, page 341.

25 See Appendix, page 341.

26 See Appendix, page 341.

27 See Appendix, page 342.

28 See the "Story of Dirce," Appendix, page 342.

29 See Appendix, page 345.

30 See Appendix, page 343.

31 See Appendix, page 345.

32 She was also known as Ilia.

33 See page 74.

34 See Appendix, page 346.

35 See page 76.

36 See Appendix, page 349.

37 See Appendix, page 351.

38 See Appendix page 350.

39 See Appendix, page 347.

40 Appendix, page 357.

41 See Appendix, page 352.

42 Also called Erinnys or Eumenides. Their names were Alecto, Tisiphone, and Megæra. See Appendix, page 353.

43 See Ovid, *Metamorphoses*, Book XI, line 590, etc.

44 See "Story of Ceÿx and Halcyone," Appendix, page 355.

45 Two gates of sleep there are: one of horn, through which pass the true dreams; the other of shining white ivory, through which the spirits send false dreams up to the world.

46 Pale Death steps with the same foot to the huts of the poor and the palaces of kings.

47 See Appendix, page 356.

48 See Appendix, page 357.

49 See page 36.

50 See page 230.

51 See Appendix, page 356.

52 See page 110.

53 See Appendix, page 359.

54 See "Story of the Dragon's Teeth," page 121.

55 See Appendix, page 359.

56 See page 164.

57 See page 113.

58 Old name for Naxos.

59 See page 299.

60 See page 40.

61 See Appendix, page 360.

62 "Pactolus singeth over golden sands."—GRAY.

63 See Appendix, page 361.

64 See Appendix, page 360.

65 See Appendix, page 361.

66 See Appendix, page 362.

67 Here in a vast cave, King Æolus keeps under his control the struggling winds and roaring tempests, and holds them chained in prison. They, chafing at restraint, surge against their barriers with the great rumbling of a mountain. Æolus sits in a lofty stronghold, holding a scepter, and soothes their feeling and softens their wrath. If he did not do this, they would surely carry with them in rapid course the seas and lands and the deep sky and sweep these with them to the high heavens.

68 See page 269.

69 See Appendix, page 362.

70 See Appendix, page 362.

71 See Appendix, page 362.

72 See Ovid, *Metamorphoses*, Book XIV, line 645.

73 See Ovid, *Metamorphoses*, Book XIV, line 655.

74 See Appendix, page 363.

75 Some authorities state that Hippolyte was not killed, but lived to marry the hero Theseus. See page 301.

76 See page 155.

77 See Appendix, page 364.

78 See page 6.

79 See Appendix, page 365.

80 See Appendix, page 365.

81 According to some stories, Atlas was the father of the Hesperides and owner of the Garden.

82 See page 302.

83 See page 35.

84 See page 155.

85 See page 145.

86 See Appendix, page 366.

87 See Appendix, page 366.

88 See Appendix, page 367.

89 See Appendix, page 367.

90 See Appendix, page 367.

91 See page 243.

92 Hawthorne's *Wonder Book*, "The Chimæra."

93 See Appendix, page 368.

94 See Appendix, page 368.

95 See page 121.

96 See Appendix, page 369.

97 Sometimes given as Glauce.

98 Sometimes given as Milanion.

99 Ovid, *Metam.*, Book X, line 610.

100 See Appendix, page 370.

101 See page 218.

102 See Appendix, page 370.

103 See page 179.

104 Some authorities say that it was Hippolyte whom Theseus married, and that she was therefore not slain by Hercules. This is the story that Shakespeare adopted in "Midsummer-Night's Dream."

105 See page 74.

106 See Appendix, page 371.

107 See page 229.

108 See Appendix, page 371.

109 Sophocles, *Œdipus the King*.

110 See Appendix, pages 371, 372.

111 This was the same Creon whose daughter Megara had married Hercules.

112 See page 234.

Milton Keynes UK
Ingram Content Group UK Ltd.
UKHW040838141024
449705UK00006B/351